DIAMOND IN THE DUST

MEL A ROWE

The Following Is Written in Australian English

I consider the ELSIE CREEK SERIES a love
letter to the unique individuals that continue to
shape the Northern Territory into a truly
amazing part of Australia.
My dad would've loved it.

ONE

Over teeth-chattering corrugations and rocks, Verily navigated the small scooter through the treacherous terrain. Her smile grew, as the wind whipped her sun-bleached hair free from the edges of the bike helmet. It was as if she was the only person alive in this place. Inhaling clean air, zipping along the red-dirt road that contrasted with the biggest of blue skies.

Cattle, with wide handle-bar sized horns, grazed in the wide-open paddock. Across the road, rows of barren mango trees followed the curve of the land belonging to Verily's aunt.

Suddenly, the ground shook and vibrated through her seat like an earth tremor as a low earthy rumble grew to a roar behind her. Her eyes widened at the reflection in her side mirror and her heart jumped to her throat as fear spiked to an all-time high.

A devil's dust storm of explosive, churning red soil spewed high into the air.

Its cause was a mountain of metal that led the tornado, and it was the biggest truck Verily had ever seen—charging straight for her.

If I can get through my Aunt's front gates, I'll be safe. Verily twisted the throttle, forcing the bike to go faster, trapped between two barbed wire fences that shone under the afternoon sun that could seriously damage some skin.

But the dust demon barrelled toward her. The ground shook, and the noise was horrendous.

'NOOOOO!' Her scream was lost in the deafening roar as trailers taller than houses passed by, one after the other, after the other.

The more she tried to ride through the storm, the more it dragged her along with the truck—straight for those towering tyres.

She hit the brakes. The bike skidded, her ears rung, and the train on wheels engulfed her in an apocalyptic world of red rain and thunder.

Buckets of gritty red powder showered over her, filling her ears and nose, crunching grit in her teeth, while her tongue was like sandpaper. It was suffocating.

Then, like a summer's monsoon, the walls of red dust fell, and the cloud moved away.

'What the hell?' Verily spat out dirt, wiping at her gritty eyes. She was completely covered, rolled, and basted in a coat of red grit.

She scowled at the mobile storm that slowed down with a hiss of its brakes. It then turned right—straight into her Aunt's place, tumbling past the main house, then down the track and disappearing into the mango orchard.

How does a truck that big, just vanish?

It wasn't any of her business because Verily was only the visitor. She was always the visitor.

Rolling her left shoulder, ignoring the dull ache, she gunned the dust-spluttering bike and slowly rolled back to Molly's, hoping to blow away the dust she wore. It was everywhere.

She steered through the thick fallen layers of dirt that had erased all other tracks on the road, it was like riding on freshly fallen snow. Everything in this place was new ground, ever since she'd returned to this country. It was a land she had once called home, yet she felt like an alien. A red dust covered alien.

Why did she come here at all? There were far better places to holiday than being stuck in the middle of the outback.

* * *

Alex steered over fifty metres of moveable metal to the centre of the mango orchard and parked the prime mover behind his cottage. It snaked around the building, shielding it from the rows of trees as the smell of cattle wafted from the empty trailers.

On the veranda, he tossed his Akubra on the hook by the back door, ripped off his long-sleeved shirt and chucked it straight into the washing machine. He dusted down his jeans by the laundry tub, and splashed water to rid the dust and dirt from his face and hair. There was no time for a shower, so the pommy powder shower would have to do and he let the deodorant can do its worst.

He snatched a fresh shirt from the clothesline that stretched across his veranda, he took a mouthful of milk from the old beer fridge, then sighed at the sight of the bottled beer calling to his taste buds. 'Soon fellas, soon.'

He held up a labelless bottle to the afternoon light. There was minimal sediment with a promising clarity to the pale ale. Would this be his winning brew?

He spotted the clock on the wall. 'Crap, I'm late.'

Shoving the t-shirt over his head, he snatched his duffel-bag from the old armchair. Small dust clouds stirred beneath his boots as he headed for his ute and followed the dirt track that ran through the mango orchard, to Molly's house. Their stout trunks and sturdy branches were naked and ready for fruit bearing. Alex was looking forward to their flowering, hoping his new pruning technique would work on the next crop. A crop that would pay for his dream future.

He pulled up to Molly's stone house with its deep verandas, where he'd spent many an afternoon. The place was his second home.

In through the back door and into the large open kitchen, he grabbed the water cooler from Molly's pantry. Its shelves were stacked with jams and preservatives, and where the bickie tin called his name.

With a sweet biscuit in his mouth, Alex filled the water bottles at the sink. 'Hey, Molly, you ready?'

No answer.

He chomped on his biscuit as his boot-steps echoed along the wooden floorboards. 'Molly, you about?'

Voices carried down the corridor as he stepped through

the doorway and stopped. His eyes widened, his jaw dropped and his head tilted.

And his heart stopped, but only for a second…

Then it hammered.

Fast.

Mouth dry, it was impossible to swallow the tasteless biscuit as he stared at the heavenly vision at the end of the hallway. Long, messy sun-bleached hair. Sleepy eyes the colour of raw umber. The rest was athletically toned perfection in matching bra and bootyliscious-briefs where the word sexy just wasn't a big enough word in his vocab to define the perfection.

'WHAT THE HELL!' She screamed at him, covering herself with her arms, and dashing into the spare bedroom.

He gave a slow lopsided grin as his eyes followed that great arse through the doorway, then found himself frowning at the mash of red, angry scars that ran down her left shoulder and upper arm.

The door slammed, snapping him back to reality.

'Um, sorry,' he mumbled to the closed door. *Not really.* It'd been the best perve he'd had all bloody year. 'Oi, Molly? Did you finally find your magic potion and turn young again?'

'I wish,' replied Molly, coming out of her room at the far end of the corridor.

'You always look the same, except for the hair.' That changed colours and styles all the time, but Molly's warm smile never changed. 'So, ah. Who's…' —*the goddess behind door number one?* He pointed to the closed door.

'Verily. Remember? I told you my niece was visiting.'

'Wasn't she supposed to be here last week?'

'She got hung up. Talk about being late…' Molly tapped on the closed door and sung out, 'We'll be waiting outside, Verily.'

'Won't be a sec, Aunt Molly,' came the muffled reply from behind the door.

'Aunt Molly, huh?' Alex leaned his broad shoulder against the wall. 'It's been a long time since I've heard anyone call you that.'

'I've only got one niece,' said Molly, walking past him. 'Are you coming?'

He'd rather wait for the mystical creature to come out from behind that shut door. 'Ah, yeah.' He followed Molly and grabbed the esky and water coolers off the table.

Flicking through her vast umbrella collection from the rack he'd made her way back in school, Molly plucked a blue one that matched her dress. 'Now, do me a favour, Alex. Don't tell Verily where we're going or what we're doing.'

'Why? It's not like it's a secret. The whole town knows about it.'

Entering the kitchen in a pair of sweatpants that hung low on her hips, Verily threw her hair into a ponytail and asked, 'The whole town knows what?'

That a goddess had moved into town. She looked like someone who'd just jumped out of bed, but sexier.

'Nothing,' said Molly, pushing open the creaking flyscreen door. 'Come along, hon, we're late.'

'Sorry, I had to take a shower because some idiot in this massive truck covered me in dust. I nearly got sucked under the tyres.'

'Ah crap,' mumbled Alex, and headed for the safety of his ute.

'Then,' continued Verily, 'that monster tore down your driveway and disappeared into the mango orchard. How does a truck that big disappear?'

'Sorry, Molly,' said Alex, wincing at Molly raising her eyebrow at him. 'I didn't want to be late.'

'That was you?' Verily narrowed her eyes at him from the other side of the rear tray. 'You—whoever the hell you are—almost sucked me under those tyres. I almost suffocated in all that dust.'

'Were you walking, hon?' Molly asked Verily.

'No, I was having a great ride on your scooter, until I swallowed enough sand to make my own Bondi Beach.'

'No need to be so dramatic,' said Alex, shaking his head. 'I thought you were some kid who'd pinched that bike, the way you were wobbling.'

'I was learning! It's not easy riding in that powdery red dirt.'

'It's called bulldust.' *Typical tourist.* 'Most people pull over to let a road train pass on dirt tracks, but you were trying to outrun me. Weren't you?'

Her dainty chin lifted and her lips tightened. She was mad at him—but those bedroom eyes of hers were damned sexy.

He grinned for a moment, then matched princess-drama's frown. 'Welcome to the Territory, Princess, where red dust is part of everyone's daily diet in the dry season. Get used to it—' *Or leave.*

She just sneered at him, digging the soles of her shoes into the dirt.

He shouldn't—but he liked that look.

'You know,' he said, 'those scooters would be lucky if they do eighty clicks, and they weigh less than a road train's tyre with your weight included.'

'Did you just call me fat?'

Hell no! He re-admired the figure he'd seen near-naked, but stopped at her fiery eyes boring into him. 'What I'm trying to say is,' *before I get my face slapped,* 'I'm hauling up to 200 tonnes when loaded, while you're sitting on a postage stamp on wheels. Do the math, sweetheart, of course, you would've got dragged along for the ride.'

'Can we argue on the road, please, Alex,' Molly said, climbing into the cab from the passenger side.

'Yes, Molly.' Alex obediently climbed in and started his ute.

'Who the hell are you, and why should I go anywhere with you?' Verily stood with hands on hips and a focused fire in her eyes.

He *really* liked that look.

'Sorry, hon,' said Molly as she scooted to her spot in the centre, her familiar floral perfume filling the cab. 'This is Alex, who lives in the Picker's Cottage at the back of the property. Alex is managing the mangos this year.'

'Oi, Molly, that's a secret, remember,' mumbled Alex, shifting in the driver's seat, ready to go.

'Pfft, I've never seen the trees looking so healthy.' Molly

waved as if swatting a fly at Alex, then turned to the hottie hovering by the open door. 'Hon, I trust Alex's driving, he's a road train driver who hauls cattle from the stations. The trailers are a rarity.'

'I didn't have time to unload them.' Normally he'd park them up at his dad's, but not today. 'Are we going, or are you staying, Verily?'

'So glad you know my name, when it took half the conversation to learn yours.'

'Of course, I know your name, you're all Molly talked about these past few weeks.'

'And here you are. Now get in, Verily, I don't want to be late.' Molly beckoned from her seat.

'To where?' Verily asked.

'Where else but Elsie Creek, hon,' replied Molly.

'Are you sure *he* won't speed like some maniac?'

'My name is Alex.' *Stuck up city snob!* Although her accent was a bit odd, for an Aussie, it was almost American.

'I trust Alex, he's been driving me for years. You'll be fine,' Molly said, patting the passenger seat.

Verily climbed into the cab and stared straight ahead as if hiding behind her Aunt. They were soon out the driveway in what Alex suspected to be the tensest trip into town ever.

TWO

Verily tried to be nice—but the guy had almost killed her with his truck-storm. Shame he looked so good with his toned chest, muscular shoulders, and with ice-diamond-like blue eyes. He also had strong hands. They were the type that'd make any pitcher proud, she just couldn't stop staring at them.

So, who the hell is he?

And what was so special about this place, that was nothing more than a tiny speck on a map?

They drove past the sign that read *Welcome to Elsie Creek,* where one set of traffic lights stood in the centre of the main street waiting for non-existent pedestrians. There was a small supermarket, a butcher shop, a bakery, a post office next to a craft shop, and a hardware store that was more of a big shed saying drive-thru feed store. What kind of feed? It didn't look like any fast food drive-thru she'd seen before.

Although, they had the cutest little fire-station, reminding her of a doll's house replica behind the shopfronts, all overshadowed by a mighty two-storey pub.

It looked identical to all the other towns she'd driven through to get here. Some, if she blinked, she'd miss. This town was only an extra blink bigger and in the middle of nowhere.

'What makes Elsie Creek a town?' Verily asked to break the silence. 'Why build here?'

'It's a train stop,' replied Alex, keeping a strong grip on the steering wheel while focusing on the bitumen road ahead.

The Stuart Highway stretched out like a long black carpet. To the south, it led to Katherine then onward to Alice Springs and the rest of Australia. North was Darwin city, but once she'd crossed the border into the Northern Territory, it was all this space between a few tiny towns, surrounded by the vast and lonely outback.

'What train?' Verily looked around for train tracks.

'Over that way.' Alex thumbed to his right.

'Alex and his father cart cattle from the outlying stations to the Elsie Creek Railway Station, driving those trucks that nearly sucked you under their tyres,' said Molly.

'Thanks for the reminder, Aunty.' Verily rolled her eyes as her aunt giggled. 'What do you call that kind of truck? A transformer's monster truck?'

'Road train,' replied Alex with a chuckle.

'So, you're a truck driver.'

He frowned at her. 'Anything wrong with that?'

'Did I say there was?' His attitude irritated her, along with his sinful stocky looks that were definitely a danger to her pumping pulse.

Molly leaned forward to cut them off, saying, 'Did you know Elsie Creek started as a train stop for people to get out and stretch their legs?'

'It was just a piss stop,' blurted out Alex. 'Still is.'

'It's not that bad,' Molly said. 'Don't mind Alex, he's just in a mood.'

'Your niece isn't helping.'

She hated to admit it, but Alex was right, Verily wasn't making a good impression with her poor aunt playing peacekeeper in the middle. 'You could say sorry, you know, for covering me in dust.'

Alex arched his eyebrow at her. 'You were on a road and I was driving on the same road that's made of dirt.'

She leaned past her aunt, frowning at Alex. 'Are you kidding?'

'I said sorry.'

'Not to me, you didn't.'

'What am I sorry for? You're alive and sitting here arguing with me, aren't you?'

Her face dropped along with her heart as the prickles squirrelled across her skin. She most certainly was *alive*.

'Now, Alex didn't mean it, hon,' Molly said, rubbing Verily's arm.

Verily hugged herself tighter and stared out the window as the world slowly moved by.

'What didn't I mean? I swear Molly, some days you have your own language,' Alex said, steering them through town.

Verily sighed with relief, Alex didn't know. *Good.*

'Shush you, keep driving.' Molly waved her hand at Alex and put her arm around her niece's shoulders. 'Anyway, Elsie Creek is like most of the towns and rivers around the Top

End, they're named after a woman. There's Adelaide, Victoria, Mary, and Elizabeth Rivers. The Katherine River runs through the town of Katherine. Elsie Creek may seem like a creek in the dry season but she's a river in the wet season. They say, every fifty years she floods.'

'So, what made this woman so special they named the town after her?' Verily asked.

'The first Elsie was the wife of the first railway station manager,' explained Molly. 'Elsie grew watermelons out the back of the station house which she then sold by the slice, to the passengers. She made a killing, and that's how she started the pub, that all began from a tiny roadside stall, then the pub, with the town growing around it.'

'A woman started your town pub?'

'It's still owned by Elsie's great-granddaughter.'

'Who is someone you don't want to mess with,' said Alex.

'Why, ex-girlfriend?' Verily said.

Alex screwed up his nose at her. 'No. It'd be like dating my sister.'

'What is that?' Verily pointed to the wide road where a few dusty utes and assorted four-wheeled drive vehicles were parked in front of the shops. But what looked out of sorts, was the four-legged mound of black fur walking down the centre of the road.

It had black horns bigger than any beast she'd ever seen, with a red hen resting on its broad back. Her eyes widened at the sight of its beefy black sides painted in pink chalk with the words: *Dusty Dingoes Season Begins Today.* 'Is that a cow?'

'That's Cecil,' replied Molly.

Alex slowed down, unwound his window and tapped on the outside of his ute's door. 'Get off the road, ya bloody menace.'

The beast looked up at him as if to give him a nod, then casually clip-clopped in front of them and onto the pavement waving a pink ribbon wrapped around its tail. On its back, the red hen spread out its wings and squawked at Alex.

'What is Cecil?' Verily asked, watching the huge beast pass them by.

'It's Esther's pygmy water buffalo,' replied Molly.

'It's not a pygmy, it's just short,' said Alex, chuckling to himself.

Verily stared at the beast wearing pink paint. 'It's huge. What about that red hen on its back?'

'Who knows where Cecil picked that up from, hon, but they're always together.'

'It's a crazy bird too. I heard it took on the ranger the other day,' said Alex.

'As in a council dog catcher?' Verily asked.

'There's no dog catcher here, only park rangers. Kakadu National Park is just over there.' Alex thumbed to their left as he resumed driving them through town.

'Aunt Molly—'

'You can stop with the Aunt, you make me sound older than I am, hon. Molly will do.' Molly patted Verily's hand while Alex smirked at the road ahead.

Molly looked amazing for her age. Tall and slender, wearing a tailored blue dress, her hair a modern blonde blunt bob. Her aunt's glamorous style didn't fit this place of outback dust.

'Molly, why is there a water buffalo walking down the main street of town?'

'Cecil is our town's walking billboard. We wouldn't want him confused with being a feral buffalo so Esther puts ribbons on him. She likes her art.'

'Esther's crazy,' mumbled Alex.

'Aren't you mates with her grandson?' Molly asked.

'Yep, and he'll tell you she's nuts, too,' replied Alex, 'but Esther is colourful, I'll give her that.'

'Don't mind our town-downer over here.' Molly patted his arm, then faced Verily and said, 'Everyone knows everyone's business around here, which can be both a good and a bad thing.'

'Everyone knows everything?' Verily asked.

'Yes.' Molly nodded, then widened her eyes. 'But I didn't tell them about you, I know how shy you are—not that anyone listens to me anyway. Look, there's my shop.' Molly pointed to the hairdressing salon next to the Post Office. It seemed to be one big building with a craft shop attached.

Oh great! Verily had somehow, again, found herself in the land of crafts and cooking—when she did neither. How was she expected to fit in?

Story of her life.

Good thing she was only here for a holiday.

'You're free to visit anytime. Shame you're not a hairdresser, I'd give you a job,' Molly said, reaching for the ends of Verily's hair. 'We'll do something about these split ends. I'll give you a proper pampering with the girls at the shop.'

'I'm okay.' Verily never bothered, it was easier to wear it in a ponytail to hide her helmet hair. Why fuss when make-up sweated off in seconds, and panda eyes were not an attractive look, especially when she appeared half asleep most of the time.

Then again, she was finding a whole new way of life she'd been forced into. 'Um, thank you for the offer. I could do with something new.'

'That's the spirit, hon.'

'What do you do?' Alex asked Verily.

'I'm on holiday.' What could she say? That she was recovering from life-changing surgery? Trying to avoid depression? Searching for answers of who she was and what she wanted out of her new life? Because all of her goals and dreams had been lost the day her arm was almost torn free from her body.

Yet she'd give ten arms, or her life for the others to have survived, instead of being one of the few left standing.

Verily swallowed down her tears and stared at the side mirror that reflected the black water buffalo covered in pink paint with a matching ribbon at the end of its tail. It was so ridiculous it made her smile. 'What are the Dusty Dingoes?'

'You'll see soon enough,' replied Molly.

'Is it a dingo playground where they do tricks like you see at dog shows?'

'No, but they are around,' said Alex. 'So please, don't let the chooks out at night or we'll lose the lot.'

'What about that hen?' Verily craned around to point back at the red feathered bird riding high on the back of the buffalo.

'It's the safest spot up there, I reckon.' Alex chuckled, and his lazy grin made her breath catch. 'Who'd want to tango with a buffalo and his lady?'

'Like most men around here with the manners of a bully buff,' scoffed Molly.

'Are you still single, Molly?' Verily couldn't remember her uncle.

'Widowed. Don't worry, hon, I like how I live. Not how the typical male around here would expect me to play housekeeper if they moved in with me. Bah! It's my house, why should I clean up after them.'

'You don't clean up after me?' Alex said.

'That's because I've trained you well, hon.' Molly patted his muscular arm as Alex drove them into a large dusty carpark. 'Well, here we are. You're gonna love the girls, Verily, and they'll love you too. Welcome to our town's sporting arena,' announced Molly.

Verily peered through the insect splattered, dusty windscreen to a large field and pointed to the white railing that ran around a large oval. 'It looks like a racetrack?'

'It's where we have our annual picnic-race day and rodeo,' explained Molly. 'It's our footy field in the wet season when the monsoons help the grass grow.'

'Isn't football a winter sport they're playing now, down south?'

'Most of our footy players are busy working the musters

or on shift for the local mine,' Molly said. 'Are you going to play this year, Alex?'

'Dunno? Depends on the mangos and you'll want a hand with your dragon fruit this year.'

'The dragon fruits are looking fabulous. Thank you for fixing the trellis.'

'No worries. I checked the irrigation too.'

What the hell is dragon fruit?

And who was this Alex, to suck-up to her aunt like that?

How come her Aunt never mentioned Alex before?

Verily gritted her teeth, straightening in her seat, it shouldn't matter. It wasn't her place to interfere when she was only here for a holiday.

Verily peered up at the cloudless sky, it was like summer with its mild weather. 'So, this is your winter?'

'Dry season,' replied Molly. 'The wet season is our summer.'

Verily felt every part the tourist when she asked, 'What's the difference?'

'Heat. Humidity. Hell.' Alex mumbled, parking the ute.

'Don't scare the girl,' said Molly, patting Alex on the arm. 'Dry season is now where we have no rain for months. It's the best weather, so nice and cool without the humidity. It's like an Aussie southern summer — which is our winter.'

'Okay.' Not that Verily had seen an Aussie summer since a child. 'What about spring?'

'Mango Season,' said Alex. 'Also known as the *Troppo Season* where people go loopy.'

'Is that true?' Verily asked Molly. She was here to see

her aunt, not the guy who lived on the property like some caretaker.

'It's called the *build-up* also known as the *Troppo Season*, where people do the craziest things that time of the year,' said Molly. 'We blame it on the intense heat and humidity, but it all settles down when the rains come.'

'I see.' Nope, Verily didn't have a clue, and nodded towards the racetrack that outlined a drying oval. 'So, what do you use the dust bowl for when the men aren't playing football?'

'It's—'Alex started.

'Why don't you see for yourself, hon. Let's go.' Molly opened the door and half pushed Verily out of her seat.

'What's the rush?'

'We're late,' said Alex, taking the esky off the ute's back tray.

Verily had to admire his biceps and his strong hand-grip that made her bite her lower lip.

Molly popped open her blue and white polka dotted umbrella and hooked her arm through Verily's. 'Come along, Verily. Stop daydreaming.'

'I was not.' The heat rose in her cheeks as her aunt led them toward the ancient wooden grandstand, its shade stretched across the greying grass.

'What the hell?' Verily's sneakers skidded to a stop, creating a tiny dust]'cloud that soon dispersed with the breeze.

'What's wrong now?' Alex put down the esky by the bleachers and headed back to the ute. 'I swear your three favourite words are: *What the hell.*'

'Are not.'

'Are too. They're the first words you said to me.'

'Because you were perving on me in the corridor.'

'You were standing there in your underwear and that was…' Alex stopped and sighed. Tilting his head, his eyes followed her figure as if picturing her naked, all while wearing that lazy grin of his.

He'd done that twice now.

Verily wrapped her arms around herself. 'I didn't expect some random guy to walk through my aunt's house when she said she lived alone.' She was used to walking around in various states of dress in changerooms filled with women only. 'Do you mind?'

'Not at all.'

'What the h—' She caught herself. *The prick was right.*

His grin grew. 'You were saying?' Alex chuckled to himself as he carried the water coolers to rest beside the esky, then returned to his ute.

She frowned at the irritating cretin before her. Why was he affecting her so much?

If he didn't speak, Verily could watch Alex haul cargo all day with his strong hand grip, and that great arse in those jeans.

'Come along, hon. I want you to meet the girls.' Molly tugged on her arm, again. 'We could use someone like you.'

'Are you playing, Verily?' Alex asked, lifting a large duffel bag from the back tray.

'Playing what?' Half dragged by Molly, Verily

approached the barrier that bordered the large open field. One woman had a long tape measure, followed by another woman with a spray can painting a white line and dropping white plastic mats on the corners.

Verily recognised it straight away.

It was a diamond in the dust.

'Softball.'

Shit.

* * *

'At least you didn't call it baseball, so you've got that going for you.' Alex spotted the colour draining from Verily's face. 'Hey, I was only joking. Are you okay?'

'I… I…' Verily stepped backwards and stumbled.

'Hey, steady on.' He caught her and felt her trembling. 'What's wrong?'

'Molly, you knew. Why?' Verily savagely wiped at a stray tear.

'I thought it'd be good for you, hon.'

Alex stepped back, adjusting his baseball cap while looking at the pair of women. 'Molly, what's going on?'

'It's softball,' Verily said, pointing to the oval.

'It's just a game. So what?' He shrugged.

Verily whirled around with pure fire in those eyes. It was one dangerously sexy look, except for the tears that tore into him.

'What?' He stepped back from the anger emanating from her in invisible waves.

'Softball was never *just* a game. It was my life. *Was…*'

Verily turned on her heel and stormed off.

'Where are you going, Verily?' Molly called out.

'Back to your place.'

'It's a two-hour hike from here, hon.'

Alex leaned on the corner of his back tray, watching Verily's hips sway in those sports pants of hers. They cupped her behind beautifully.

Verily stopped and looked up and down the dirt road. 'Which way?'

Alex chuckled. 'Stick by the ute and I'll take you both back when I'm done with practise.'

'ALEX LANDERS!' The voice boomed like a shotgun blast echoing through the near-empty carpark.

'Great, I've ticked-off the coach already.' Alex hoisted his duffel higher on his shoulder and looked at the two women he'd brought with him. Something was going on between them, but he had enough of his own baggage without adding more—especially over someone on a holiday. Still, she was Molly's niece. 'Molly, will you and Verily be okay?'

'We'll be fine,' Molly said, twirling her bright umbrella and grabbed her niece by the arm. 'Come along, Verily. You're not playing, just observing.'

'I don't want to be here.'

'Well, you are.'

'You tricked me.'

'We need you.'

'I don't play anymore.'

'Neither do I,' said Molly, dragging Verily to the bleachers.

Alex watched the two women argue like mother and daughter in hushed voices.

'ALEX LANDERS! DO YOU WANT AN INVITATION COURIERED BY WHISTLING KITE?'

'No, coach.' He rolled his eyes at yet another person telling him what to do. Why did he have to promise to play for another season? Yet, he obediently took his place on the field.

THREE

Trapped on the bleachers, Verily hugged her knees to her chest. With the sun a red sinking fireball in the cloudless sky, it was too risky wandering on an unfamiliar outback track in the dark. 'This isn't fair.'

Molly patted Verily's hand and switched her umbrella to rest on the other shoulder. 'Listen, hon, your father and I thought this would help you.'

'I'm only here because Dad wanted his couch back.' And to re-define her normality in life.

'That's not true.'

'If I'd known this was going to happen, I wouldn't have come.' She nodded to the group of women gathered on the field wearing softball gloves as the only sign of a uniform. It made her own palm itch, missing the feel of leather.

'Did you know your mother loved this game? We played every season. This year's team has such a great bunch of girls playing. See that sexy one?' Molly pointed to the third base.

'In the hot pink short-shorts?' Was Alex perving at those hot-pants on the woman slathering oil on her long legs? No, he seemed preoccupied putting out practise gear.

'Tess is here to work on her tan. She works at the Post

Office, along with her craft-mad family. Then you've got Bella in the outfield, she's our resident stoner.'

A woman in loose cargo pants, boots, a tie-dyed shirt and straw hat, dragged a large hessian bag onto the field. Bella looked like a farmer, not someone about to play softball.

'What do you mean a stoner?' Was Bella going to pull out a bong on the field?

'Bella grows hemp for clothing.'

'So, there is another industry in Elsie Creek beside mangos, cattle, and mining.'

'We had a few banana plantations, but we're still under quarantine from the banana freckle thingy. We have the tourists from the train too, hon, which is Lucy's thing. Shy thing she is, it's good to see they got her out here again this year. Lucy helps out at the pub and does the train's tea-house for lunches on train days. Then you've got Karen Kimble, our rabbit-mummy. She's our shortstop.'

'The what mummy?'

'She's got seven boys and finally got her baby girl. We think she's trying to breed her own softball team. Karen insists on playing, she loves the break. The money we raised from last year's Rosella Festival paid for all that new equipment the Kimble's mob of littlies are playing on. We're hoping it'll attract more marvellous mummies to join us.' Molly pointed her brolly at the children playing on the swings, a slippery dip, and a small wooden fort. 'Which it has as we now have Kat Jones, don't know if she's taking on her new husband's name. I must ask her. But it's her daughter, Kaytlan in the tutu, she started a new trend in town that little girl has.

It's so cute, all these kids in tutus and none of them dance.'

'Who?'

'Kat, Katlyn's mother, married to Kyle.'

'That's a lot of K's.'

'All part of the Kat and Kyle show. Kat's a brilliant handywoman and artiste who only used to stay for summer holidays. She's the niece to my marvellous friends Frank and Bea. Sadly, Frank passed away not that long ago, although he stubbornly stuck around for the wedding, everyone cried.'

'For the wedding?'

'For Frank too. It was what he always wanted, to give Kat away, and he did. Sadly, the poor man passed and we all miss him.'

Verily just sat there unsure what to say, she knew all about the burden of loss, as the breeze carried a fine layer of red dust across the deserted bleaches.

Molly reached over and gave Verily's hand a squeeze while staring out to the field where more women entered the grounds. 'Oh good, Jenny's here too. She's our bush clinic's head nurse, as the centre fielder. Then we've got the jillaroo sisters, Amanda and Melinda, everyone calls them Mandy and Mindy. They're our first and second basemen. They drive two hours to do this, mad keen they are.'

'Two hours?'

'That's one way, hon.'

'Four hours for a practise? That's commitment.' But then it took almost an hour—while arguing with Alex—to come and watch from the deserted grandstand.

'Mandy and Mindy come here for the female company

because there are no other women on their family station. I think they also do the mail and stores run for the stations in their area while in town.'

The sisters wore dusty denim jeans, boots, and long-sleeved shirts. Wide-brimmed cowboy hats shaded light brown hair that trailed down their back in matching plaits. They looked like they should be on horseback whirling a stockwhip, instead of tossing softballs on the field.

'Then there's Speedy, our team's pitcher,' Molly said, pointing to the centre of the diamond.

'Who?' Verily narrowed her eyes at the petite lady, chewing her nails on the pitcher's mound.

'Adrianna, but everyone knows her as Speedy. She works at the feed store when it's not fruit-picking season.'

Verily watched Alex playfully nudge the smaller pitcher on the field. Was Speedy Alex's girlfriend?

Yet, she just couldn't stop admiring the way those jeans cupped his backside. His long easy gait toward the home plate was breathtaking. His tight t-shirt showed off his muscles as he grabbed a set of long leg pads and a helmet from his duffel bag. 'Why is Alex out there?'

'He's our catcher and number one home-run hitter. They're all good hitters, but lousy chuckers.'

'Chuckers?' Verily raised her eyebrow at her aunt.

'Y'know, tossing the ball around.'

The team tossed the softball like it was a paperweight. 'So, it's a mixed softball team?'

'Yes. We have a few men who play when they can, but Alex became our catcher before he hit puberty.'

'So, you're close to this guy?'

'Not that close, hon, I'm no cougar.' Molly giggled, patting down her perfectly styled blonde hair, highlighted by the blue of her umbrella. 'Alex's mother was our neighbour and a close friend. When she died, Alex stayed with me for school terms, then he'd be with his father in the truck for holidays. His father has high hopes for Alex to become a partner in their trucking company. Neville will be devastated if Alex doesn't take the job.'

'Why wouldn't Alex want it if he's driving those big things now?' Why should she care?

'Alex is a homebody like his mother. But the boy didn't have a choice. You see, when he was young, on school holidays he'd spend all his time sleeping in the truck with his dad. Kind of like you being on the road all the time with your dad. I don't know how Alex does it, working three jobs.'

'Three jobs?' How does he have time to play softball then?

'Alex is busy driving, cleaning up the Picker's Cottage, and it's his first season managing the mangos and then there's the rest of the farm to manage, too.'

Yay for the outback's Superman, Alex—not! 'Why don't you manage them? It's your farm, isn't it?'

'I don't do manual labour,' Molly said with an eye roll, 'I prefer to just lease the orchard. I've let Alex do it this year.'

'Isn't hairdressing manual work?'

'But it's done in air-conditioning and out of this relentless sunshine. Make sure you wear a hat and sunscreen, our outback sun is very ageing, you know.' Molly daintily dabbed at the side of her eyes as if tapping the minimal wrinkles away.

'So, you don't live on your own?' Verily asked.

'I do—well now I have you here, finally.'

Verily winced, she'd been too busy to visit, until now.

'Alex lives out the back. Don't worry, he won't be a bother.'

'I'm only here for a holiday, so it won't bother me. Although, I'm hoping you might tell me more about my mother.'

'That's why I've put you in your mother's old room. In the closet, you'll find her scrapbooks of her school life. Rose loved her craft stuff; she was always making something. She handmade the quilt on your bed.'

'I didn't know she liked crafty stuff. Do you have a hobby?'

'Playing with people's hair is my creative outlet. What about you?'

'Don't have one.'

'Why not?'

'We never kept stuff that didn't fit in the suitcase.' Just like she never got attached to places and people, always ready to move on.

'You can unpack now, the farm is your home, hon.'

'No, it's not.'

'Yes, it is,' said Molly, with a nod and a twirl of her umbrella. 'When your grandparents passed away, your mother and I inherited the farm. Now you have your mother's share. Didn't your father tell you?'

'Dad never mentioned much about this place, except to tell me I was born in this town where mum lived her whole life.' What would it be like to grow up and live in the same place all your life?

'I bet it was because of all the wonderful memories of this place. Memories your father didn't want to share,' said Molly.

'Right…' Memories so good, her dad never talked about them—ever.

'Your father loved your mother so much and they were so happy together, they were that lovey-dovey-cutesy couple that made you want to retch.'

'Really?'

'Ah-huh. They lived down in the cottage where you took your first steps.'

'Why did we leave?'

'Because everything was a reminder of your mother. Your poor father kept expecting Rose to walk through the orchard, he was so heartbroken. I think he would've given up if it wasn't for you. I can show you Rose's gravesite if you like? Your baby brother is there too.'

'Not today.' Verily had a sudden urge to call her father and tell him how much she loved the man who'd given up so much for her. She also wanted to hit him with a whole load of questions too. 'I can't own half your house, Molly.'

'Your name is on the Trust, where we share two hundred hectares.'

'In mangos?'

'A quarter is. Besides the dragon fruit—'

'What is dragon fruit?'

'It's a tropical cactus fruit that produces these wonderful pink dragon eggs. It's a superfood, more powerful than Kale, and so much prettier. It's also higher in Vitamin C and lots of other fabulous stuff. More importantly, they're full of these wonderful anti-ageing properties.' Again, Molly dabbed at the corner of her eyes as if to pat away her non-existent crow's feet. 'As for the rest of the property, it gets leased for agistment. Alex says we should plant crops, hops, and feedstuff or something. Now you're here, you can help me decide.'

'I know nothing about farming'

'Have you ever been on a farm?'

'Sure, all kinds. When I got billeted out, I went to this horse ranch in Texas, an orange orchard in Florida, a sheep farm in Ireland. I even did rice paddies in Japan.' Now here she was visiting a mango farm surrounded by cattle country in the middle of the outback.

'I loved my annual holidays, travelling the globe to watch you play. Canada was too cold for me and I've never seen so many mountains, compared to this place.' Molly waved over the wide-open flatlands surrounding them.

'Dad still lives near the border, with his family.'

'You know, you're my only family.'

'Am I?'

Molly put her arm around Verily. 'There are a few distant cousins who live in the southern cities, but if you treat me nice, I may leave you my half of the farm too.'

'I don't know how to manage a house or a farm. I only

know…' Again, her eyes were drawn back to the diamond in the dust.

A diamond that used to shine for her.

Now, it only brought heartache and a sense of loss.

'I don't know anything anymore, Molly.'

Molly gave Verily a squeeze around her shoulders. 'Oh honey, you know me and there are those magnificent women on this team, too.'

'Do they play for a trophy?' Did Verily have the heart to befriend another team?

'The Rosella Cup. It's part of this huge town festival we have, all about Rosellas. You'll love it. I think you're flying back to the States a few days after it.'

Verily shrugged, surprised she was having her holidays over another softball season. *How did that happen?* 'Where are the other softball teams?'

'They come from neighbouring towns. Some travel six hours to play.'

'From where? Mars.'

'Tennant Creek, Mataranka, Victoria River. We had a team travel from Alice Springs one year and we played there too, it was brilliant.'

'How often do you play?'

'Once a month. We're not as organised as the city. Sometimes the towns don't have enough players to make a team, like Gove. Sadly, now their mine's shutting down, so we don't think we'll see another team from there again. We only do it for fun. It's not like we're going to the Olympics now, are we hon,' Molly said, nudging Verily with her elbow.

'No, I guess not.' Verily peered at the field surrounded by scrublands stretching further than the eye could see. A rodeo ring stood to one side with railed stables that made up part of the horseracing track. On the inside, a set of Aussie-rules football goal posts stood on either end, and in the centre was the newly painted softball field.

Verily pointed at the wave of white galahs that flew in to cover the oval like a dotted blanket. 'Why is that woman feeding the birds?'

'Bella gets free grass seeds,' replied Molly.

'If she's the stoner, what kind of grass is that?'

'Bella's theory is, if it survives the birds who eat it, it'll then be pooped out in perfect fertilised packages. Then the rains come and voila—a perfect footy field for her husband and sons to play on. Also, Bella swears if she feeds them here, they'll steer clear from her property when she's planting her hemp.'

'Why don't you water the softball field now? The sport can be played on grass, you know.'

'We used to have a caretaker who lived in his van out the side. He'd paint the rails and keep the gardens and lawns in top-nick. He'd be grumbling in his grave at the sight of the place.' Molly dusted the peeling paint off the small barrier fence. 'We should have a working-bee for the Festival.'

Tall grass, with seed tops grouped like spear-heads, lined the edge of the field where a light tan dog peeked out, it blended perfectly with the long grass stems. Verily pointed to the animal. 'Is that a dingo?'

'Yep. Just like the team's name, The Dusty Dingoes,'

replied Molly. 'I'll take that as a good sign for the upcoming season, shall I?'

'I'm surprised your town hasn't tamed a dingo for a team mascot.'

'We did, a long time ago. But Cecil, the water buffalo you met earlier, he has that honour as our town's billboard.'

'Ah-huh.' What was this place, some alien planet of dust?

She turned her attention back to the team. They weren't practising softball. It was more like hens scratching in the sand, with wild dogs on the perimeter, watching galahs being fed like a day in the park!

A sports whistle screamed sending the flocks skywards and the dingo disappeared into the tall spear-grass.

With a death grip on her whistle, in the centre field stood a short, stocky woman. Her squinty eyes were hidden beneath a mono-brow highlighted by a yellow duck-bill sun-visor. Her black hair ran in a thick shiny plait down her back, like a horse's tail hanging way past her bum. She wore a baggy t-shirt draped over a pair of glow-in-the-dark pink board shorts with orange and brown striped football socks that blended into her black thongs to complete the look.

Verily cringed. 'Who is that?'

Molly frowned. 'The coach.'

'Scary.'

'She is. *The cheat*,' Molly spat out, spinning her umbrella like a propeller—while seated in the shade.

'Friend of yours?'

'Never. Ever. Again.' Molly lifted her chin higher,

pursing her lips into a tight line.

'And does this coach have a name?'

'Bitch is good.'

Verily giggled as she hooked her thumb towards the coach who'd make dried paint curl up in fright. 'I understand that coaches have to be hard-arses but...'

'ALL RIGHT YOU MONGREL MOB, LISTEN UP,' hollered the coach. 'TIME FOR PLAYING PRINCESSES IS OVER!'

'Do they volunteer to play?' Verily half-whispered to avoid the coach's death glare.

'We pay to play to cover umpire fees and stuff,' replied Molly, rummaging around in her esky for a soft drink can, then wiped off the excess ice from its sides.

Verily grinned at the day-mare with a whistle. 'You're kidding. They're paying to get shouted at like that?'

'Oh, you wait and see, she's just warming up,' said Molly, screwing her nose at the field.

'Who? Why was it so hard to name people in this town? I can't call everyone *mate*.'

'So sorry, I forget you know no one.'

'Story of my life,' Verily mumbled.

'That's Agnes Pickett. Menopause has been unkind to that cheating wench.' Molly cracked open the soft drink can and drank a few good mouthfuls, then from her handbag, she produced a shiny pink diamanté covered hip flask and added a decent dash. 'It's vodka. I'm not driving.'

'Why are you here when you don't play?'

'I'm retired with a dodgy tossing elbow and I don't run,

so I keep Alex company on the drive. I'm also here to offer support as the secretary to the team and to the Rosella Festival Committee.'

'Dad always ended up being team treasurer.'

'Is he still an accountant?'

'Only for his courier business.'

'How come?'

'It's the easiest job Dad could get, especially with us moving around all the time. He used to drive our bus…I wish he'd driven us that day…' She rubbed her arm feeling the foreign steel pins that held her shoulder and arm together.

'I'm so sorry about your stepsister. Were you close?'

'She was my best friend.'

'I was like that with your mother. Days like this remind me of her.' Molly sipped her drink and sighed with a dreamy smile, staring at the softballers. 'When we were young, we'd count down the sleeps to the start of the softball season. Rose would reek of this oil she used to rub down her glove.'

'Was my mother any good at softball?'

'Nothing near your level, hon. The team could really use you. Our last star player was Agnes, the coach who's a real stickler for the rules—for *a cheat*.'

'I don't play anymore.'

'But it'd do you good to have fun with the game again.'

It was never just a game—it was her everything. 'I don't have a catcher anymore.'

'What?'

'My sister was my catcher. There's no great pitcher without the perfect catcher.' Verily missed her more than anything. 'I'm going for a walk to call Dad. How long does practise take?'

'An hour. How long did you practise for?'

'Too long.' And for what? Dust collecting knick-knacks she never saw.

Verily kicked at a stone that tumbled in the red dirt as she turned her back to the field. A familiar whack of a ball belted by a bat echoed behind her like a rifle blast. It was soon followed by the slap of leather against leather that she recognised as the ball being caught in the glove. She used to love that sound of the ball safe in the catchers' mitt and the umpire shouting *strike*.

Sounds and sensations she used to dream about—now they were the start of her nightmares.

How could she ever be expected to play a game that had almost killed her?

FOUR

Music played in the shed disguising the creak of the shifting corrugated roof, as a cool breeze weaved in from the orchard, carrying a fine layer of red dust across the cleaned concrete. At the large bench, Alex lined up a row of empty beer bottles and started to measure out the sugar.

'What are you doing?'

'What the—?' Alex knocked the bottle. It slapped and tinkled as he tried to catch it, spilling sugar crystals across his clean floor. '*Damn.*'

Verily gave a sly sideways grin as she approached the bench. 'Sorry. Didn't mean to scare you.'

'Didn't expect anyone down here.'

'Why, is this area out of bounds? Molly said you're managing the mango orchard or something?'

He winced. 'Ah, we don't tell too many people I'm managing Molly's mango trees.'

'Why, because you're a truck driver?'

He frowned at her. 'You make that sound like it's a second-rate job.'

'I don't mean to.'

'Sure, you don't, *princess.*'

'Ugh, as if. My father owns a courier company, and I used to drive for him in the off-season, or whenever he needed a hand. So, no, I'm no princess, *mate*. I'll admit I know nothing about mangos, but I assume it has nothing to do with putting sugar into empty beer bottles,' she said, pointing at his bottles.

'I'm brewing beer. Craft beer.'

'Why?'

'To make my hair curly—what do you think?'

'That's a lot of beer, so you must be after the all-over curl then?' She nodded toward the boxes of beer lining the inner walls of the shed. 'Ever hear of perming? I'm sure Molly can help you with that in her shop.'

Cheeky wench. He grinned at her as he tried to concentrate on his measurements. 'I want to create a micro-brewery.'

'You really must like the stuff.'

'I got sick of the same yeasty brew they sell at the pub and made my own.'

'What has that got to do with mangos?'

'I'm hoping for a bumper crop where the profits will pay for my micro-brewery system, then I won't have to do this fiddly stuff.'

'Here, in the middle of an orchard.' Verily waved to the trees covered in fresh green shoots that surrounded the shed. From the other side of the table, she looked over his simplistic operation set up like a factory line—for one.

'It's a good buffer for when I brew.'

'What do you mean by that?'

'In case of exploding bottles, and fermenting yeast does

attract flies. I'd better clean up this sugar before the ants move in.' He grabbed the dustpan and broom and swept up the crystals.

'Are you talking from experience?'

'I've had a few misses, but I'm getting closer to the perfect ale.' He washed his hands in the sink and frowned at the large stack of empty bottles waiting to be filled. He'd only just started. 'Stuff this.' He dropped the sugared bottle in with the sterilising solution, then sterilised a tall bucket and poured in the sugar. Using a sterilised hose, he syphoned the wort from the fermenter into the bucket.

'I thought you drove trucks?' Verily asked from the other side of the table.

'I help my old man with his business. But...' He sighed, stirring the wort as he checked his brew blend.

'Would you rather be playing farming-brewmaster?'

'I've got my diploma as a brewmaster to prove it.' It took years to get, but it was a necessary part of his long-term plan.

'Is that like a beer sommelier?'

'I'm not a wine waiter, I'm a brewmaster. Or, are you like every other Aussie bloke in the pub who are all bloody beer connoisseurs?

'I know nothing.' She shrugged.

He admired her honesty even if she did say it with a shrug, and she shrugged a lot. 'Are you going to today's game?'

She shrugged.

'You haven't gone to any practises, and we could do

with someone else out there as a backup.'

'What did Molly tell you?'

'Why don't you tell me yourself, so it's not second-hand like most of the tales told in this town.'

Again, she shrugged.

Alex sighed. 'You have this annoying habit of not saying anything when people talk to you. Remember, you came over here, and oi, don't blab what I said about the mangos and this beer operation.'

'Why not? Are you ashamed of it?'

His head tilted as he looked at the bottles. 'I won't be judged until I've got it right.'

'Fair enough.'

'You're kidding. No snarky remark, nothing?'

'Who am I going to tell, when I see no one.'

'What do you do in the house all day?'

'Molly kept some of my mother's things and I've been going through them.'

'Rose died a few years before my mother, I don't remember her.'

'I don't remember you.'

'I don't remember you either. But I knew whenever you sent a postcard or Christmas card to Molly. It's good you're here for her, she's thrilled to have you around.'

'Why? I'm this third wheel of nothing around the place. I have no idea what to do without getting in the way.'

'You can help with this if you want?'

'And do what?'

'Can you cook?'

'No.'

'You're kidding?'

She shrugged. 'I can cook two-minute noodles or toast. Most of the time I ate out or stayed with families that cooked for me.'

He lifted the last of the amber liquid from the glass fermenter and into the bucket while he stirred it gently with a long paddle. This was a much simpler way. 'Where?'

'Japan was my last place, and I was in the States for a long time.'

That explained her slight American accent. 'Doing what?'

She shrugged.

'Why do you do that? It's really annoying.'

'Because I can.'

He winced. *I'm such an idiot!* 'I'm sorry. I saw the scars on your shoulder. Didn't mean to…' He sighed and put down the hose. He deserved that fierce frown of hers, even if they were arguing, again. Which was unusual, when he got on with everyone, mainly because he avoided confrontations if he could.

But he had to make more of an effort because this was Molly's niece and he adored Molly. 'Look, can we start again, please?'

'Why?'

'Technically, I think you're my landlady.'

Her eyes widened as she grinned as if she liked the thought of having the power to evict him. 'Oh, really?'

'And we're neighbours. So…' He dusted his hands on

his shirt and held it out. 'Hi, my name is Alex Landers. I pretend at being a truck driver hauling steak during the day, while I dream of being a brewmaster and snobby beer connoisseur after hours. Now it's your turn.'

She grinned wider at him as her eyes caught the sunlight; it made his heart warm. Her hand in his was so small and soft, yet incredibly strong. As he clasped it, an electrical hum ran beneath his skin, squirrelling a pleasure-punch all the way up his arm. It was a whole new experience for him.

'Hi Alex, I'm Verily Wayfaren.'

'Verily is an unusual name?'

'It was meant to be Verity, but it was a typo on the birth certificate that stuck.'

They shared a grin as he kept holding her hand. It felt so natural. 'I bet you got called names because of it?'

'Only the usual on-field sledging, but I was okay with that.'

'Verily means truly. Doesn't it?'

'How do you know?'

He was so tempted to shrug but just held her hand. 'And...'

'And what?'

'Job? Work-life skills?'

'I'm in-between jobs.' She tugged her hand free and rubbed her shoulder.

'Is the shoulder thing recent?'

'A few months back, yes.'

'Okay, I won't ask. If you're looking for something to do, I could use a hand—if they're clean. But all I can offer by way of payment is a beer once this lot is done.' He liked holding her hand, but he shouldn't. He'd never bothered holding anyone's hands before.

Not to mention this was Molly's niece who was only here on holiday. Even if the short time span was tempting, he didn't want to complicate things. He liked his life simple and stress-free from all female-family-drama. 'I'll make this simple, it's a yes or no to assist.'

'Sure.' She rolled up her sleeves and washed her hands in the sink. 'What do I do?'

'We're bottling without spilling, so don't rush it.' He was surprised she'd agreed to help. 'It's a new recipe, so let's hope these bottles don't explode from gas or end up like flat lolly-water.'

'I didn't know there's so much sugar in beer.'

'There's little in the beer itself, but I'm aiming for a fruity IPA this time. I've got this batch of organic sugar-free variety in that fermenter I want to bottle next. I've been experimenting with local bush honey for that unique flavour. Although, I reckon this might be too sweet. I prefer the sour IPA myself. What's your favourite brew?'

'I wasn't aware there was such a specialty to beer. What is an IPA?'

Alex had to admire her honesty and held up a bottle to explain. 'This is an India pale ale, a beefed-up hoppy styled beer that has more flavour. Are you a wine person?'

'I rarely drink. Couldn't.'

'Why? Are you allergic to alcohol?'

'I was always in training, but we had our benders. Shots

were a specialty.'

'Training, for what?'

'Um…' Her teeth gnawed on her bottom lip.

'Don't make me Google your name, now I know it.'

'Is that how you know what my name means?'

Busted. Turning his back to her, he tapped the end of the syphon hose free from the emptied fermenter and dropped it into the sterilising solution. He pulled out another hose and dropped its skinny end into the bucket he'd syphoned his wort into, turned its tiny tap and began to pour it into the bottles. 'Here, you take over while I get the bottles from the oven.'

'What do I do?'

'Lay the hose on the bottom of the empty bottle so it doesn't cause a head, fill it up, and stop a finger width from the top. I'll do the capping.' He passed the hose to her and showed her how to man the tap. Satisfied, he transferred a tray of sterilised bottles from the oven onto the cooling racks. The next set of bottles went into the oven, setting the timer on his tablet. With any luck, he'd get both batches bottled today.

'You've got me curious about what you did before you came here?' He'd prefer to hear her story first hand.

'Softball,' she whispered.

'What did you say?'

She cleared her throat and croaked, 'Softball.'

'You played softball?'

She shrugged, and he arched his eyebrow at her.

So she shrugged again.

He frowned harder.

She shrugged as her grin grew, shrugging again, and again—just to tick him off.

Instead, he laughed at her grin and had a sudden need to make her smile all the time. 'What was your position?'

'Pitcher.'

'Were you any good?'

'I dunno, some people said I was,' she said with such a low voice. 'Not anymore.' Verily poured the wort into the bottles and stopped it at the top. She then moved onto the next one and didn't spill a drop of his precious brew.

Good girl. 'Your hands are nice and steady.'

She shrugged.

'Is it because of your shoulder, you don't play?'

She shrugged.

He frowned.

'I'm retired.'

'Thank you, for replying. So, how good were you?'

Her face reddened as she lowered her head and focused on bottling his beer.

'Well, if you won't tell me your side of the story, I'll find out myself.' He snatched his tablet off the bench and typed in her name. 'Bloody hell—'

'HEY!'

'Well, you won't answer my questions. Blimey, Olympics. Did you get gold?'

'Bronze in Beijing that was the last Olympics they had for Softball.'

'How old were you?'

'I'd just turned seventeen.'

'World championship winner...' Then he frowned at the images of a bus crash with the headline *Women's softball team killed*. He dumped the tablet face down onto the bench. 'Sorry, I shouldn't have done that.' At least not in front of her.

'So, you've spotted the accident's headlines.'

He nodded as he picked up one of her filled bottles, put on an aluminium cap, then pulled down the handles of the bottler to punch the bottle cap on top. He stored it in an empty crate, then repeated the process with the next one as Verily resumed filling the bottles. 'I was with my mum when she died in a car accident.'

'I'm sorry,' she whispered, but he heard her. It wasn't a *sorry* people tell a stranger; this was a genuine sorry he read in her eyes. She didn't ask about the details, not like the others, and that was such a rare gesture it spoke volumes to him.

'I'd snuck out of school to watch the cattle getting loaded onto the train,' he said. 'I saw all these cattlemen cracking their stockwhips and the dust created from over a thousand head of beef, it was amazing to watch. It was like this whole tide of cattle shifting the way water spills over the riverbank when a boat cuts downstream.'

'I've never seen that many cattle.'

'Now it's all I see. Back then, those things were the holy grail, the backbone to this town, and Dad's job.' He punched down another cap, slid the bottle into the crate, grabbed the next one and repeated the action. 'At the rate we're going, we'll put this batch to bed early.'

'Glad to help,' she said with a smile.

He almost sighed at that smile, but it wasn't quite

shining in her eyes like he'd seen before. He also wanted to show her he understood, in his own simple way. 'My mum had this mini-car she and Molly used to dress up for the Easter bonnet parade at school.'

'Sounds like fun.'

'It was,' he said, grinning at the memory. 'They'd park it in the middle of the school oval and we'd try to squeeze as many kids into it as we could. We were going to break the world record.'

'How'd you go?'

'There weren't enough kids in the town to make a quarter of the record's numbers, but we all fit into the car.' He smiled with her. 'Anyway, that same day I'd snuck off and there I was on the fence line watching the cattle get loaded onto the train when Mum found me. She clipped me round the ear and we were going back home to fetch Molly when it happened.' He put the bottle into the crate with the others and stared at them.

'You don't have to tell me.'

'In this town, it's better hearing it from me first.' Telling her had to be better than reading about his life as a headline like he'd done to her. He winked at her and she gave him a slight smile as she filled another bottle.

But he soon sobered up as the memory replayed in his mind. 'There was this cranky steer who'd escaped by hiking over the railing at the railway yards. It rammed through the gates and straight into mum's car, piercing its horns through the driver's door like ripping open a soft drink can. He rammed us so hard his horns got stuck spearing through the door, straight through the side of Mum's chest and out her throat.'

'Oh my god.' She gasped, covering her mouth with her hands.

'It was a freak accident. Mum wouldn't have been there if it wasn't for me, she was supposed to be at softball practise. Instead, she was out looking for me.'

'Is that why you play now?'

'Yep. You? Molly said your mum used to be keen on it.' Yeah, he knew her history from Molly, who had a habit of over-glamorising things. It's one of the reasons why he'd learned it was always best to hear from the source itself.

'Apparently so.'

'Did you stop because of that?' He cranked his thumb towards the tablet on the bench, hoping she'd answer instead of shrugging.

She sighed and said in a soft voice, 'It was a team trip in Japan. One of those pre-season bonding sessions, where the old players meet the new players. We'd gone professional that season in corporate teams.'

'We?'

She stopped and stared at the half-filled bottle on the bench before her. 'My step-sister, Kylie. She was my catcher, and we were a great team. I wouldn't take the contract to play without her.'

'Did she go everywhere with you?'

'Kylie didn't make the Olympics or Nationals, but she made State with me. I got her back on the team when I went professional.'

'And now you're blaming yourself for it?' It was obvious she was from where he stood.

'If I hadn't gotten Kylie the job, or if I'd given her my seat on the bus, she'd still be alive and so would most of the team. I should've driven that bus—I've got the licence, but I wanted to catch up with her. We had so many plans together, but now…'

'Did you force her to get on the bus? Chain her up and drag her on like a stubborn sow.'

Verily's frown was ferocious. 'No, Kylie was so excited to have a change because she'd just broken up with her boyfriend.'

'Can I offer you some advice?'

'Do I have any choice?'

'Sure, you can choose to listen or not.'

'Go on,' she said, rolling those sexy bedroom eyes at him.

'Time does heal that guilt you've carrying—and it's just guilt. Believe me, you can't change the past.'

'Like what happened with your mother?'

'Yep.' He capped another bottle and placed it into the crate for fermenting. 'I bet you've played it over and over in your mind, all these miniscule detailed moments of what you could've and should've done to stop the accident. Including everything leading up to that one event. If I hadn't skipped school—if you hadn't got on that bus.' He stood directly opposite her with the bench of bottles separating them, but her sadness was suffocating.

He knew that feeling only too well.

'I know my mum forgives me. But it was harder to forgive myself for what I'd done, even though it was an accident. Do you think your sister would forgive you too?'

She faced him as an errant tear trickled down her cheek and he reached over and wiped it away with a fingertip, surprised he'd dared to do such a thing. How would she react if he hugged her?

'Kylie would be kicking my arse for moping,' she mumbled while using the heels of her palms to swipe away her tears. She inhaled deeply and with a steady hand, she began filling more bottles.

He had to admire her focus for keeping to the task. 'What plans did you have with your sister?'

There it was, another annoying shrug.

'Come on,' he whined at her. 'Conversation—it helps to talk.'

'I'm used to keeping my mouth shut.'

'Rare for a woman,' he mumbled with a grin as her lips curled into a fleeting smile. He took the bottle from her, their fingers brushed and the hairs on his skin prickled like a warm shiver. He'd never been so aware of any female like this before.

She cleared her throat as a slight colour feathered her cheeks.

Damn it was pretty.

'So, what does your father think of this?' She asked, waving her hand over the bottles, only to snatch up another empty.

'I haven't told him.'

'Why not?'

'Dad would think it's a stupid waste of money when it's easier to buy a slab of beer.'

'What do you want to do with it?'

'Are you going to tell me what your goals are?'

'I have none. Not anymore,' she whispered with eyes so sad, his heart crumbled to ash, sprinkled over his boots and littered the floor.

'I want to supply the pub.' It was the first time he'd told anyone that.

'Here, in Elsie Creek? Is this the kind of clientele you're after?'

'The mob in town wouldn't care if they're drinking vinegar after a few. The front bar crowd are all about getting blotto. I'm talking about the restaurant side of things.'

'What about in the city?'

'I dunno?' He wasn't no famous athlete, he was just a simple bloke, a dumb-arse truck driver bottling homebrew in a shed. What must she think of him?

'If you're going to all this trouble, you must have a plan?'

Alex had many, but he wasn't used to telling anyone. Yet, with a swallow, he couldn't stop over-sharing with this complete stranger. 'The town's publican owes me a few favours, so when the time is right, I'll ask her to do a tasting session for the feedback. I'm pretty sure she'll say yes.'

'When will that be?'

'Once I've perfected this brew. I need to get the alcohol content standardised and find my unique flavour that sets me apart from the rest of the market. That's why I'm using the local bush honey in this batch.' He pressed down the handle that capped the bottle and raised it up to the light where the fine sediment stirred inside. 'Here, take one of this new batch,' he said, holding out the bottle.

'To drink?'

'Not for another few weeks, it needs to ferment.'

'Does it have a name? A label?' Verily asked, turning the bottle in her tiny hands.

'Nope, just a brewer's batch number. Here.' He plucked the bottle back from her and with a permanent marker he wrote the batch number and date on the lid, then handed it back. 'I hope you'll like it. I haven't shared it with anyone, and I did say that's how I'd pay,' he mumbled.

'Thank you. I'll try it when it's ready.' She put it aside on the bench like it was some trophy, making his inner pride shine.

'Tell me what you think of it when you do.'

'Sure, but I'd better warn you, I know nothing about beer and stuff,' she said, giving another shrug.

'But you'd know all about softball.'

'It's all I lived and breathed once.' Verily returned to her spot on the other side of the table and resumed bottling.

Alex scribbled on the bottle lids of the full crate, stacked it alongside the other brews he'd created and started filling the next crate. 'Did you have any plans beyond playing softball? Like coaching?'

'I was starting to run coaching clinics in Japan as part of my contract. Kylie and I had trialled it back in the States where we'd used our little brothers as guinea pigs. Kylie was the brains behind it.'

'And you?'

'I'm not a people person. Kylie had the talent for people and could talk them into anything, but me…' Her nose screwed up, shrugging, she said, 'I'm a player.'

'Hey, saying that to a bloke means lots of different things, you know.'

'I meant, I take directions from my catcher and the coach who lead the plays,' she said, picking up another bottle and poured with steady hands and clear focus.

She was beautiful to watch, and no doubt impressive on a softball field with that focus of hers. 'Why not come to today's game, as a spectator?'

'Don't ask me to pick on other players, that's not my thing. I only look for faults in an opposing batter's swinging frame to get by them.'

'Huh.' Hearing her speak with a level of professionalism was impressive, which he didn't think was possible for a sport like softball. 'I imagine our simple bush game is nowhere near what you're used to.'

'I don't judge, not when it comes to anyone playing a sport.'

'But you can tell us where we suck—and we do suck—so you won't be telling us anything new. You could tell us our strengths. Although, I might have to give you a pair of binoculars to find any, except for my outstanding skills.'

'Oh, please.' She rolled her eyes at him and giggled.

He was stoked to hear her laugh. 'Come on, get out of

the house and see the team, they're a great bunch of girls.'

'I'm not going anywhere near your coach, Agnes,' Verily said, shaking her head, 'and you'd better not tell them what I was. I won't share your secret and I expect you and Molly to keep mine.'

Molly had mentioned Verily was shy over her achievements. Why? 'You know that's quite an incredible feat within itself.'

'What is?'

'No one knowing who you are, especially when Molly's salon is the biggest gossip shop on the planet. Although, most people never listen to what Molly says.'

'That's not nice.'

'I agree, but it's true. Have you walked down the main street, yet?'

'Nope.'

'Why not?'

She shrugged.

Alex stared at her with tilted head, waiting for an actual verbal response.

'I'm scared of that buffalo,' Verily said.

'Cecil will only come up to you if you've got flowers.'

'Flowers?'

'We reckon it's the scent or the colour that attracts him, which is what flowers do.'

'So, this town's walking beast of a billboard has a thing for flowers.'

'Cecil's harmless. The kids at the school spoil him at lunchtime, but that new chook of his is trouble. It'd wanna behave today because last time that hen attacked the umpire, Agnes threatened to turn it into a roast Sunday dinner.'

Her tinkling laughter, again, made him smile.

'I can't believe the Dusty Dingoes have a water buffalo for a mascot.'

'Welcome to the Territory, mate.' He held out a cap-less bottle of unfermented beer.

She raised her half-filled bottle of wort and said with a smile, 'Cheers.' Their bottles clinked over a table of empty stubbies and they didn't drink a drop.

FIVE

The sporting grounds carpark was filled with dusty utes and assorted beefy four-wheeled drives. The aroma of onions and sausages cooking on barbecues filtered through the air as the many gathered spectators carried various styles of eskies to the grandstands. Seated beside her aunt in the stands, Verily asked, 'Is this the whole town, Molly?'

'It might be. It's always like this for the first game of the season, then nothing until the Rosella Festival when this place is packed. We're aiming for a rodeo this year and the pub's agreed to help us get a liquor licence to run a bar for the day.'

'So, it's not just about the softball.'

'The Dusty Dingoes haven't won anything since Agnes and I played ten years ago.'

'Are they that bad?'

Molly rolled her eyes and nodded. 'Some of the teams are great. And then there are those who are only great because they've got these dodgy cousins.' Molly leaned over and whispered, 'They get in professional players, hon.'

'Can they do that?' Why would they want to do that out here?

'Yep, these dodgy cousins,' Molly said, with

punctuated air quotes, 'come in for the musters, but we know they wouldn't know one end of a cow from the other. It sucks, but at least they bring in the crowd.'

'Why do it if the Dusty Dingoes never win?'

'For the town.' Molly, with her brolly over her shoulder, sitting higher to face the crowds. 'Elsie Creek only has a few things to look forward to on our social calendar. Besides the bake-offs and the Billabong Barbie Bash, we have our annual race day using the local stations' stock horses. We also have a rodeo using their bulls, but that's only one weekend of the year. We do have the footy too, but games get cancelled regularly because the roads are flooded and we're flat out trying to make numbers for a team.'

'Like your softball team.' How many bake-offs and barbecues were there?

'It was your grandmother who loved this game so much, she started the Rosella Festival. She was the one who paired it with her softball team to create the Rosella Cup.'

'Really?' More history Verily had never known about her mother's family. It was hard to find that connection to a woman who was just a face in a photo.

'Your grandmother got the publican and the female deputy mayor involved, and together, they gathered all these local committee women into our packing shed.' Molly smiled with a dreamy stare across the field. 'It was my first taste of wine too.'

Verily knew the packing shed well, having hung-out there all morning helping Alex bottle his beer. He was a nice guy, more than nice, and she felt guilty for being so judgy and jealous over a guy who probably saw her as damaged goods. 'How old were you?'

'Nine or ten, I think,' Molly said with a wide smile. 'Your mum and I pinched this half bottle of plonk and hid in the rafters to watch them. That year, the Regional President of the CWA wanted to do a jam festival as the town fundraiser.'

Verily screwed her nose up at her aunt. 'A whole festival on jam?'

'Jams, preservatives, chutneys and pickles are a big thing out here, you know.'

'No, I didn't.' Verily forced herself to not laugh at Molly's seriousness over jam.

'I bet it's the same in many country towns who have their own shows. Unfortunately, Elsie Creek was never big enough for a town show. The carnival people travel from Alice Springs, Tennant Creek and Katherine annually, but they drive straight past us on their way to Darwin. So that night, those women decided we'd make our own annual town show. And that year we had our first Rosella Festival where our softball team, the Dusty Dingoes, won the first Rosella cup.'

'All this for some fairy floss and Dagwood dogs?'

'I like fairy floss.' Molly popped open her soft drink and sipped on her soda. She then rummaged through her bag for her sparkly diamante-encrusted hip flask and added a decent drop to her can, stirred it with a straw and sipped again. Shaded by her bright pink polka-dotted umbrella that matched her dress, she waved at a familiar face in the crowd.

'What else is at this festival?' Verily asked.

'They judge local foods and craft.'

All the things she didn't know how to do! 'Like a town fair?'

'Yep, but it's all about the rosella fruit. We have rosella jams, rosella chutneys, rosella tea and rosella cupcakes. I believe they're having a rosella wine this year, someone made it up from a mango wine recipe.'

'Do you make mango wine?'

'Me, no, but I won for best Rosella jam five years in a row until someone *cheated*.' Molly's umbrella spun like a plane's propeller, as she scowled down at the assembled team on the field. She sighed and the spinning brolly stopped as she sipped on her spiked soft drink. 'Anyway, you must use the rosella plant as a core ingredient to enter, and we're always open for new products. I think our resident stoner wants the kids to weave baskets using the stems as a school craft project.'

'I see.' Verily giggled, shaking her head at the thought.

'Do you?'

She shrugged. Now, thanks to her morning with Alex, she was conscious every time she did her shoulder shrug.

'Tomorrow morning, I'll make pancakes with rosella jam to prove how good it is,' said Molly. 'I'll invite Alex, he loves the stuff. Were you helping him with his beer earlier?'

'Yes.'

'You know Alex's beer thing is a secret.'

Alex was the first person she'd told about the accident, could he be trusted not to blab? 'He said it's because he wants to have the perfect brew before he gets judged.' She understood that, it was the same reason why she used to secretly practise all the time for that perfect pitch. Now she had nothing to aim for.

The crowd pointed at the field and laughed.

'What on earth—' Verily blinked at the elderly woman with a large hat, strolling past in a pink ballgown and work boots, leading the water buffalo, Cecil, onto the field. Today they'd painted the buffalo's beefy black body in orange with the words: *Go Dusty Dingoes*.

'That's Esther, she's Cecil's owner,' explained Molly.

'I've never been to a softball game like this.' It had a country fair atmosphere. Beer cans were raised in a chorusing round of cheers as the town's team took their places on the dried-up field. Bella dragged her bag of seeds onto the outfield and fed the birds. Tessa slathered more oil on her legs, hoisting up her short-shorts. In jeans, boots and Akubras, the jillaroo sisters took their places at the plates while the painted water buffalo cruised past the gathered crowd with the crowing red-hen on its back.

Children laughed in the playground, wearing different coloured tutus over their jeans. She'd never seen so many tutus without a ballerina in sight.

The rest of the spectators were made of groups cheering from the bleachers, along with a group of men watching the meals being cooked over by the barbecues.

It appeared disorganised, chaotic even, yet they'd all come to the game and greeted each other like old friends.

Agnes stood in the centre by the pitcher, Speedy, pointing at her team to get into their positions. The coach's monobrow was once again highlighted by her yellow duck-bill sun visor. The thick, black plait that trailed down her back was longer than the water buffalo's tail that cruised past her. Wearing black-and-white striped board shorts, red and white football socks that meshed with her black thongs, the coach was a fashionista's nightmare.

But Agnes was the coach who'd volunteered to be out there, and Verily always respected that. Like her dad and the thousands who'd volunteered every weekend so others could play sports, Agnes was no different and deserved respect.

She shouldn't even be picking on Agnes's dress sense. Not when Verily only dressed for comfort herself. Sweatpants, t-shirts and running shoes. It's all she had in her wardrobe, still packed in her bag in the cupboard.

Was she ever going to unpack her bags and find somewhere she felt connected enough to call home?

* * *

Alex checked over his leg and chest padding and slid on his helmet. Already feeling the sweat from his catcher's mitt, he crouched into position behind the home plate with the umpire shadowing him.

He nodded at the incoming batter, his eyes travelling up long legs, over her tight softball uniform to the gaping buttons on her shirt, showing off her lace bra. She smiled at him. *Crap*—it was Sherice!

'Hey, Alex, how you doin', sugar?' Sherice patted his arm and gave his bicep a squeeze.

'All good.' He stepped away from the bleached blonde and her suffocating perfume of overripe oranges. 'Heard you got engaged to Tim from Rigby Down's Station?'

'I did,' Sherice replied, adjusting the strap on her batter's glove then gripped her aluminium softball bat.

Alex spotted no engagement ring on her finger.

'Why didn't you tell me you were with Tim? He's a mate of mine, you know.' Tim also had a stash of shotguns and lived on an expansive cattle station that could hide a man forever. 'You've put me in a shitty spot, by not telling me you're with Tim.'

'I didn't want a conversation, Alex, I just wanted a good time with the truckie.' She walked her manicured nails up his chest plate to grab his helmet's face mask, dragging him closer he could smell the mint from her gum. 'If I remember, you said you don't do commitment when it comes to work and women, which suited me just fine, sugar.'

'I like breathing too,' he said, pulling her hand free he stepped back from her. *What was I thinking!*

Sherice raised her bat over her shoulder, her hips shifting as she stood at the home plate and looked over to the pitcher. 'Can Speedy throw to the plate yet?'

'Nope. Get ready to walk.' Alex sighed as he got back into position and nodded at Speedy waiting at the pitcher's plate. She was the only one who volunteered to pitch. The jillaroo sisters were great throwers over-arm, but doing the underarm slingshot, they couldn't work it out. The bird-feeder Bella only chucked out birdseed. Hot-pants Tessa was good at distracting the umpire while working on her tan and for batting like the rest of them. They were a strong batting team—they were just lousy when it came to pitching and fielding.

Agnes was great at coaching them to hit. But their throwing was so bad Alex didn't need to wear his catcher's mitt because it was like catching feather pillows. That's if they had something to throw because the opposition normally walked the plates without ever hitting a damned softball.

He glanced at the grandstand filled with people. Typically, the first game always had a good turnout. How many would bother sticking around for their normal after-game carpark party? Which he was looking forward to, even if it meant suffering a hangover in the morning, it was always a good time.

He spotted Molly's umbrella amongst the crowd, but it wasn't Molly he was watching, it was Verily. Her messy just-got-out-of-bed hair matched her dreamy bedroom eyes. She was a woman who didn't fuss with her appearance and didn't need to.

What would it be like to wake up next to her and see her bed hair for real?

He couldn't, it'd be too complicated on so many levels. Verily was only here on a holiday, she was Molly's niece, and both women were his landladies. And, Alex wanted to lock in a long-term lease on the place, once he proved himself with this upcoming mango season. That meant no risky romantic rendezvous that could jeopardise his future plans.

Yet, Verily's smile did wonders for his heart rate. He could feel those bedroom-eyes of hers watching.

Why did he ask her to come to the game today? The woman was a professional athlete—which explains the hot bod he'd reminisced about many times, while home alone.

Agnes's shrill whistle snapped him out of his daydreams and he prepared for the pitch behind the home plate.

Speedy stood at the centre of the diamond on the pitcher's plate. Breathing fast, lifting her skinny shoulders, her flat chest went up and down, up and down. It reminded him of a paper bag being used to stop someone from fainting.

'Is Speedy gonna hurl the ball or chunder all over the pitcher's plate?' called out Sherice.

Speedy swung underarm. *Bugger.* She'd let go of the ball too late and the softball arched high in the air and dropped two feet from her shoes.

'Oh man.' The umpire groaned beside Alex, shaking his head. 'Tell your pitcher I'll let that one slide as a practise throw, just the one, Alex.'

Alex met Speedy where her toss landed and scooped up the softball, facing his cousin. She was such a tiny thing.

'I suck, I do,' said Speedy.

'You're getting better.' She couldn't get any worse than last season. Could she? 'Just remember to take a deep breath, hold it, and then throw, okay.' Not that he was an expert, but they'd searched YouTube together for tips on pitching last season, and the season before that.

'I can hardly grip the bloody ball.'

'You can do this, Speedy.'

'Yeah, right. I have the hands of a kid, I do. Can't we get a smaller ball?'

Alex placed the huge softball into Speedy's tiny hands. He blinked at the memory of holding Verily's hand, and he'd liked holding her hand—shame he couldn't go there. 'I know this woman who played Olympic Softball, and she's got smaller hands than you.'

'Great, get her number and we'll do lunch out here in the middle of bloody nowhere, we will. And we'll practise pitching cow pats and dodging dingoes while the wallabies laugh at us, we will. Wait until the plovers come back and we'll duck from their aerial attacks together...' Speedy mumbled her way back to the pitcher's plate, turned around and waited.

Alex squatted behind the home plate with the umpire bedside him. 'Let's try this again, shall we?' He nodded to Speedy with the hope that maybe, this once, her pitch would make the plate.

Speedy let rip with a wild under swing and the ball went east.

'*Foul ball,*' cried the umpire.

'It's gonna be a long bloody game,' said Sherice, flicking the dirt off the batter's plate with her shiny boots.

'You're telling me.' Alex hid behind his catcher's mask and settled in for an annihilation.

SIX

The crisp morning had a sweet scent coming from the orchard, budding with new leafy growth. The last of the mist lingered as Alex strolled down the path and smiled at Verily seated on Molly's veranda. She was a vision worth waking for.

'I see you survived your carpark party,' she said with an amused expression.

'You could've stayed on.'

'I don't know anyone.'

'You know me.'

'Like I'd brag about that in public.' She kept a straight face but her eyes shone.

'Bitch.' He chuckled as he took a seat beside her and inhaled her warm honeyed macadamia scent.

Verily leaned back in the cane chair, turning the pages of a large scrapbook. The table was set for brunch with some school albums sitting on the side table.

'What are you doing?' Alex asked, finding the perfect excuse to lean in closer.

'It's my mother's scrapbooks from her school days.'

'Hey, that's my mum, there.' He pointed to the images amid colourful hand-drawn flowers and stickers. 'And that's my old man. They were sweethearts from school like most people in this town. How did your parents meet?'

'Dad's accounting firm used to send him on the rural rounds for tax time, and he met mum while he was staying in town. Hey Molly, how did you meet your husband?'

The screen door creaked as Molly exited the kitchen carrying plates on a tray. 'Your uncle was Elsie Creek's Railway Station Master. Morning Alex, you're just in time for brunch.'

Alex sat straighter and picked up his fork. 'Yum, pancakes and rosella jam. I knew there was a reason I got out of bed this morning.'

'How's the head?' Molly asked.

'Good, now you've brought me food.' He eyed off the feast on the plate before him and eagerly reached for the jam-jar. 'Your aunt's jam won the Rosella Festival's blue ribbon, five years in a row. It'd be more if she'd enter again, because everyone knows it's the best jam in Elsie Creek.'

'I don't enter anymore because we need to let the others win, hon.' Molly smoothed down her apron, sat at the table and poured tea from the pot.

'Have you ever tried making beer with rosellas?' Verily asked.

'Eh?' Alex froze with a loaded fork halfway to his mouth.

'Molly was telling me they're having rosella wine at the Festival.'

'The committee wants to try it, now we've got a liquor licence this year,' said Molly. 'We're hoping to get a band too for the aftergame party.'

'The Rosella Festival is supposed to be about softball, Molly.' With his tea, Alex washed down the fruity tart flavour of the rosella jam mixed with cream and fluffy pancakes. Sweet, but oh so good, and a food favourite he grew up on.

'Do you think we'll win this year?'

'Not after yesterday's effort. We'll be lucky to win a game.' He shook his head at their shocking loss. Across the table he locked eyes with Molly, then they both side-glanced at the world champion softball pitcher seated at the table.

* * *

'Can you make beer with rosellas?' Verily blurted out to change the subject.

Alex raised an eyebrow over his teacup, muttering, 'I don't think it's been tried before.'

'You're trialling local bush honey for that sweet lite beer, why not rosellas?'

'What a fabulous idea, Verily.' Molly then said to Alex, 'You're always telling me you're chasing that uniqueness to your craft beer, hon.'

'True.' He sat back and toyed with his teacup handle in thought.

'And you could launch it at the Festival,' said Verily.

'What!' He frowned at Verily.

Molly sat up with eyes wide. 'Another fabulous idea, hon. We could have a stand for his beer and sell samples—'

'Oi, wait on a second 'ere ladies, I'm not ready to go public. Bad enough we're failing at softball, without having my beer judged in front of everyone before it's ready.'

'How would you do your taste testing then?' Verily asked.

'I told you already, it'd be a closed session at the back of the pub with only a select few—not the entire town.'

'There's a wild rosella patch fruiting by the chook pen if you want to try it in your next brew, hon,' said Molly.

'But it's a weed, isn't it?' Verily took a dainty bite of her pancake tasting the foreign preserve.

'It's a bush tucker like Kakadu plums,' replied Molly.

Alex chuckled while shovelling food onto his fork. 'Rosellas are an introduced weed from South Africa that clog up our waterways and savannahs.'

'They've never proved where, or how it came to be,' said Molly, 'except that the rosella has been here a long time. But by doing our bit for the Festival, we're actually helping the environment and our town.'

'I'd read somewhere that they use rosellas for champagne, and it's also known as the Florida Cranberry.' Verily tasted a forkful of fluffy pancakes with tarty rosella jam topped with cream. *Yum.* 'It's tart, like raspberry rhubarb. I like it.' Molly beamed at her with pride from across the table.

'I'd forgotten it's used for the bubbly,' said Alex as the cream dripped from his fork hovering above his plate.

'Are you going to try it, Alex?' Verily asked. 'I'll help.'

'Are you that bored?'

She shrugged and Alex inhaled deeply while frowning slightly at her shoulder shrug.

'Come down to the hair salon tomorrow and we'll give

this mop a cut,' said Molly, fingering the straggly ends of Verily's ponytail.

'I've never bothered before.' Verily knew her hair was full of split ends and in dire need of some form of treatment.

'I like the no-fuss look on you,' said Alex between mouthfuls.

Embarrassed and flattered, she hung her head as the heat rushed to her face. 'Helmet hair has never bothered me.' Like her dress sense, it was all about comfort first.

'I'll take you to work with me tomorrow for a pampering, and, after this morning's brunch, we'll go pick some rosellas for Alex to create a fabulous new master brew.'

Alex wiped his mouth and asked Verily, 'did you mention you can drive a bus?'

'Yes.'

'Are you licenced?'

'I've got an international car licence.' It took a bit to get used to driving on the other side of the road, but the cross-country road trip in the hire car to Molly's helped.

'How about a simple yes or no, can you drive a bus, or not?' Alex asked.

'Yes, I'm licenced for both the States and Japan.' Again, damning herself for not driving the bus that day. *If only…*

'Have you ever driven a truck before?'

'Only the short box trucks that are part of my father's courier business. Not like the beast you drive.' Was Alex going to tease her for being a female driver too?

'Would you like to drive a road train?'

'Sure,' she said with a timid nod, 'if I ever got the

chance, I would.'

'Really?'

'I don't mind trying new things.' Alex was right, she was bored.

'You should take Verily with you when you go out on the road, Alex,' suggested Molly.

'Why?' Again, Alex arched his eyebrow at Verily. 'It's nothing but lots of dusty dirt roads.'

'I dunno, perhaps to visit a cattle station and see more of the remote outback. Remember, I'm the one on holiday.' Was she annoying him by hanging around too much?

'Go on, hon,' said Molly urging Alex.

'All right then,' he said with a huff. 'If you don't whinge about the music and don't get bored on long drives with nothing to see, and only if you'll do me a favour,' he said with a sigh.

Not if it was that much a hassle for the guy, she wouldn't go. 'What favour?'

'I've got to spend the day on the irrigation, it's blocked somewhere. I could use your help to water and fertilise until I get the system back online.'

'What do I do?'

'You'll drive the tractor with the sprayer on the back, it's wider than a bus but not as long. How much practise have you had driving a large vehicle?'

'My dad and I shared the driving of this Winnebago we had for travelling the States. I can drive big things.' But she'd driven nothing big since the accident.

'Good. You're hired.'

Did she dare do it? 'What about the rosella picking with Molly?'

'Come and find me in the shed after you've picked your weeds. It'll give me time to get the tanks ready. I'll pay you in beer.'

'You *only* pay me in beer, that I have yet to taste because you tell me it's not ready to drink.'

The last case of beer she'd earned was stored in the spare room waiting to ferment. What would she do if she didn't like his beer? She didn't want to hurt his feelings.

'It'll be worth the wait.' He picked up the jam-jar from the centre of the table. 'Rosella beer, huh? I might try it.' He gave her a nod, sharing his lazy grin, she had to smile back. 'I'll take you for a ride in the truck on Tuesday.'

'Why Tuesday?'

'Aren't you getting your hair done on Monday at Molly's shop?'

'She is, thanks for remembering, Alex. We'll find the best rosellas on the property for your beer.' Molly turned to Verily and said, 'I'll show you my dragon fruit too. When the other patch is ready you can help me make this year's jam batch. It's a family recipe.'

'I don't know how to cook,' Verily muttered, chewing her bottom lip. She was sick of being a loose end on this never-ending holiday. There was only so much relaxing she could do—but to cook?

Yet, a small bud of excitement blossomed in her chest, finally she had something to do, and hopefully, her shoulder would hold.

SEVEN

Alex was enjoying himself playing the tour guide for Verily, who sat in the passenger seat of his prime mover, sharing a grand view of an endless sea of olive-leafed gum trees divided by a simple red dirt road. He pointed out ant mounds as tall as two men, built like mini spherical cathedral-roofs of mud, or the flat tombstone varieties where she took plenty of photos with her phone.

Verily leaned toward the windscreen and peered out. 'When I landed in Sydney, I'd thought the sky there was big. But it just got bigger the closer I got to Elsie Creek. But this,' she said, pointing to the sky, 'is huge. It's amazing. And not one cloud anywhere, except the dust cloud behind us.'

Alex steered the truck, with its four long trailers snaking behind them for over fifty metres. 'Believe me, the novelty of being on the road wears off.'

'Only because you've done this all your life.'

'You'd be the same, travelling from game to game in foreign countries?'

'We went wherever the contract sent me. Some days I felt like we'd sold my soul to the highest bidder.'

'Why?'

'Some new teams or places were bitchy.'

'Wouldn't they want someone of your skills to play on their team? My team would.' He'd love to see her pitch in real life.

'Most clubs have their prize pitchers who've been with the team for ages, that is until I come along where they're then forced to become my back-up. So of course, some feel cheated and accuse me of stealing their spotlight.'

'Surely not all of those places were like that?'

'No. Some places I never wanted to leave.'

'Why did you?'

She shrugged.

He hated that shrug. 'Come on, gimme a reason?'

'There were plenty. The season was over, the contract was finished, or I'd outgrown the team and had another too-good-to-refuse contract to fulfil.'

'You could've said no.'

'Okay…' She inhaled deeply, sitting straighter in the passenger seat, she faced him squarely. 'I wanted to see how far I could go. Just one more game, one more team, one more country. I didn't think it'd end so suddenly.' She looked away to the scrub that spread endlessly into the distance. 'Hey, what do you do while you're driving and not taking in this amazing countryside.'

Nice change of subject, babe. 'I've got movies on my tablet for the long straight hauls, or I listen to audiobooks or podcasts. On dirt, I need to concentrate to dodge the roos, cattle, donkeys, camels, emus, buffalo and whatever else wants to take a nap on the track in the sun.'

'You dodge?'

'No, they run, or get sucked under a dust cloud.' He grinned at her frown, guessing it was from having swallowed his dust the day they'd met. 'Tell you what...' He slowed down the massive vehicle and with a hiss of the air brakes, he stopped the truck.

'What's wrong?'

'Something must be wrong with my head for what I'm about to do.' He climbed out of the driver's seat and onto the bunk bed that made up the back of the cab. 'Go on, get in.' He pointed to his vacant driver's seat.

'Are you serious?'

Her smile was so wide, he swallowed hard at the beautiful shine in her eyes that made up that smile. 'Didn't you say you wanted to drive a road train?' He'd seen how easily she drove the tractor on Sunday through the orchard and was willing to take a risk on her driving today—as long as his dad never found out.

'Yes, please.' She scooted into the seat before he could change his mind.

'Don't rush. Even if there are no speed limits out here, it is a dirt track.'

'I won't.'

'You're hauling empty trailers that float.'

'Okay, okay.' Wearing that dazzling smile, she adjusted her seat and mirrors. Verily rubbed her fingertips together, wiped her palms on her tracksuit pants, then gripped the steering wheel.

He'd seen her do that on YouTube before letting loose a screaming slingshot throw in a game. Yes, he'd cyberstalked her past. How could he not! Verily was the most famous person he knew, and she'd been the world's best. Now…

'So, what do I do?' she asked with the world reflecting in her eyes.

It was beautiful.

'We've got a straight run through to the first cattle grid.' He forced himself to look away and point at the road ahead. 'That'll give you time to get a feel for it, so there's no need to rush.' He explained the gears, and they were soon on their way as he sat back and watched her. He liked watching her.

'How come Molly cut-off so much of your hair?' He was tempted to touch her sandy sun-bleached hair that barely brushed past her shoulders. It still had that messy look he liked, and it still suited her sexy bedroom eyes.

'Split ends. Being in the sun all day and suffering from helmet hair, all I ever did with my hair was wash-and-wear-it.'

'So, you wore your helmet all the time?'

'Practise five days a week, then gameday.'

'And out of season.'

'I was always practising my pitch, every single day.'

'Do you miss it?' Her sadness filled the cab, and he kicked himself for asking, but he had to know. 'Have you thrown a ball since the accident?'

'Yeah.'

'And?'

'I'll never be the same.'

'You were clocking an average of a hundred and thirty clicks. That's faster than the average Aussie cricket bowler.'

'How do you know?'

It was his turn to shrug and grin. 'I wanted to be a full forward for the Saint's Football Club, but I can't kick and run that well.'

'You throw and bat fine and run the plates.'

His chest rose at the compliment coming from a woman of her calibre. 'Only because Mum and Molly dragged me along so they could practise in the orchard, over some wine. Hey, you never said what you thought of our first game, and don't reply with just a shrug. I dare you to answer.'

'Are you sure you want my professional opinion?'

'I'm not asking the Pope, now am I?'

'I'm no Mother Teresa.'

'No, you were the terror on the pitcher's plate letting off *Satan's Screamers*. That's what those American commentators called it.'

'Are you like my groupie or something? Are you going to sprout off my stats too?'

'No, numbers aren't my thing, but I saw the footage of your pitch, it was amazing. Poor little Speedy can't chuck for peanuts and there's you slamming speedballs at the catcher.' He sat back in his seat and said, 'I've never caught anything that fast.'

'Sure, you have.'

'Nope. Don't you ever worry about hurting the catcher with that speed?'

'No. You guys are padded-up and I trusted my aim. Back then I did.'

'And now?' Molly had told him Verily had broken her

upper arm in several places, where pins held it together. A plate ran across her shoulder, which had been ripped out from its socket and crushed in the accident. Her pitching arm was ruined. Just like that, the star of her future…gone. It had to be soul-crushing when the experts had claimed Verily was only starting to reach her prime.

'Please, Alex. I'm driving.' She side-glanced him with a pained-fear in her eyes that made his stomach plummet.

'I'm sorry'—for being such an idiot!

She faced the road ahead and her beautiful smile returned. 'Look at this, I'm in charge of a big-arse semi!'

'Road train, princess, and your Yank accent gets pretty thick with some words you say?'

'Southern. I spent a lot of time in the south, in Atlanta. I love their accent.'

'Do you miss the States?'

'I'm enjoying this.'

He was stoked he'd given her the opportunity. 'The best road train driver I know is a woman.'

'Really?'

'Yep. There's plenty around. Well, wherever the work is… Dad's been managing the runs this side of Elsie Creek. Now he's got his new truck, he's been sticking to the main highway letting me do the small station runs.'

'Small? This truck is huge and I can't see the end of that road.'

Through the bug-splattered windscreen, shimmering heat waves gave the red dust a glossy appearance. But it was just like every other dirt track cutting through the outback.

Nothing changed out here. 'Would you go back to the States, to your dad?'

She shrugged.

'I hate that shrug.'

'What do you want me to say?'

'Anything to keep up the conversation, because we have a loooong drive ahead,' he said, pointing to the endless red road. 'It's another hour to the station, an hour to load up, two hours back and then we do it again to the next one.'

'How many loads?'

'Dad's got us booked in for three trips to cart cattle into the holding yards. They like them settled-in and well-watered before tomorrow's train.'

'Where are they going?'

'Darwin harbour for exporting.'

'You don't drive to Darwin?'

'Only if the client pays for it. Dad does the longer hauls. I prefer short runs so I can crawl into my bed every night.' He thumbed behind him to the cab and said, 'I got sick of sleeping in these bunks and living off roadhouse food a while back.'

'Can you cook?'

'Yes, I can. Unlike you.'

'I've been learning how to make beer, that's cooking right?'

He chuckled. 'I should call you my brewer's apprentice.'

'Well, you can't call me slave labour when you're only paying me in beer.'

'At least I'm paying you.'

'So, I'm cheap labour.'

'Hey, that beer will be top shelf one day.'

'I believe it.'

'You do?'

'Yeah. The few you have let me taste are nice.' She grinned, giving him a fleeting side-glance while steering the road train.

She looked good in that chair.

'But I can't compare if it's exceptional beer, when it's been a while since I've drunk any kind of beer.'

'You haven't been to the pub yet, have you?'

'No.'

He sat taller and shuffled in his seat. 'Tell you what. Um, how about, um, Friday night—I'll give you an education?'

'On town politics, or beer?'

'Both. We'll have dinner.' Would Verily want to go on a date with her truck-driving-tenant? Would Molly allow it?

'Sure. We should see if Molly would like to join us, to give her a night off from cooking, too.'

'Great,' he mumbled, sinking into his seat again. 'Molly can drive us home, if we can keep her flashy hipflask in the car.' Shame, it wasn't a date, but they could be mates hanging out in the bar, maybe.

He leaned over and checked the gauges on the dash, inhaling her warm honeyed macadamia aroma. 'You're a natural at this.'

'I had a good teacher.'

'Thank you, I do my best.'

* * *

'Not you. My dad taught me first.' Her father would be so proud to see her driving this massive truck.

'You really know how to flatter a bloke, don't you?' Alex shared a wink that made her shoulders hunch and skin tingle to the top of her head.

All day, stuck in the cab with the guy—how could she drive without falling into a drooling pile of fan-girl mush? It'd be more challenging than driving a road train down a dirt track, through the middle of the outback, going to a cattle station.

Wow, she was driving a monster truck!

If someone told her she'd be doing this a few months ago, she wouldn't have believed them. Best of all, it had nothing to do with softball.

'Slow down, and park by that row of sheds.' Alex pointed ahead.

Having survived the challenge of passing through skinny gateways and over the many cattle grids Verily steered into the large clearing. She manoeuvred the truck toward some corrugated sheds that sat opposite a few scattered buildings, utes, and various other machinery and lots of fenced fields. It reminded her of a farm plonked onto the dust in the middle of nowhere.

With the hiss of the air-brakes, the massive road train stopped without creating a dust storm. 'How's that?'

'Perfect.'

Her jaw ached from smiling and her hands were stiff

from gripping the wheel so tight. She rolled her aching shoulder, only feeling it now they'd stopped. But it'd been worth it.

'Keep the engine running. Someone will show up and tell us where they want us to load the trailers. I reckon it'll be that yard over there.'

She squinted against the bright sun shading her eyes with her hand. The railed yard was filled with live cattle—and they were huge! They had thick horns, pale coats, with black noses and big dark eyes belonging to the Brahman breed, so explained Alex earlier.

Alex jumped out of the cab and helped Verily climb down. 'From that smile you're wearing, you enjoyed driving, didn't you?'

She couldn't stop smiling. 'It was fun. Thanks for trusting me enough.'

'No offence, but I'll take it from here with a full load. Cattle shift.'

'Well, hello, sugar,' said a woman's voice from behind them.

'Sherice?' Alex turned with a frown and stepped back into Verily. 'What the heck are you doing out 'ere?'

The woman, with great blonde hair, stepped in closer to Alex. 'I'd heard you were coming and—'

'Hi, I'm Verily,' she said, peeking around Alex's solid torso.

'What is *she* doing here?' Sherice demanded with a scowl at Alex.

'G'day Alex,' called out a man in an Akubra, long

sleeved shirt and jeans with his boots stirring up dust as he strolled over from the sheds.

'Hey, Tim. Congratulations on your engagement, mate.' Alex and Tim slapped hands in a hearty handshake.

'Thanks, mate.' Tim smiled, his teeth so white and bright against his sun-kissed skin. 'Who's the lady?'

Wow, a real-deal cowboy. Verily could almost melt from the heat as she stared at the ruggedly delicious male specimen. 'Hi, don't mind me I'm just the tourist.' She was getting used to not being introduced in this town and calling everyone *mate*. They all did it. *G'day mate, ol' mate said this,* and *had a mate who'd done that,* and *she'll be right, mate.*

Right now, none of that mattered, when what she really wanted was somehow to make Tim turn around so she could check out his denim derriere and take a photo? *Helloooo cowboy.*

'Guys, this is the lovely, Verily.'

'Huh?' Verily stopped her perve to peek at Alex, stunned at his politeness.

Alex put his arm around her shoulders and whispered, 'Please play along. I'll explain later and pay you in beer.'

She tensed all over at the weight of his arm. It was strong yet gentle and his aroma wove around her like a spell. Why was she drooling over an engaged cowboy for when Alex was right here?

'Hey there, Verily, I'm Tim,' he said, dusting off his hand on his jeans, then held it out to her

'Hi.' She shook Tim's dry, callused, strong hand. Working man's hands. A real man's hands. Just like Alex's hands, she'd admired many times from steering the truck to cutting up pancakes with his fork.

Well, that confirmed it, she was a hands girl.

Yet the texture of Alex's shirt brushed the back of her neck and brought back her focus—what she'd do for some skin. Why was Alex doing this? 'Is this your cattle station, Tim?'

'Yep. It's been in the family for a few generations now.'

'Did Alex pick you up hitchhiking on the road?' Sherice asked, while sneering at Alex.

'Close, through the mango orchard,' replied Verily.

'Verily is Molly's niece,' Alex said with a chuckle that travelled through her body. She couldn't stop her goofy grin.

'Molly's a good sort. Welcome to Rigby Downs station, Verily.' Tim nodded his sweat-stained Akubra, giving her another smile.

Her temperature soared but was it from Tim or Alex? 'Thank you, it's my first station.' *That sounded silly?*

'You should've given us some notice and Sherice could've shown you 'round the place. She'll be moving in soon enough,' Tim said, sliding his arm around Sherice's shoulders.

'Wedding first, sugar.' Sherice patted Tim's toned chest.

'You should bring Verily out fishing, Alex. There's plenty of Barra jumping in the billabongs from the decent Wet this year.'

'I can do that, mate,' said Alex. 'Do you like fishing, Verily?'

'Not that I know all, but I do know the basics of a simple tackle box. My dad was into it.' *Just shut up!* She was such a tomboy compared to the shiny feminine Sherice.

'Sounds like you've got a keeper there, mate,' said Tim.

'Who dresses like she's on her way to the gym,' snarled Sherice, flicking at her hair with manicured nails.

What was Sherice's deal? Verily looked down at her sweatpants that blended with her t-shirt topped off with a grey hoodie. She was in a truck—not going to some red-carpet event. Although she was standing on a sea of red dirt.

Yet, compared to the shiny Sherice who was a striking figure in her tight bootleg jeans that suited her American cowboy boots. Even Sherice's belt buckle shone below her tailored shirt with its collar up and buttons low, showing off the delicate pink lace bra. Sherice was stunning. And shiny.

While Verily was as dull as the dust on her sneakers.

Is this what Alex liked in a lady?

Why was she worrying about Alex's taste in women when she was just a mate? He was just like every other guy she'd met, always nice at first, until their fragile male egos got threatened by a female who could throw a ball faster than the average male. She was used to them not bothering with her after that, so why waste her time now? Besides, she was only here on a holiday.

Verily used to want more, but with her career gone and her shoulder damaged, she'd given up all hope. There was no guy buying her flowers or waiting at her bedside in the hospital. There was no one. And she'd never been able to shrug off that level of loneliness until she'd started to spend time with Alex.

'We'll load up over there, Alex,' Tim said, pointing to

the railed yards.

'I'll show you where,' said Sherice.

'I'm good thanks, Sherice.' Alex pulled Verily closer to his side. 'Come on, honey, I don't want you getting trampled by the cattle.'

'Verily can come with me if she wants?' Tim said, 'Being her first time at a station we'll find her the best spot to watch and take photos.'

'Really? I wouldn't want to interfere or put you out. This is Alex's job.' *Ramble-much?*

Tim's smile was so amazingly bright, she could almost drool. 'It'd be a pleasure.'

'Ah huh.' For her, *hell yeah.*

'Don't worry Alex, we'll keep the lady safe,' said Tim. 'Come on, Verily. It's not often that we get to show tourists around.'

'Okay.' She'd follow Tim anywhere and skipped forward and Alex's arm dropped. Now cool away from his body heat, she shuddered. *No way!* It was Alex she was reacting to, not the cute cowboy.

'Sherice, you coming?' Tim asked.

'Nah, seen one cow, seen 'em all,' snarled out Sherice, staring daggers at Verily.

What was that woman's problem?

'Do you play on Alex's softball team too?' Tim asked Verily.

'Molly and Alex are trying to get me to play. Were you at last week's game?'

'Nah, I was busy with the muster. I'll be there for the

Rosella Festival though. Hey, have you seen Cecil yet?'

'I have,' Verily replied, laughing. 'I've never seen a water buffalo like it.'

'Esther keeps Cecil painted so we don't mistake him for a feral-buff and put a bullet in him.'

She gasped. Woah, these guys had guns. How wild west were they?

'Right now, let's get you sorted. You'll need a hat, wouldn't want you gettin' sunburnt. Hey Sherice, can you grab Verily a hat, please? There's a spare one inside by the door of the office.'

'Sure, sugar, whatever, I'll play fetch for the little...' On her boot's heel, Sherice spun around muttering to herself with a hip-swinging walk that'd make traffic stop, unlike Verily's dust-stirring-clomp through the yard.

Verily felt like a common cow compared to the shiny Sherice. 'What did she say?'

'I dunno. She does that,' replied Tim with a shrug. 'Anyway, have you had your fill of dust yet?'

'I got swamped on day one from this passing road train—the driver was a menace.'

'Oi, I am not,' called back Alex as he headed for the driver's side of the massive truck that threw as much shadow as a house.

She watched Alex's denim stride. Should she take photos of his great arse? Did she dare step back and compare cowboys' bums while both were in view?

'Have you ever been dusted by a herd of cattle before?' Tim asked.

'Um, no. Will it wash out?' She held up her phone's camera aiming for that perfect shot.

'Heh, you're a good sort. About time Alex found himself a lady with a sense of humour, he's just as bad.' Tim laughed loud and patted her back so hard, it pushed her forward.

'*Oi*, watch the back-slapping, Tim. The lady has a sore shoulder,' shouted Alex, with a fierce frown.

'Sorry, mate, I didn't mean to rough up your girlfriend,' said Tim humbly, then looked down at her wincing. 'I'm sorry, Verily.'

'It's all good.' *Not good!* When they were lying about being a couple.

She caught Alex's pleading face, silently begging her to keep up the scam. Even if she didn't understand why, she'd do it for Alex. Its what mates did, right?

* * *

Cattle loaded and with a blast of the air horn that punched through the air, Alex steered the road train out of the station's yard. 'So, what did you think?'

'Tim's great, and the guys he works with are fun too,' replied Verily with a wide smile and a touch of dust across her pink skin. She sat in the passenger seat watching all as he drove them back to Elsie Creek Railway Station.

'Ah-huh.' Should he be jealous of his mate, who got on very well with Verily. Her smile was impossible to miss when she was mucking around with Tim. She'd taken her photos and joked around with the ringers in her oversized cowboy hat, managing to look both cute and comfortable amongst the stockmen. All while Alex was busy loading cattle and trying hard to avoid Sherice

'Hey, what was Sherice's problem?' Verily asked. 'And why did you let them think I'm your girlfriend? I don't like lying to strangers, especially nice ones.'

Who did she think was nice, Tim? 'We didn't lie, I only put my arm around you.'

'Which implied something was going on when we're just mates.'

Well, he stuffed that up, didn't he.

Alex wiped at the layer of dust from his face as he slowed to cross over a cattle grid. Through the side-mirror, he eyed the long trailers he was towing like a snake in the red sand where the truck-churning dust plume could easily be seen for miles.

'I'm waiting.'

'For what?'

'The conversation, when we have a long slow road ahead of us.'

Now the clever woman was using his words against him. He liked that. 'Can you notice the difference in weight dragging?'

'Yes. And the smell of cattle, or is that you?' She waved the hand in front of her face.

The cheeky thing. 'You got sunburnt.'

'I'll be okay, I've been worse. I'm always wearing sunscreen, a habit of playing an outdoor sport.'

That explained why she never complained once about

standing in the sun in the cattle yards. Tim was right, Verily was a good sort and had said his girl was gold.

But she wasn't his girl, and they'd lied to Tim, who was a good mate. But he had to do it or he would've had Sherice in his face. 'Is that why you dress like that?

'Like I'm going to the gym? That's what Sherice said.'

'Oi, don't worry about Sherice, she's not the kind to break out the bikkies and tea for guests.'

'That explains why she ignored me all morning.'

He wished Sherice had done the same to him, too.

'What I don't get is, is Sherice like that to me or all people in general?'

'Would it matter?'

'No. I'm okay when on a playing field, sledging happens, but I don't play in this town and I've never met that woman until today. Yet, I got the distinct impression she didn't like me.'

'Girls doing the on-field sledging? You're kidding.' His team never did it.

'Believe me, it's a nasty bitch-fest.'

'How? When you hardly talk or did you shrug your way out of it?'

Her lips pursed tight as if to stop smiling and she shrugged, freezing her shoulders high. 'Then I'd hit them with my fastball.'

'Ouch. I've seen how fast you throw.'

'*Used* to.'

It had to hurt to be in your prime and lose that overnight. 'I saw this YouTube clip—'

'While cyberstalking me?'

'Nah…' *Yeah.* He faced the road ahead to avoid that focused stare of hers. Batting against Verily would be scary. 'I saw this young girl with one arm, who went back to playing after losing it in a bike accident. You've still got your arm and a spare, and they both seemed to move just fine.'

She sat back in her seat, arms crossed over her chest, looking out the window. 'I'll never be as good as I was.'

'What does it matter. Are you scared of failing?'

'I have failed, don't you get it.'

'How do you learn if you don't fail now and again? Hey, I bugger up with my beer too.'

'Should you be telling me that when you only pay me for my labour in beer?'

'I'm getting better. Practise makes perfect, so they reckon.

'I used to believe that.'

They drove on in silence with the steady engine roaring in the background. The long red road ahead of them cut through the spindly scrub across sandy plains and through to spring-fed creeks. Paperbark swamps led to cool monsoonal forests with thick canopies that blocked the sunlight. They passed billabongs with pink lotus lilies that followed the sun as long-legged birds waded along its edges. Wallabies lay beneath shady trees just behind the pink, flowering turkey bush that lined the track like hedges as they headed closer to town.

Breaking the silence, Verily asked, 'What was going on with you and Sherice?'

'Damn it.' He dropped his head and pushed up his sunglasses. 'Was it that obvious?' He hoped not.

'No, I took a guess. Sherice wasn't shirty at me, she was jealous at what you did *with* me. You said you'd explain.'

'Do I have to?'

'You said you would.'

'Don't judge me.'

'What's the big deal?'

'I slept with Sherice.'

Her eyebrows rose, and she faced the road. 'So, she's an old girlfriend then?'

'A month ago,' he admitted sheepishly.

'No way,' she said, staring back at him. 'Tim told me he got engaged to Sherice four months ago, on their second anniversary as a couple.'

'I honestly didn't know.' Alex sighed heavily, leaning on the steering wheel. 'I'd only found out about it the other week. Sherice is from Lavell's station on the other side of Katherine. I had no idea.'

'Did you tell Tim?'

'And get my head punched in. Are you crazy?'

'That poor guy is going to marry a woman who's cheating on him—with you.'

'Great, make me sound like a loser when I already feel terrible. Tim's a mate and we go way back.' The kind of mate you didn't see for years, where you'd pick up the conversation as if it was only yesterday.'

'How did you *not know* if he's such a good mate?'

'Tim's been working out west for a bit and my dad's

been doing this side of the station runs. I don't go to the pub much anymore not since I began brewing back home. *I don't know* how I missed it? I just know I did, and if I'd known I wouldn't have touched her. I swear.'

'And how long have you known Sherice?'

'I only met her late last year doing the truck hauls. That's it, and softball.'

Verily pointed her finger at him. 'I bet it was a carpark party, right?'

Was he that transparent to the woman? 'Oi, just because I play with the girls—'

'You sleep with them too.'

'Nick-off. Those girls on my team are my mates, and I've never slept with any of them. Do you know how much crap I get put on by their partners, boyfriends, big brothers, and new husbands? I've even had fathers on my case about being near their girls playing softball. All throughout school, they teased me over it.'

'But you still played.'

'It's a game.' He snatched up his water bottle and took a deep swig while keeping an eye on the road ahead. 'I hate what I've done with Sherice. If I'd known she was with someone I wouldn't have touched her. I'm not like that.'

'You're saying you don't cheat?'

'I've had plenty of married women throw themselves at me, but I won't.'

'What special moral code do you live under?'

'My own. My dad cheated on my mother and I remember her crying with Molly over it in the mango orchard, getting hammered on the wine. I was just a kid helping Mum stagger home and putting her to bed, while Dad was out on the road, like always. My mum made me swear to never do it, and I've kept it that way, until that…' Alex gripped the wheel tighter, hating himself.

The road weaved and bent as he followed the trail that looked the same as always. It was as if time stood still out here across the outback. Shame he couldn't turn back time himself.

'Do you think I'm a rotten bastard for what I did with Sherice?' He asked Verily.

Again, she shrugged.

'Oh, come on, I've just bared my soul! That deserves more than a shoulder shrug.' He snapped at her. He'd never been like this with anyone. Yet, Verily was so easy to talk to about things he'd never dare share with anyone else.

'Okay, okay,' she said, holding her hands up in surrender.

'Okay, what? I'm an idiot?'

'You got tricked. It happens.'

'It wasn't meant to happen.' He'd been so careful. 'Has it ever happened to you?'

'Yeah. I hooked up with this assistant coach from another team during the playoffs. I didn't know he was married, but as soon as I found out—courtesy of his wife—I confronted him about it.'

'Jeez, that's ballsy.' He hated confrontations.

'I didn't like being in the middle, either. You know, this guy then told me they'd separated, but his wife had a different story. Although, technically, he may have been right, because

I'd heard they both filed for divorce soon after that.'

'Because of you?'

She shrugged.

'So, you're not an old maid, then?'

'I think I might be,' she said, wiping some dust off her thighs. 'Do I dress like I'm going to the gym?'

'What you're wearing is fine.' What he'd give to see her in her underwear again. 'I already told you not to worry about Sherice, she's not in your league. You're so much better than her, so don't worry about Sherice.' He did not just say that! Heat crept up the back of his neck.

'She's gorgeous.'

'She's ugly. Inner ugly.'

'That's not nice to say about your ex-bunk-buddy.'

'My what? That saying had some real southern drawl to it.' Her mixed accent was cute.

'You sound like a bitter, jilted lover.'

'I wouldn't even call it that.'

'What would you call it?'

'A dusty booty-call in the carpark.'

'No way. What happens at rodeos then?'

'We've got buckle-bunnies for that.'

'What?'

'They're like groupies that follow bands.'

She slapped her hand to her forehead and said in a dramatic tone, '*What is this strange world I've landed in?*' They shared a laugh between them, then she said, 'If you were in Tim's position, would you want to know if your partner was cheating on you?'

Damn. He glanced at her with a frown. 'Maybe I shouldn't have pushed for the conversation.'

She shrugged.

Again, he sighed heavily, leaning over the wheel and stared at the long road ahead. 'I remember what Mum was like, and I'd wondered back then if it was better to not know because it tore our family apart. I don't think Mum ever truly trusted Dad after that.' Neither did Alex, and he used to idolise the man—until then.

'Did your parents separate?'

'They had this big blue where Mum threw things at Dad, who hit the road—like always. Then, I fell off the motorbike and broke my ribs, punctured a lung and they kissed and made-up over my hospital bed.'

'Aww, how romantic.'

'I was in a lot of pain and thought it was the drugs, myself.'

'Drugs are good for pain.'

'Are you on hard drugs for your shoulder?'

'What?'

'I heard Molly talking to Jenny after the game, about you needing medicine. Jenny's going to talk to the town doctor about shipping them in. Is that true? I mean, it must be pretty serious medication to ship it in.'

'My painkillers. I don't use them much, only on bad days. Don't worry, I won't be asking to drive on those days.'

'So, the good stuff, eh?'

She shrugged staring out the window.

'Have you seen the town's doctor yet? The women in

town are all gooey over the fancy guy from some city hospital.'

'Gooey?' She giggled at him.

'Not my word, it's my teammates who call him the Hot-Doc.'

'I like to avoid all things medical, thank you, especially doctors if I can.'

Good. 'Do you exercise it?'

'Excuse me?'

'Well, you must do something the way you look… fit, I mean, do you do exercises for your arm to make it better, like physio?'

'I exercise daily.'

'What else do you do?'

Again, she shrugged.

'Is shrugging part of your exercise routine?'

'Should be, huh?' She sat there shrugging at him. 'So, are you going to tell me all the ins and outs of your medical condition too?'

That was fair. He was being nosy and blurted out, 'What would you do if you were in Tim's position?'

Without hesitation, she said, 'I'd want to know the truth. Even if it meant the risk of getting my head punched in, I'd say something if the guy was my friend.'

'Why?'

'Well, Tim hasn't married Sherice yet. She hasn't moved in, so they have time to sort these things out now, instead of later. Do you think Sherice is the type to sleep with other men if she's done this with you?'

'Who let you out of your box?'

'You asked.'

'Yeah, I did.' And the truck hit the bitumen road leaving the dusty trail behind them. 'Thanks for the conversation, and for being honest with me, and for playing along before.'

'All good. Not that I've helped any.'

'But you've got me thinking. I'll let you drive the truck to the next station.'

'Really?' Her eyes lit up, and the smile was pure sunshine in his world.

'Sure, when we're well away from all chances of cops and transit police.'

'You're on.'

Alex steered them back to Elsie Creek, unsure if he'd ever tell Tim. But what worried him more was that he'd been friend-zoned by Verily for what he'd done with Sherice. And that just sucked.

EIGHT

olly stroked the last slash of colour across Verily's fingernails and put the lid on the bottle of polish. 'I like this colour on you.'

'I've never worn this colour.' With her sneakers up on the small dividing fence that surrounded the oval, Verily blew on her painted nails where the sun caught the sparkly blue. Her nails had never been this long before. 'I like the colour of your hair today.'

'I like this red. Blonde makes me look washed out after a while,' said Molly, patting her new hairstyle.

'ALL RIGHT YOU MOB OF MANGROVE MIDGIES, GET INTO POSITION,' shouted Agnes to the straggly crew of Dusty Dingoes as they practised on the field.

'Did you ever have a coach yell at you like Agnes does?' Molly asked Verily.

'No. They believed in building on your strengths with the help from their assistant coaches who were all about positivity. Although, we were all too scared to go against the head coach in fear of getting benched.'

'Did you ever get benched?'

'Yep, for being a smart mouth. The team lost and they hated me after that, so I learned to shut my mouth when on-field.' Strangely, Alex and Molly seemed determined to make her talk more.

'I spotted you at the fence line this morning, what were you doing?'

'Walking.' She'd finally found the courage to leave her room and do more. She didn't have a club curfew. No scheduled practices. No team rules to follow on tour. This was her first holiday. Hers.

It was a strange feeling to be free from routines and training schedules in between games. She used to have her daily exercises on the floor before she left whatever room she was living in, then she'd follow it up with a run around the hotel or suburb she was staying in. It's the only thing that remained the same no matter where she was.

'You didn't spot any broken fences on your travels?'

'I wasn't looking.'

'That's what I used the scooter for, to check the perimeter fences and fire breaks. Careful lighting fires, it is bushfire season.'

'Guess I'll have to keep the smoke signals to a bare minimum.' She didn't know about riding that scooter again after being bathed in red dust. 'What do you do to fix a broken fence?'

'Alex can fix it when he has time. I don't think he'd appreciate cattle wandering through his mango orchard.'

'I can just picture his face if they did.'

'Mango leaves are poisonous to stock, hon.'

'I'll remember that.'

'You and Alex are getting along.'

'Just being neighbourly.' She didn't dare wish for more, but there was no harm in looking, and she adjusted her cap to covertly perve on him practising softball.

'I had this young jackeroo come into the shop today,' said Molly, slow-twirling her brolly over her shoulder.

'I'm sure it's not the first time a jackeroo has walked through your door. After all, it is cattle country,' said Verily with a giggle. 'Did he book in for a mani-pedi?'

'He was looking for you.'

'Me?'

'Word's out there's a new female in town.'

'What?'

'Haven't you heard about the male to female ratio out here?'

'Do I need to?'

'It's about ten men to one woman. More if you count the miners.'

'How do they even know I'm here when I go nowhere?' She looked at her Aunt smiling away while twirling that brolly over her shoulder, watching the women practise on the field. 'You didn't...'

'I told him we were having dinner at the pub on Friday. I'm driving. Alex said he's giving you a beer education. So, it'll be like a coming-out-gala for you to meet the locals. Have you got a dress?'

'It's the pub, not a debutante ball—isn't it?'

'We should have one of those at the Rosella Festival, after the rodeo, if we can find a band. We should have fireworks too.'

'How big is this Festival? Next, you'll want to get a marching band to lead the parade down the main street.'

Molly's eyes widened. 'What a fabulous idea. We could have a cavalcade of players in the back of utes for each attending team, all following our newly crowned softball sweetheart.'

'Like a homecoming queen.'

'Or our very own Miss Rosella.'

'I was only kidding, Molly.' Verily grinned.

Molly dug around in her bag, pulling out her notebook and pen. 'I'm not. I'm meeting with the committee on Friday night at the pub, I'll ask then. No harm in asking, and it's something to consider for the future.' A softball landed at their feet. 'Toss it back, hon.'

Verily bent down and plucked up the large ball, her hand moulded around the leather as her fingers gripped, it was so familiar.

'Come on Verily, we haven't got all day,' shouted Alex from the catcher's plate on the far side. 'Unlike you, holidaying and painting your nails.'

'Why the cheeky bugger, aim for his balls, hon,' said Molly, pointing her pen at the catcher.

'Bastard.' Verily reacted with reflex more than thought. Her arm side-winded like a windmill, and in one lifelong practised move she let go. Like a catapult, it propelled the white leather ball across the field, blindingly fast.

WHACK! The ball slapped hard against Alex's open glove. He just stared at her, then at the ball in his mitt.

'*Were you aiming for my balls?*' He shook his hand free

from the catcher's mitt as if it stung, while the girls on the field stared with open mouths.

'Oh no, no, no, no. *No.*' The pain tore through her upper arm and shoulder and Verily dove for the esky to grab an ice pack. She'd thrown a fastball without even warming up. 'I'm so stupid.' What possessed her to show off like that?

'Are you okay, hon?' Molly asked, holding hesitant fingers to Verily's shoulder.

'Why did I do that?' Verily slapped the ice on her sore shoulder where the stabbing heat of pain speared through to her hand. 'I'll be paying for that. I'll try and walk it off.' Repeating the mantra of many a coach, she snatched up a water bottle.

Why did she do that when her arm was doing so well?

It was another reminder she'd never be at that elite level again. It was nothing but a downhill slide from here, no matter how much she might want it.

Who was she kidding? She couldn't play or get involved with anyone or any team, because she didn't want to disappoint them as much as she was disappointed in herself.

Like always, painfully, she ran alone with that familiar weight of loneliness bearing down on her shoulders and headed back to Molly's.

* * *

Alex jogged over to Molly and reached into the esky for a chunk of ice. 'Where did Verily go?'

'Home.'

'Is she okay?'

'I think she threw her shoulder out. How's your hand?'

'It stings, I wasn't expecting that.'

'I don't think Verily did either. She just threw it so effortlessly.'

'I knew she could do it.' It was the fastest ball he'd ever caught.

'Verily said she'll pay for it.'

'Is Verily okay, was she upset? I should go pick her up—'

'Let her be. Maybe she needs to clear her head. Don't worry, Verily is one of those runners who used to run every day like religion.'

'I'd seen her walking the boundary track.'

'Her father said she'd do sit-ups and stuff as a morning ritual. I guess that's why she's got such a flat tummy.' Molly patted her own stomach.

'What else did Verily's father say about her morning training?'

'She'd do her exercises, then run for an hour, then throw the ball for an hour, all before school. Now that's commitment.'

'To get to that elite level you'd have to be,' mumbled Alex, calm on the outside, but inside, his guts ached in a knot. He was so tempted to jump in his ute and chase after her.

When Speedy dashed over, spitting her fair hair out of her face, she then punched Alex on the arm.

'Oi, what did I do to you?'

'That wouldn't hurt,' said Speedy. 'Why didn't you tell me Molly's niece could throw? Did you see that? Did you see,

Molly? It was huge. It was the most supersonic ball I've ever seen and the distance, it flew all the way from here to all the way over there. Did you see it, Molly?'

'I saw it Speedy. Well, I didn't actually, it flew so fast. I heard you catch it, Alex.'

'I'm still feeling it.' Alex sucked on the chunk of ice cooling his palm.

'I've seen nothing like it. Will she play, Molly? Will she?' Speedy jiggled around like she was about to pee her pants.

'No.'

'Why not?' Speedy's shoulders slumped and her jittering stopped.

'Verily's recovering from shoulder surgery and a broken arm.'

'The one she threw with?'

'Yes.'

'No way. Can you imagine what she was like before the break, can ya?' Speedy thumbed up the brim of her baseball cap, with her eyes widening at Alex.

'You have no idea, Speedy.' What Alex would give to see Verily pitching in another game.

'D'ya think she'd teach me to chuck a screamer like she let loose across the paddock? None of this mob can chuck half as good, not even the blokes. She'd have tips, wouldn't she?'

'It wouldn't hurt to ask, Molly?' God knows his cousin could do with the help.

'Do you think she would, Molly? Do ya?' Speedy's jittering started up again as she bounced on her toes. 'I'll pay her with chocolate or —'

'Not beer, that's my bartering tool.'

'Typical bloke and their mates-rates in beer currency.' Speedy nudged Alex in the ribs with her skinny elbow, then she faced Molly and begged. 'D'ya reckon your niece would, huh? I'll do her washing and ironing, and I'll clean your house, you name it, Molly.'

'Can we book you in to manage the picking crew this mango season?' Alex asked.

'Why? Who's managing your orchard, Molly?'

'I've got a new manager this year, and the trees look fabulous.'

To stop smiling, Alex sucked on the dripping chunk of ice soothing his stinging palm.

Speedy shook her head. 'Dunno? I don't like working for people I don't know.'

'I know you, and Molly knows you,' said Alex.

'But I've promised the Cobbs who are offering me a bonus to work their crop.'

'Damn… I can't afford that and you deserve it, Speedy. Good for you.' Alex patted Speedy on her skinny shoulder, proud of her.

Speedy pointed up at her big cousin. 'You're the one managing it, aren't you?'

'We haven't told too many people; you know what my old man is like.'

'I won't say nothin', not that anyone listens to me anyway.' Speedy then squinted up at him. 'Tell you what, *cuz*, if you can get Verily to teach me, I'll work for you at last year's seasonal rates, I will.'

'Don't tease me like that.'

'It's the family deal. But only if your mate coaches me and I get to strike someone out once this season. I'll do it, I will.'

'You're on.' He held out his hand and his cousin shook it with a wide smile.

'Hey, is this that sheila you said was a professional player with hands smaller than mine? She sure chucked a pearler, she did.'

'I don't think Verily would appreciate throwing cowpats in the paddock, Speedy.'

'I don't care if it's mud pies. Did you see her throw! Did you see it?' Speedy skipped off across the field.

'I could learn a lot from Speedy this picking season, and at the rate she's offered, I can afford her.' Alex leaned his hip against the boundary fence where he let the iced water drip between his fingers. 'What do you think Verily will say?'

'No harm in asking,' said Molly.

'Can you ask her?'

'No. You can.'

'Me, why?'

'Verily likes you.'

He straightened his back as he arched an eyebrow at Molly. 'She does?'

'You two get along, don't you?'

It was his turn to shrug and act cool. 'I dunno, Molly, I swear she was aiming for the crown jewels.' Thank god he caught that softball or he'd have been knackered—literally.

Molly giggled. 'Only because I told her to. How fast was that throw?'

'No idea. Sorry, I didn't bring my speed camera with me. I let the cops borrow it to sit on the highway and hassle the tourists. My bad.'

'You cheeky bugger. I can see why you and Verily get on so well together.'

'I wasn't expecting her to throw, not like that.'

'Neither was Verily.'

'The only problem is, Verily wanted to keep who she is on the quiet, but she's got their attention with that throw,' he said, throwing his thumb back at his teammates out on the field.

Molly twirled her umbrella like a propeller over her shoulder and said, 'I'd love Verily to teach Agnes a lesson.'

'I'm not getting in the middle of that one, not when the coach hates me enough already.' Palms up, he stepped away from Molly and the melodrama.

How could he convince Verily to coach his cousin? Because getting Speedy on board would increase his profits as a first-time primary producer, giving him more money to invest in his micro-brewery.

But what nagged him most as he strolled back to the home plate, was whether Verily was okay?

NINE

Everything ached, from the tip of her toes to her fingertips where Verily lay perfectly still in bed, staring at the ceiling fan's large blades catching the morning sunlight like an inverted helicopter. It'd taken ages to get used to the tick-tick-ticking turns of the fan. Just like the geckos that dashed across the internal walls at night, chasing bugs.

She glanced out her open window to her view of the orchard that was once barren with its skeletal limbs now flush with dark glossy green leaves. A curlew couple, with their long stork-like legs, foraged amongst the tree roots accompanied by a few white ibises.

Verily shifted, and a moan escaped. She had sore feet, blisters, shin splints, tight calves, achy thighs and her shoulder throbbed.

But still, she smiled.

She'd done it.

Exhausted, hot, sweaty and thirsty, she'd done it—ran all the way home, beating Alex and Molly back.

Once she'd left the town's main street, free from whistles that came from the pub, there hadn't been a car on the road anywhere, and thankfully, no stray pygmy water buffalo to follow her.

But then she'd chased the sunset.

Amid open country, on a red dirt road, passing ant mounds that someone had dressed in clothes like outback garden gnomes, and without another soul to bother her, except the odd grazing cow, she'd pushed herself.

It was so different from jogging suburban streets that looked the same, no matter which country she was in. She'd run in city streets, through smog, yet rarely through fog. After all, softball was a summer sport, and she lived a never-ending summer, chasing the sun around the world. To here.

Knock. Knock.

'Are you alive in there, hon?' Molly called out from the other side of the bedroom door.

'I'm awake,' and most definitely alive.

The door opened and Molly's corked wedges squeaked across the floorboards as she carried a small pile of folded clothes. 'I just wanted to check on you and bring in your clothes.'

'You don't have to do my laundry, Molly.' As far as Verily's skill levels for domesticity went, laundry was her greatest talent. She'd hung out in many laundromats and had hand washing down to a fine art using the tiniest of sinks in hotel rooms. It was cooking skills she lacked.

'I needed to fill the machine,' said Molly. 'Your feet look sore.'

'I'll survive.' And knew it. She'd pushed beyond her comfort zone and won.

But she'd never achieve that elite level again and lay

back on her pillow, defeated.

Molly pointed to the pile of pills on the bedside table. 'You could start a chemist shop there.'

'I could.' Verily realised she hadn't had any painkillers, nothing—but then again, she hadn't gotten out of bed, *yet*.

'Is your shoulder okay?'

'It's swollen and sore, but manageable.' If she laid in bed forever. Then she spotted the worry etched in the deepening crow's feet around Molly's eyes. 'I'm fine, Molly. I swear it.'

'Okay… It's late-night shopping tonight, will you be right to fix yourself something for dinner?'

'Late night shopping? In a one street town?'

'A few of the girls want their hair done, it's gonna be a big night at the pub tomorrow night. Are you going to wear shoes on those feet?'

'No stilettos in a hurry, that's for sure.' She giggled, wriggling her painted toes that Molly had attacked. 'Go. I'm sure I'll find something to eat. It might be my chance to learn to cook.'

'Well, call me for anything.' Molly caught the door jamb on her way out and asked, 'Hey, hon, what do you think about cleaning?'

'I don't. If I was rich, I'd hire a cleaner.' That was one of the advantages of living out of hotel rooms—room service and housekeeping.

'Someone offered to be our house-cleaner last night.'

'How much were they charging? Not that I'd know the going rate.'

'Um...'

'Hey, my pitch didn't cause too much of a stir yesterday, did it?'

'You've got Speedy's attention.'

'Speedy?'

'The Dusty Dingoes pitcher.'

'The one who can't throw?' It'd been painful watching a pitcher unable to pitch near the home plate.

'Yep.'

'Oh, that poor kid.' Why did she show off like that?

'I know, little Speedy tries so hard, too. Well, call me.'

'I will, thanks.' Verily lay back and stared at the circling ceiling fan.

She remained there until Molly's SUV had long disappeared down the driveway.

The birds shared their morning songs as the breeze carried fresh earthy scents through the window. Beneath it, pages flipped open from the scrapbooks that sat on the spare chair. Up and down, the pages flapped and shifted like a fan as the breeze picked up.

With a groan, she forced herself to roll off the bed and onto the floor mat. There, she started her daily Yoga-like slow stretches and sit-ups, too sore to do any push-ups today.

Everything ached.

As she lay there, she forced her arm slowly above her head, stretching her spine and her arms and smiled. It hurt, but she could do it. Even with that hot throbbing pain in her shoulder and arm, she could cope without the painkillers. Also aware, if she pushed it further, she'd be swimming in a world of pain.

She rolled over and used the bed to sit up, drank some water from the bottle on her bedside table and stared down at her red, blistered feet. She shouldn't have gotten blisters in those shoes. When not that long ago, running had been part of a lifelong habit.

Sure, she got blisters every time she got a new pair of cleats for the start of the season. It happened with every new uniform when starting with another new team, all supplied by sponsors. Along with bats, balls, helmets, and protective padding, even mouth guards and sports underwear came from sponsors.

Only one thing remained the same—her glove.

Once you found that right glove you moulded it to your hand like it was a part of your skin. Checking over the stitches, tightening the webbing, working it until it became a part of the player. And Verily had her glove restitched and the webbing replaced annually.

She also hadn't seen it since the bus accident.

Meanwhile, the pages on the scrapbooks flapped in the breeze on the chair. It was irritating.

She opened her closet and slipped her laundered clothes into the suitcase that had seen countless hotels and airports. She hadn't unpacked, she never bothered anymore and it'd been years since she'd put her case away. Would she ever unpack permanently?

Again, the pages flapped in a fan formation with the breeze.

She stared at the scrapbooks that belonged to her

mother that told the tale of a young girl, a stranger in one sense, when Verily had hoped for something more to connect them. Unfortunately, it was like looking at a foreign magazine where you didn't know the models, the places, the language, or the reasons.

Although, she now recognised her mother Rose, and Molly, when younger.

If her mother hadn't have died, would Verily still be living here in this house or the cottage? Would she have gone to the local school that was only one building which didn't have enough kids to fill a mini-car?

How different would her life be today if her father had decided to stay?

Why was she bothering with the past when she was still trying to work out her future?

She scooped up the scrapbooks from the spare chair and with one hand she slid them onto the top shelf where they hung over the edge, as if stuck.

Angry with herself at not being able to do the simplest of tasks, she raised her achy left arm. A heated spike of pain from her shoulder travelled down her ulnar nerve and through to her fingers. Resisting it and through gritted teeth, she shoved the scrapbooks back on the shelf as if shifting a massive board of solid stone.

But she'd succeeded.

Relieved, she lowered her achy arm and rubbed it, flexing her hand. The fourth finger was a little numb, and the pinkie tingled like teenage growing pains.

Since the accident, the ulnar nerve had been a constant

electrical-humming ache, always playing its tune, but there were bigger contenders who demanded her attention—like the upper arm and shoulder with its throbbing heated pain.

DONK!

'*Ow!*' She rubbed the sharp pain from something dropping on her head, as a softball rolled across the floor and under her bed.

'What the hell.' *Stuff you, Alex!* Why should she change for him? It was her saying and her shrug.

Donk. Another softball rolled off the top shelf. Then another, and another, and then it started raining softballs.

Grabbing the spare chair, she opened the cupboard door wide against the window. With achy feet, she climbed up to catch another two softballs while more spilled across the floor and rolled under the bed.

On tippy toes and with nose to the shelf, she peeked over to discover a cotton sack with another ball caught in the bag's mouth. It rested against the pile of scrapbooks.

Wood and leather rustled in the cotton bag as she pulled it down. She sat on the floor amongst the spilled softballs and opened the simple rope line that made up the mouth like a sailor-sack. There, she peered inside and grinned. 'No way.'

Three ancient wooden softball bats of different sizes were retrieved from the sack. Unlike the aluminium ones of today, these looked handcrafted. There was writing on the handle at the base like she'd seen many times, and the name read: *Rose.*

Verily blinked at the name and at the differing bat sizes before her. They were her mother's.

She lay them down on the floor like matchsticks. Softball mums she'd known, would have them displayed on walls in their homes like decorative antiques. Coaches would hang them in their office like trophies, while she had them lying on the floor.

Inside the sack, she pulled out more balls wrapped in tissue paper. They appeared to be brand new. Unlike the grey, scuffed ones that fell across the floor, these antique, soft leather balls were white. She recognised the detail in the hand-stitching set amongst the finest of leather, made of cork and no synthetics. How rare.

If Verily's past teammates and other pitchers saw these, they'd be oohing and aahing over the balls alone as if they were national treasures.

Carefully, she dusted the floor and placed them onto the tissue paper next to the bats as the sunrise streamed over them like gems in a jewellery store.

Having spent years playing with cheap substitutes, Verily recognised quality when she saw it and sat back admiring them.

As a small kid, she'd instantly fallen in love with the sport when she'd learned to play it in class one day. Her teacher showed her how to catch and throw and she loved it. She'd told her dad, who helped her to throw. While other fathers took their sons to the football or their daughters to ballet lessons, Verily's dad spent hours playing catch with her in the tiny driveway of their apartment block after work.

They couldn't afford the equipment to practise with and Verily's first glove was a cheap plastic knock-off. It gave her blisters, and she suffered terrible sweat rash from wearing the nasty vinyl, but she looked after it because that was all they could find for a left-handed pitcher.

For pitching practise, she'd scavenged busted tennis balls and filled them with lead and other scrap metals. She then wrapped the tennis balls with electrical tape to make them the same size as a softball.

From amongst the scrap on the side of the road, she'd dragged an old car tyre home after school. An onion bag she'd foraged from the kitchen to make a net to cover the back of the tyre. Then when her dad came home from work, he'd helped her tie it to the tree in their small yard, making it the same height as the catcher's mitt. That's what she aimed for, the hole in the tyre that would swing. Every single day, all summer long. For years.

She'd gotten so used to that solid, weighty ball that when she'd finally found the courage to pitch at the try-outs for the school softball team, the weight was nothing, her aim was perfect and she was instantly put into the senior's team at ten.

That silly tyre and those lead-filled tennis balls travelled with them everywhere. They were the first things she unpacked at a new town, a new school, at the start of every new softball season.

Now here she was, in another new town in her first season as a non-player.

She squeezed the softball in her hands, seated on the floor in her mother's old room.

She'd never throw these softballs. The stitching had

never touched dirt, nor had they been gripped by sweaty hands, or dusted with chalk.

'What else is in here?' There wasn't a mound big enough for a helmet in the black sack—if they had helmets back in those days.

Digging around in the bag she pulled out a glove. 'Huh?' Old, dry and brittle, the stitching had deteriorated on the unknown brand of glove. Verily checked the inside along the heel of the glove and found a name written in pen, *Rose*.

She slid her hand into the scratchy stiff leather and grinned. 'What do you know, Mum, we're the same size, and both lefties?' She giggled at the glove. It desperately needed a good oiling, and she remembered how perfect the fit of her own glove was.

She put it down beside the bats and pristine balls and reached into the sack for the last item and pulled out a tiny glove. It was so soft and small it sat in the centre of her palm. She'd never seen one so small.

Inside, on the wrist of the leather glove, she read another name. *Verily*.

Tears formed as the lump stuck in her thickening throat. She clutched the tiny glove to her chest, and even though her body ached, her heart ached more.

Was this what she'd been searching for?

Had she found her answers in a black sack, inside a room that was like a shrine to a woman she didn't know.

Now she knew a connection, a shared a love for softball.

And that's all Verily knew… softball.

She re-wrapped the balls back into their tissue paper,

and along with the bats, she returned them to the cotton sack with her mother's glove. With the swipe of her arm, she dumped all of the pill packets and painkillers into the top drawer and placed her baby glove on the clear bedside table.

On hands and knees, she gathered the old well-worn softballs together and dumped them into the sack. She then wriggled under the bed to tackle the dust bunnies for the last one.

'What the Hell!'

With her shoulder aching along with the rest of her body, she dragged out the final ball and the handle of the biggest monster under her bed.

It was a large black duffel bag she dumped in the centre of the room.

'How did you get here?'

It was her gameday bag.

A large, rectangular bag with wheels on the bottom that she'd dragged through many airports and bus stations from England, the Netherlands, El Salvador, Taiwan, Canada, China, Venezuela, New Zealand, and all over the United States. The tags and stickers showed the many countries and Championships she'd attended. It was well worn, yet so big and modern, compared to the simple cotton sack that lay beside it.

She pulled down the zip and opened the mouth wide, exposing her bats that lay on the outer, just like she'd packed them. She was a hopeless hitter and those bats had never been used. Her helmet, training shoes, and cleats were hardly worn. Her batting gloves, shin guards, mouth guards, and protective pads were all there. It even contained the strapping tape, liniments, and heat pads for her pitching arm, along with her string bag of balls she slammed with daily.

It also had her uniform from the last game she'd ever played which was the World Championships, held in Chiba, Japan, where she'd broken the world record—twice.

Heartbroken, she started to zip it shut when she spotted the soft towel she used to wipe sweat and dirt off the balls during the game. It was clean, and it wrapped around her most prized possession.

Unwrapping the soft towel, she revealed her glove, holding a spare ball.

The leather glove's stitching was new, ready for the start of another season. The fingertips scuffed but oiled just right, and she slid her hand inside.

A tremor squirrelled up her arm, her skin prickled and her scalp tingled as she slid on the glove and punched it with her fist, wincing at the pain. *'Damn.'* She inhaled slowly and exhaled, forcefully willing the pain to pass until it was manageable.

Opening her eyes, she stared at the glove in her lap. No matter how much money sponsors offered her to wear their glove, she only had one… and it was priceless.

Her father had it specially made for her as a birthday present when she'd turned thirteen, it was so big and sloppy but it became her lucky glove. The day her father had given it to her was the day she'd won the State Championships in Tasmania and was rewarded with a contract to play in America. She used to sleep with the damn thing and grew into it. She was always gripping a ball to help mould it just the way she wanted it—her way—the pitcher's way.

It was Verily's version of home.

The wind blew pushing the open cupboard door against the chair that stood in its way. It ricocheted hard back against the wall. From the top shelf a scuffed-up softball rolled off, it bounced along the floorboards to stop at Verily's blistered feet.

'No way.' Fear spiked along her spine as if a ghost was in the room.

She swallowed the lump in her throat, picked up the ball and gingerly tossed it into her glove. It fit perfectly.

She threw yesterday.

Could she dare do it again, today?

There was only one way to find out.

She groaned at the aches and pains as she scrambled to her sore feet. Scooping up her string bag of balls, she popped an anti-inflammatory and washed it down with water. All while wearing her glove, still holding the ball.

No one could see her and she didn't need to prove it to anyone, she just wanted to see for herself and went in search of a target.

TEN

Alex leaned against the open shed door, with hands in his pockets, Akubra on his head, staring at Molly's house. Molly was working late in the shop and he hadn't seen Verily.

How could he convince Verily to coach Speedy, who was beyond help?

But most of all, he was worried about Verily and needed to know how she was after running home last night.

He shoved off the shed's corrugated wall, scooped up his small esky from the bench behind him, and with heavy boots he trudged down the track.

'I'm just doing the neighbourly thing.'

He liked her, a lot. He'd gotten to know her this past month, but sadly he'd also been friend-zoned. She was Molly's niece and that kind of made her family and his landlady. Pity.

'Oh no.' His heart dropped at the sight on the veranda where Verily sat on the outdoor chair with an ice bag strapped to her shoulder and her arm in a sling. 'I'm so sorry I made you throw that ball.'

'Hello, Alex.'

'I am so, so sorry.' He winced, climbing the steps to

slink into the chair with the small round table between them.

'Not your fault.'

'Yes, it was. I hit that ball your way.'

'Did you tie my hand behind my back and force me to pick it up too?'

'Of course not, but…' Hesitating, he nodded at her sore arm.

'I threw out of reflex and didn't think.'

'Obviously, you're paying for it now.'

'It looks worse than it is.'

'Ya think!' It looked pretty bad from where he was sitting.

'The sling just takes the pressure off the shoulder, so don't stress. I know it doesn't look pretty or smell too great, but my sinuses are all clear.'

He smelt the liniment's eucalyptus aroma, but underneath there was her warm honeyed macadamia scent he adored. 'Are you okay, besides being sore?'

'Walking around with a wet t-shirt, while balancing a block of ice on my shoulder, I'm lucky it isn't winter.'

'It is winter.' His eyes flicked over her t-shirt that covered her perky breasts. *Why isn't it white?*

'I meant a winter with temperatures in the single digits. Hey!' She crossed her good arm over her shirt and pulled down the towel to cover herself.

Oops. 'Um, here.' He held out a bottle of beer to her.

'What are you trying to pay for now?'

'I've just brought these as a sorry thing.'

'To store in the cupboard?'

'No, to drink, they're cold. Do you want one or not?'

'Okay.'

Alex narrowed his eyes at her. 'Are you on any medications this brew might affect? My mate, Johnny, blames being drunk while on antibiotics as the reason he woke up married.'

She giggled with shiny eyes and a pretty smile. 'I'm okay, just a bit sore.'

'Are you sure you're all right?'

'Are you going to keep asking that?' She gave him a slight frown.

'Okay, point made.' He held up his hands to back off. He'd happily fuss over her if she'd let him. 'I'll get the glasses and we'll do this taste-test properly. It'll be good practise for tomorrow, at the pub.'

'Is this a new batch?'

'Yep,' Alex replied, opening the kitchen's flyscreen door and before it creaked shut, he'd returned with a set of beer glasses.

'Is this your new rosella brew?'

'No, I've got the rosellas soaking to plump them up. Did you spot any on your travels along the fence line? I might need more.'

'How big a witch's brew are you concocting?'

'I'm trying different techniques; I went for the dry hops this round. I'd love to try using a wet hops ferment next. I'm thinking of putting down a crop of hops among Molly's dragon fruit trellises next Dry. If she'll let me.'

'Molly is very protective over her dragon fruit. She can't

wait until they fruit, she really must love eating them.'

'Molly doesn't eat them.'

'Why not?'

'She uses them like cucumber slices for her eyes. She grows it for the anti-ageing properties, not for food but for cosmetic purposes only.'

Verily giggled, and it made him sigh with relief to see she was okay as he cracked open the lid of what he hoped was a good batch of beer.

'What are you trying to do with the rosella beer?'

'I'm trying to marry the spices and sugars to combat the tartness while aiming for a true sour IPA.' He poured his beer into the glass and held it up to the sunlight. 'This is my first Belgian Sour IPA.'

'So that's a beer, huh?'

He appreciated her honesty at not being a beer connoisseur like every other beer-loving bloke in the bush. 'Looks good. It's a little light in colour, the bubbles are in straight lines and the froth is clean. Here,' he said, holding out the glass to her, 'try it.'

'Um, okay.' She took the glass, their fingers brushed and her eyes dropped to her lap.

He shuffled in his seat, swallowing hard, trying to steady himself while pouring his own glass. What would happen if he held her hand, like really held her hand for a long time? Would she let him? 'And?'

She sipped.

Alex held his breath, waiting…

'It's nice.'

'Nice, huh?' He cocked an eyebrow at her. 'Just nice?'

'Oh, come on, I don't know the words you're looking for, except that this isn't as sweet as the last one. It's drier.'

He sniffed at the hoppy aroma, then sipped a little and allowed the crisp flavour to wash over his palette. 'You're right."

'I'm always right.'

'Even injured, she's still cheeky.' Her smile was reward enough; he could watch it all day.

This has to stop!

She was out of bounds and just a mate, nothing more.

'What was I right about this time?' Verily asked.

'It isn't as sweet, it's drier, yet with a crisp lightness to it which is unusual for an ale,' he replied, choosing to focus on his beer and not the babe. 'Although it has an acidic after-taste I'm not too fond of. What can you taste?' At least it wasn't rocket fuel like his first batch and he sipped again.

'Apples.'

'Good girl, you're learning.' Just like he did, even if he did sound a bit snobby. 'I put apples in this one for the fructose.'

'Still aiming for the calorie-free beer?'

'At this stage, this batch is organic with pure rainwater, it made a helluva difference, don't you think? Don't you dare shrug with that sore shoulder.'

'Not with this hunk of ice sitting on it.'

'You didn't throw it out yesterday?'

'No, I broke one of the cardinal rules with sports. It was my fault.'

'How?'

'I threw without warming-up or stretching. I did this to myself.'

He winced. 'I'm so sorry.'

She rolled her eyes at him. 'How's Speedy?'

He looked at her with hope. Had Molly already asked Verily?

'Isn't Speedy your team's pitcher? I hope I haven't upset her with my throw yesterday?'

'Um… I'm just gonna come out and say it.'

'Say what?'

'Speedy wants you to coach her. Poor kid can't throw, but she means well. She's always showing up to every game and practises, even though she knows she stinks. The thing is…' He took a deep breath and blurted out, 'If you coach Speedy and she strikes someone out, she's agreed to head the packing crew for my mangos at last season's prices, but only if you teach her.'

'Speedy can't even throw the distance from the pitcher's mound to the home plate.'

'I know it's impossible, and I've been trying to work out what to pay you to do it. Speedy has offered to clean Molly's house but I want her to do the…' He pointed his glass at the orchard before them.

'Mangos.'

'Yeah.'

'Is Speedy called that for her speed on the softball field?'

'I wish. She's speedy with mango picking and a perfectionist at packing unmarked fruit. Speedy is offering me family-mates-rates I can afford to pay if you coach her. She doesn't even know who you are, because you sold her on that one throw.'

'Does Molly know about this?'

'Molly was there when Speedy and I struck up the deal. I mean, no deal, if you say no or yes or… crap.' He raked fingers through his hair and readjusted his Akubra.

Verily sat back with pursed lips as her steady eyes watched him. It was an unreadable expression.

A small ute drove in and parked nearby with a flurry of dust.

'Oh no,' Alex mumbled.

'Who is that?' Verily asked.

'Speedy. She's left fifteen messages on my phone, all begging me to ask you. Look, she's kind of hyper and over keen, and she has some other challenging intellect issues, but she's a sweet kid who'd do anything for anyone.' And he was very protective over his little cousin ensuring no kid picked on her at school.

'Fifteen messages?'

'She's my cousin—and not of the kissing kind, okay?'

'I said nothing.' She giggled.

'Name your terms, I'll do anything.'

'Anything, huh?'

'Yeah. Not that I have much, but—'

'Hi.' Speedy hopped up to the veranda with a bunch of flowers, a six-pack of beer under her arm, and her hand held out. 'We haven't met officially, but I'm Speedy, I am.'

'Speedy, this is Verily. Verily, meet my cousin, Speedy.'

Verily shook Speedy's hand. 'Hi, Speedy.'

'Wow, my hands are bigger than yours. Bugger, look at the shoulder, I heard you'd wrecked it.'

'Behave, Speedy,' warned Alex.

'Well, these are for you, to help you get better and this beer is because, well, everyone drinks beer 'round here, they do,' Speedy said, holding out her flowers and beer.

'Thank you, Speedy, that's very kind of you.' Using her good hand, Verily put them on the table.

'Why'd you bring that muck over? It's sewerage water that lacks substance,' complained Alex, checking out the beer label.

'Gawd, listen to him gettin' all posh 'bout the grog coz a lady's present.' Speedy then dragged over a chair and sat directly in front of Verily with their knees almost touching. 'Did Alex ask you if you'll coach me? I want to throw like you do, coz I know who you are, I do.'

'How?' Alex asked with a frown. 'I never said a word, Verily, I swear it.'

'Alex told me nothing, it was Molly. I wouldn't leave her alone until she told me. Don't worry, I'm sworn to secrecy and I'm never allowed to badger Molly in her shop again or she'll ban me. So, I agreed, and then we Googled ya. Olympics, huh? Five-time world championship as the best female pitcher holding the current world record for the most consecutive strikes with your fastball, they call *Satan's Screamer* coz of the burrrnnn—'

'Stop.' Verily held her hand up like a traffic cop. 'I don't need to hear the stats, I was there.'

'Speedy, don't badger the lady,' warned Alex, aware Verily was very sensitive when it came to her past career.

'Lady, huh.' Speedy grinned at her cousin. 'You call no one lady.'

'I do too.'

'No, you don't.' Speedy screwed her nose at Alex, then focused back on Verily. 'Did my cousin tell you the deal, did he?'

'Alex just told me before you drove in.'

'So, ya reckon you can coach me to strike out a player? Just one. I mean three strikes to one player. Once would be bloody brilliant.'

'In practise?' Alex's mind whirled into paying another player to fake it, but it was useless because Speedy couldn't throw far enough for anyone to fake a miss.

'Nah, not havin' you fix it. I want the real deal, and only if the lady says yes to coaching me.'

'No one's called me a lady this much.' Verily giggled to herself.

'Why not? You are a lady.' His eyes widened at Verily's blush—*wow!*

'You've got the blokes in town talkin' after you jogged past the pub yesterday. Heard you're going there for tea tomorrow night, the place is gonna be packed, I reckon.'

Verily arched her eyebrow at the fast-talking Speedy. 'Why, has Molly auctioned me off?'

'What auction?' Alex demanded, sitting straighter. 'We're just going for dinner and a beer tasting session, that's all.'

'Shh, this isn't about you.' Speedy waved her hand at Alex and dragged her chair even closer to Verily. 'So, what will you want from me, huh? Just ask. Anything, I'll do it, I will.'

'Verily's injured and I'm not putting her at risk.'

'I'm not gonna hurt the lady, I'm just asking her to coach me. But look at you getting all protective.'

'Leave off. Maybe I should leave you two alone.'

'Please stay, Molly said you were cooking me dinner,' blurted out Verily with an expression he knew well.

Alex adored his little cousin, but her energy was a bit much for some at first. But then he grinned at the chance to be Verily's champion. 'That's right, you can't cook.'

'I had planned to try and teach myself but...' Verily nodded to her arm tucked up into a sling.

'Excuses, excuses,' he said with a wink.

'I'll cook. I'll even clean your dishes and inside your cupboards if you'll coach me, I will.' Again, Speedy scooted her chair closer, with palms pressed together as if in prayer.

Verily leaned back from the begging young woman. 'Aren't you doing this for Alex?'

'Only if you'll agree. I still want to learn and make the strike, it's my dream, it is.'

Verily's lips pursed together and her eyes narrowed at Speedy with that determined look Alex admired. It even forced Speedy back in her seat.

Verily picked up her glass and sipped on her beer. 'This brew is better now it's aired, it's not as bitter.'

'Acidic you mean.' He sipped on his own glass and

looked at the brew as the flavour impacted on his pallet. 'You're right about it needing that air.' But this was an ale, not a stout like Guinness, and definitely not red wine. 'So how about we make this really simple, with a yes or no, you'll coach Speedy?'

She sobered up with that focus of her eyes the colour of burnt umber; it was beautiful. 'I'm sorry, but to pitch, Speedy needs to practise with a catcher.'

'Why?' Speedy asked.

'Because a pitcher isn't any good without a better catcher who can handle the heat and they're your on-field partner. Know of any good ones in the district?'

Speedy nodded. 'Yeah, I reckon I might. Bit of a smart mouth who doesn't shut up, but I think I can find one, I can.'

'Oi, I'm sitting right here, ladies.' He frowned at the pair giggling together as the bonds of friendship formed. Verily was very easy to get along with, just like she'd been at the station talking to Tim, the ringers, station hands and other truckies at the railway yards. The lady was very approachable and he liked that about her.

'Are you committed enough to practise every day?' Verily asked Speedy.

'I finish work at four and I can be here ten minutes after that.'

'Speedy, it's over forty minutes to town, it's not a racetrack,' said Alex.

'Fine, I can be here forty-two minutes after knock-off, I can. Wait until Agnes hears.'

'No.' Verily put her hand on Speedy's shoulder to stop

the girl wriggling as she lowered herself to meet her eye to eye. 'I never interfere with coaches, especially when I'm only here on holidays.'

'When do you leave?' Speedy asked.

'A few days after the Rosella Festival.'

'But. But...' Speedy sat back, pouting her lower lip, looking at Alex with big sad eyes.

Alex didn't like the sound of Verily leaving either. 'Speedy can keep her mouth shut to not upset Agnes. Can't you, Speedy?'

Speedy nodded at Alex and whimpered at Verily. 'I swear it. Our secret.'

'Well, okay then...' Verily sat back, picked up her beer glass and sipped on the amber liquid. 'I like the slight apple aftertaste of this one, it's refreshing.'

'I agree.' Alex sat taller with chest out, pleased with his latest brew and took another mouthful. It still had room for improvement, but it was palatable.

'So, um, okay, what... Will you do it?' Speedy asked unsure.

'That's a *yes*, Speedy.'

'Don't think you've said no to me yet,' Alex mumbled to Verily over his glass.

Speedy jumped in the air. 'Yes! How soon can we start?'

'Not tonight with Verily's shoulder causing a pool on the veranda,' said Alex.

'Am I?' Verily leaned over her chair to check the puddle beneath her seat. 'Oh no, I don't want to make a mess for Molly.' She winced as she stood.

'I'll get the mop, and you should be resting with your feet up,' said Alex.

'I'm stiffening up from sitting too long.' She twisted her torso while holding the block of ice.

'Hey,' Alex put his hand over hers, the one holding the ice. 'Please, don't overdo it.'

'Um... I won't.'

'Make sure you don't, please.' He patted her hand and went to fetch the mop.

'I've got a couple of softballs in my car. I'll go get them,' Speedy called out, skipping to her ute.

'Bring them and your glove because you need to get used to pitching while wearing it. We'll start with the basics until sunset.'

Alex returned with the mop and deftly dabbed at the floor. 'Are you sure you're up to this, Verily?'

'I'm not doing anything, its Speedy who'll be doing the work. She's going to need lots and lots of practise. Just don't expect a miracle to happen overnight because she needs to build muscle in her pitching arm.'

'Did you hear that, Speedy?'

'I did, I did.' Speedy skipped over with her glove and balls, wearing the biggest smile he'd ever seen on his cousin. 'When did you practise, Verily?'

'Every day, twice a day.'

'Every day? How?'

'I had an old car tyre as my target with a net to catch the balls. I think I saw a tyre in the shed we can get Alex to hang it up for us, it's his orchard he should know the perfect tree.'

Alex mopped the water underneath her seat and the drip trails Verily left as she hobbled to the edge of the veranda. 'As long as you're okay doing this, coz your feet look sore.' Wincing at her blistered feet, wearing a pair of thongs, long shorts, t-shirt, tan and messy hair, she looked more like a surfer babe who hung at beaches, not a softball pro cruising the outback dust on the fringe of a mango orchard.

'I'm just playing spectator,' said Verily, sharing the grin that made him smile.

'Well, okay then. Speedy, we'll take it down to my place. I'll drag a chair out from my veranda so the coach can put her feet up, drink beer and drip there.' He slung the mop over the side rail to dry. 'You may as well stay for dinner, Speedy. You can do the dishes while we wait on the coach, huh?' Alex winked at Verily, carrying her beer glass as he stepped in beside her on the track that led to his place.

'I'm keen,' said Speedy, skipping like a kid through the orchard to the packing shed, while Verily limped with the ice on her shoulder and arm in a sling. Alex strolled beside her, a lot lighter than when he'd started this trek. Did he dare to even hope this scheme would work?

ELEVEN

The house phone rang on the kitchen wall and Verily picked it up from its cradle. 'Hey, Molly.'

'That's got to be the first time you've ever been wrong.'

'Alex?'

'It is.'

'What do you want?' It sounded like he was driving.

'Hello is what most people say.'

'Good afternoon, Alex. How may I be of assistance?'

'That's what I want to hear. How's the shoulder?'

'Fine, but I might have to give the trapeze act a rest.'

His chuckle made her smile.

'So, what are you wearing?' He said in a low seductive tone.

'Excuse me?'

Again, his laugh carried down the line. 'Can you put on some jeans and boots? I need a hand.'

'You want me to put on my dress boots, are we going out somewhere?' Even though her boots weren't stripper shoes, they weren't work boots, and they weren't having that kind of relationship. Or were they?

'Tracky-daks and sneakers will do. We'll have to get

you some workboots soon.'

'Why?'

'I need a hand. Are you able to help me with your shoulder?'

'I'm okay, I've suffered worse. What do you want help with, Alex?' She was sick of sitting around feeling sorry for herself.

'Can you meet me on the road by the driveway?'

'You aren't going to cover me in dust again?'

'Not today, princess, I'll be doing a drive-by. See ya in five and bring a hat, Molly's got her straw hat in the laundry. Guess we'll have to get you a decent hat to match them boots too. Oh, and grab a long-sleeved shirt or you can borrow mine, but bring a water bottle with you too, the one we take to softball training will do. Now go, we've got a schedule to keep.'

The phone disconnected, and she stared at it for a moment. What was he getting her to do today?

Whatever it was, it beat sitting around fighting with boredom.

She snatched up her shoes and socks, pocketed a few painkillers just in case, grabbed the water cooler and was soon out the door. She couldn't wait to see Alex.

Okay, he was just a friend. That's all.

Nothing more.

Even if her heart beat faster and she was bristling with excitement, waiting for him on the side of the dirt road.

She'd had a great time last night helping Speedy, who was so hyper and cute at the same time. Speedy reminded

Verily of herself when she'd met her idols as a kid, keen to glean any and every titbit of information to be that better player. It also made her forget her own problems by helping Speedy. But, Verily's main issue was she was a left-hander trying to teach a right-hander to pitch. Could she do it?

With a straw hat on her head, she peered down the wide road and soon spotted the plume of red dust that rose high in the sky as the ground trembled beneath her shoes. Led by the towering beast of metal and muscle, the dust storm barrelled down the red road towards her.

Alex slowed down the prime mover and with a hiss of the air brakes, he jumped out of the cab. 'I'll give you a hand, seeing as how you're not up to swinging off any trapeze.' He grabbed her good hand and led her to the passenger side of the truck.

She got all giddy inside as he held her hand. Did she have time to gloat or float in this daydream? When she heard it and smelled them—*cattle*. 'Why are you here with a load of cattle?'

'The train had a slight derailment on the other side of Alice Springs.'

'Is anyone hurt?'

'Everyone's fine and it happens.'

'How do you have a slight derailment?'

'The railway tracks get out of alignment from seismic shifts due to a change in extreme temperatures which happens in the red centre's outback desert. It's a scorcher in the day and as cold as dry ice at night, and it's not even summer yet.'

'How often does the train de-rail?'

'At least once a year. Normally it's when the tracks get flooded in the Wet and the rails get washed out. They still need us truckies then. Up you get.' He grabbed her by the hips and hoisted her toward her seat. 'Hey, you're not as heavy as I'd thought you'd be.'

'Are you calling me fat?'

'You haven't got an inch of fat on you, princess. Remember, I've seen you in your underwear.' He laughed, closing the door and walked around to the driver's side.

In the side mirror, her blush was so bad her face blended with the red dirt, she was desperate to compose herself by the time Alex climbed into his seat. 'What do you need me for?'

'Firstly, I appreciate you volunteering for this.'

'Just tell me what it is, Alex?' Why was he stalling?

'I need you to feed the cattle and check the troughs. Can you ride a bike with that arm?'

'A motorbike?'

'Yeah.'

'Not sure.' Not after her wobbly incident with the scooter.

'How about a quad? Don't you dare shrug that shoulder at me.' He frowned at her as he put the truck into gear and rolled the massive metallic beast down the road.

'Not sure, I won't know until I try.'

'You can use mine. I'll bring it down once we unload this thirsty lot.'

'Unload where?'

'Here, out back. Hey, you didn't find any fences down,

did you? It's been a few weeks since I've checked the boundary.'

'I didn't see any, not that I was looking.'

'Now you know why we need to keep an eye on the fences. Mango trees aren't the best tucker for livestock?'

'Molly told me. So, exactly where do the cattle go?'

'The back paddocks, this area is all feeding pasture. Speedy's bringing in a bale of hay from work to keep them happy. The owners' stockmen should be here, they're giving us a hand to unload this lot. I'll be back with more.'

'How many?'

'Two loads. We need to create a space at the railway yards, it won't hold that many cattle long-term. Twelve hours, sure, but we're unsure how long before the train's back on track.'

'So, these cattle stay here until when?'

'No idea. We might end up driving them to Darwin ourselves,' replied Alex as he easily moved through the truck's gears. 'Dad's on his way back now, to give us a hand. Have you ever worked with cattle before?'

'You know I only saw my first cattle station this week.'

'Well then, you're about to get a crash course, the good thing is they're easy.'

'How do you know?'

'I've worked on most of the stations around here.'

'I thought your day job was driving trucks?' His night job was checking on the orchard, or in the shed brewing beer where he was at his happiest.

'I did the stations during my school holidays before I

was old enough to get a truck licence. I started as a jackeroo to a stockman until I was old enough for Dad to let me work for him. By that time, I'd been hauling trucks to Elsie Creek Railway Station for years.'

'Why didn't your father hire you sooner, especially if he wants to make you a partner?' Why Alex hadn't told his father he didn't want the job was beyond her, when her own father was always supportive.

'Insurance. It would've cost Dad a fortune to insure me until I'd turned twenty-one and could prove to the insurance company I had the experience. So, I got my education working on cattle stations, driving outback roads.'

The road train pulled up where two men in wide brimmed cowboy hats and dusty jeans leaned against the side of a rugged four-wheel-drive ute towing a horse float.

'Are those cowboys waiting for you?'

'No cowboys here, unless you want to annoy them. They're called cattlemen in this country, or stockmen, ringers, jackeroos—'

'You're confusing me on purpose.'

Beneath the brim of his Akubra, he gave her that lazy side grin as his eyes captured the sun highlighting their ice-diamond blue. 'They're good blokes who are here to help sort this lot out with their horses. We need to keep the cattle separated.'

'Why?'

'Two different owners and we've got two different yards.' Alex wound down the window and shouted, 'Oi, Jacko? Catch.' He tossed out a set of keys on a large red tag that the stockman caught with ease. 'We'll be taking this lot to the back paddock. Just follow the trail to the windmill and you can park the float there, it'll be a good spot for the horses. Leave this gate open, I've got the rookie with me to let you through the next one.'

'Righto,' yelled Jacko. With a nod of his Akubra, he unlocked the padlock and opened the double gate.

Alex steered the large truck through the gates and down the slope towards a windmill standing on the far hill. 'Sorry, Verily, we might be late for dinner at the pub tonight.'

'I don't care, this is exciting. Even if it is smelly.'

'Oi, I showered.' He sniffed at his collared shirt. 'It must be you.' He grinned at her, then sobered. 'Are you sure you're okay and not in any pain with your shoulder?'

'I'm fine, I had an anti-inflammatory earlier. So, what do I do first?'

'You'll be opening and closing the gate. I'll get you a handheld radio so you'll know what's going on.'

'I've never used a radio. Do I need to learn fancy call signs?'

'Not out here. You can serenade us if you want?'

'I don't think so.' Verily shook her head, but couldn't stop mirroring his smile.

'Have you ever manned a bore pump?'

'I've never seen one.'

'Well, get ready for another crash course. I hope you like the taste of dust because cattle are messy buggers.'

For the next four hours, she helped open the gates, cleaned troughs, fumbled with the handheld radio and felt like a lollipop girl on the highway for roadworks. Too scared to get too close to the big hoofed animals, she helped Speedy roll off a large circular bale of hay while standing on her small ute and trailer.

Amid the rolling dust and rippling heat, bellowing beasts spewed down the ramps from the massive road train, where the musterers whistled on horseback, weaving through the herd. Their whirling stock whips crackled like gunshots in the air as they guided the cattle out to the large pasture. Overshadowing all was the windmill on the hill shooting specks of sunlight from its blades stirring the soupy air.

In charge of it all, Alex looked right at home amongst the cattle. Truck driver—be damned, the guy was an outright sexy cowboy/stockman/truckie-whatever, and if she wasn't surrounded by all this swirling red dust, she'd be watering at the mouth.

As the sun started to set, the mighty prime mover was the last to leave, followed by its usual thundering devils-dust storm. Alone on the hill, they'd left her with two herds of cattle, four horses, two horse floats, and a creaking windmill that churned high in the sky.

Covered in dust, she smiled at the scenery. Towering red-flowering flame trees dotted the area, their shade lengthening over cattle spread across the paddock that seemed as chilled as she was to just be standing in the paddock.

Alex rode up on a large quad bike, stopped beside her and reached into his small esky. 'I think you deserve one.' He removed the lid from the beer bottle and held it out to her.

'Cheers.'

'Pull up a pew.' He patted the back of the large quad as he swung his leg over the bike and sat facing the herd.

'How many are there?'

'Coupla hundred head.'

'I can't believe all of that came from two loads in one truck?'

'The road train carries about a 140 head each load.'

'From two stations?'

'Yep.'

'So how come you're not using that fenced paddock over there?'

'That area's resting.'

'Is that patch of dirt having a holiday too?'

He chuckled at her, thumbing up the brim of his Akubra. 'I'm letting it rest until the next dry season, where I'll try my hand at planting barley for my beer, and that paddock will be perfect for it.'

'Have you ever grown crops before?'

'Not for myself, but I have for others, besides, there's no harm in trying. If it doesn't work to the standard I want, it'll go to stockfeed.'

'You'd feed it to the cows?'

'Most of the ingredients in beer is cattle feed.'

'I didn't know that.'

'Did you know all of this area used to be mangos?'

'No.' The guy not only had plans for his future he also knew more about her family history than she did. Should she be annoyed, jealous, or listen and learn in awe?

Seriously, her crush on the guy had to stop. It was just a summer holiday thing (in winter), nothing more.

'Where did the mango trees go?' Well, she was here to learn more about her mother's side of the family. She knew her dad's side, even her step-mother's side of the family. A step-mum who was more of a friend than a mother, who Verily had known for years through the softball circuit.

Her dad had only officially started dating when Verily had gone to college with her step-sister, Kylie. A step-sister who was her catcher and best friend long before they'd officially been tied as family. They'd shared dorm-rooms and bedrooms, holidays and birthdays, it was perfect...

But when Kylie died, and Verily had flown back to her dad's house, she couldn't step into Kylie's bedroom anymore without drowning under the combined burden of guilt and grief, preferring to sleep on the couch. Until her dad suggested she come here, in hope of finding answers to questions she didn't know how to ask.

'It happened when the market price for mangos plummeted,' explained Alex, 'pickers were hard to find and the fruit just rotted on the ground to feed the magpie geese. Then, it was followed by a drought. So, your grandfather cleared this area. I think Molly's husband had a hand in that one too.'

'To chop down trees?'

'No, in telling your grandfather to diversify. Your uncle ran the Elsie Creek Railway Station. He knew if there was ever a delay, the freight company was liable and would pay for the lodgings of their passengers who stay at the pub or—'

'Here in this paddock?'

'Yep. Truckies love it when the train stops. Right now, we're getting paid to babysit beef.'

'Do you want to work with cattle? You looked the part out there.'

'I grew out of that a while ago, but I don't mind doing this.' He nodded to the grazing herd with his eyes shaded by his hat's wide brim. 'I still keep my hand in, especially when the train company is paying us for the privilege. But I'll still need your help because I have a feeling I'll be driving. Simple, yes or no if you want to help?'

'Yes.' She blurted out without thinking.

'Great.' Sharing his lazy slow grin, he handed her his phone. 'Can you put your mobile number in for me, please?'

She tapped on the keypad. 'What do you want me to do?'

'Just watch the water. Those large hay bales will keep them happy for a while plus what we've got in the pasture. You'll need to keep an eye on the fences, cattle have a habit of pushing up against them. If any of that mob do go walkabout, call me and I'll get you some help.' He pulled a shiny brass key from the stash on a red tag. 'Take this spare key for the gate to the road, the stockmen will only show up for loading the trucks. Sometimes the owners come to check on their stock, too. When that happens, I'll call you to let us in.'

'I'm playing gatekeeper?' Verily slipped the key into her pocket, beside her pain pills. Her new exercise routine was working wonders in becoming aware of her limits and improving her pain threshold.

'You bet. Although, you've got to be the cutest gatekeeper around with that straw hat on your head. I was expecting a baseball cap.' He playfully messed up her hat. 'Got enough dirt on you, Cinderella?

With back straight and chin up, Verily smiled towards the undisturbed view of the setting sun that rippled in the background of the grazing cattle. 'I'm a softball princess, thank you very muchly. My helmet is my crown, the shirt my ball gown, and the field is my castle, where you never leave the playing field cleaner than you arrived. We are the good girls who steal, playing all our bases freely, and share a love for diamonds—except you'll find ours waiting for us in the dust.'

Alex chuckled beside her. 'Knew you were a princess—whatever that was?'

'Softball mantra, one of many. But I don't think any of them mention paddocks with cattle.' She waved at a field of cows with their low moos.

'Are you going to be okay with all of this? I know it might seem like a lot to handle; just know I'd never leave you without help nearby.'

'Are you kidding? This is great, and I don't know why, but I could sit in this spot and watch these guys for hours, it's a great view. Thanks for letting me help and for taking the time to teach me.' She hoped she didn't mess up.

'Hey, I might pay you in cash for this one, as soon as Dad pays me,' he said with a sly wink. 'First, you need a lesson on riding this quad before dark. We'll go once around the permitter fences to put my mind at ease and we'll re-check the troughs. I'll show you how to work the windmill too. Are you still up for dinner at the pub?'

'Um, honestly.' She rubbed her shoulder as she looked over the cattle. 'Would it be rude if I stayed? I, ah—'

'You're not sore, are you?'

'I'm okay, I, um...' She held her arm protectively against her chest. 'I'm kind of wary being around crowds ever since the accident.'

'Oh, you don't want to get knocked.'

'I know it's silly, but I'm still a bit sensitive from the other day.' Plus what she'd done today, but she wasn't sharing that with anyone. She was done letting her shoulder stop her from doing things. She didn't want to be benched on the sidelines of life forever.

'Hey, I get it, I'd rather let you heal here at home, safely. We can go another time. Anyway, it might be best if we stuck around and kept an eye on this lot.'

'Thank you.' She sighed with relief. *Could the guy be any more perfect?* 'You can still go.'

'I reckon I'll be buggered after a few beers. I'll cook tea then, eh?'

'Sounds good.' She liked Alex's cooking and liked watching him cook too.

He tapped the quad's seat. 'You up for a lesson?'

She smiled so wide her cheeks ached. Would she be able to concentrate with Alex right behind her on a bike? 'Yeah.'

'Good. Let's put the cattle to bed then, shall we?'

TWELVE

Verily steered the quad into the packing shed and parked as per Alex's instructions, while he sat behind her. She turned off the bike, plunging them into darkness.

'Thanks for letting me drive your quad,' she mumbled over her shoulder to him.

'Hey, my pleasure.' Even better on the back of the quad, holding her against his chest, teaching her to ride while immersed in her fragrance, it was heavenly. Shame he couldn't go there. She was Molly's niece, only here for a holiday, and there were too many other risks.

Yet, her company was so easy to be around and the more time he spent with her, the more he wanted to surrender to her spell.

'I guess we'd better go tell Molly we're not going to the pub tonight.' Alex swung off the seat and helped her off the broad bike. 'We'll need to raid her pantry because there's little left in my fridge. You girls ate me out of house and home last night.'

'I can't see anything.'

'Here, don't want you tripping in the dark.' He grabbed her good hand and led her from the dark shed. The stars peeked through the tree's canopy where crickets serenaded them as the fragrance from the flowering frangipani near the house, warmed the air.

'You're doing a good thing coaching Speedy. She tries so hard that kid and she's got a great heart too. She got picked on at school, so I've always tried to look out for her.'

'I hope it works for her? I'd like to see Speedy do it.'

'Do what?' Alex asked as they walked down the track, side by side, still holding hands like it was the most natural thing to do.

'Make that first strike.'

'For me?' It would save him a fortune and ensure he had gold class pickers for his first crop. It'd make selling them easier, giving his reputation as a new grower a good head start.

'No, for herself. I remember my first strike, hearing the umpire call out, *strike three you're out!*' She pulled her hand free and waved a pointed finger through the air as if mimicking the umpire. 'It's the best feeling in the world.'

Holding her hand was a good feeling too, while it lasted. 'I can only imagine—'

'Whose car is that?'

'It's my old man's.' He entered the light to find his father sitting on the back veranda with boots resting on his esky. Molly sat at the table beside him cradling a wine glass. 'Dad. Hey, Molly.'

'Alex. You finish puttin' the cattle to bed?' Neville reached forward and shook hands with his son.

'Yep. Two hundred head. Dad, this is—'

'Rose?' Neville sat back and blinked at Verily with mouth ajar.

'Um, no, Rose was my mother, I'm Verily.'

'Jeez, you're the spittin' image of your mother.'

'I know,' said Molly.

'G'day, I'm Neville, Alex's old man.' Neville stood and shook Verily's hand.

'Let me guess, no pub tonight after your adventure out the back?' Molly asked.

'Yeah, no. I mean, sorry about the pub, Molly, but the afternoon was brilliant.' Verily took a seat, smiling wide, with her eyes sparkling under the veranda's lights. 'I've seen nothing like it. I had a lesson on how to ride a quad, work the bores, windmill, troughs, fencing, radios, and basic animal husbandry,' she said, ticking off each task with her tiny fingers.

He hadn't overwhelmed her, had he? Although honoured to show her these things, which was easy due to her willingness to learn, it was her shining self-confidence that was his best prize. 'How was the trip, Dad?'

'Usual. Heard you had a backpacker in the cab with you out at the stations earlier this week. I've told you about having girlfriends in the truck when working, they're distracting.'

Alex frowned. 'It wasn't distracting, Dad.'

'It was me playing tourist,' said Verily, raising her hand in the air like she was in school. 'I'm sorry, I didn't mean to get Alex into trouble.'

Alex frowned at his father, who'd made him feel like he was ten years old all over again. 'It's fine, Verily, you weren't a bother, and we were well ahead of the schedules.'

'Obviously, Verily's settled into the place then,' Neville said, barely giving her a side-glance.

Verily replied with her signature shrug, and for once it didn't bother Alex.

Neville narrowed his eyes at Alex, then gave Verily a fleeting glance only to scowl back at his son. 'I hope you've got nothing planned this next month, son, coz we start clearing out what's stranded at the Elsie Creek Railway yards tomorrow morning from four. We've scored the contract to haul that lot out the back of Molly's on Sunday, so there'll be no partying for you.'

'Good thing we weren't planning to visit the pub and tie on a big one,' Alex said to Verily.

'Blimey, pretty girl like you at the pub? Place'll be bloody crawling with blokes.' Neville shook his head, then sipped from his stubbie.

'Molly, weren't you meeting your committee tonight, for the Rosella Festival?' Verily asked.

'It got cancelled. The pub's booked out because of the derailment. It might be a good thing we're staying home; those ringers get rowdy and I wouldn't want them to knock you about, hon.'

'Agreed,' said Alex, protectively over Verily.

Neville's brow creased at his son, then he pointed his stubbie at Verily. 'You're the softball champion.'

Verily winced in her seat. 'Was.'

And in the blink of an eye, all the shining self-confidence she had before, disappeared.

She was still a champion in Alex's eyes, who should be proud of her achievements.

'Nah, you're that bronze medallist,' said Neville. 'I remember looking after this place while Molly went to the Beijing Olympics.'

'You remembered?' Molly giggled, fidgeting with her necklace.

'I'm one of the few people in this town who does remember what Molly has to say,' said Neville, sitting back and giving her a wink.

'Well, I'll find something for dinner. You'll be staying then, Neville?' Molly stood up from the table and smoothed down her dress.

'I never say no to a home-cooked meal, Molly.'

Molly again giggled as she headed for the fly screen door with wine glass in hand. 'Alex?'

'Sure. Although, we were planning to raid your fridge and cook for ourselves.' He'd pictured cooking for two at his place and who knows from there.

'I'll give Molly a hand. You and your dad catch up.' Verily patted his shoulder like a mate as she went past.

This friend-zone sucked!

Molly looked at Verily in her straw hat and long-sleeved shirt hanging off her shoulder, covered in dust. 'If you think you're getting a cooking lesson in my kitchen, young lady, think again.'

Verily slipped off her filthy sneakers, held the creaking screen door open and bowed to Molly in her sports socks. 'I'm trained to have quick showers, even faster now I have less hair to wash.'

Alex grinned at Verily, her fun mood was infectious to be around.

'Verily is just like her mother,' said Neville, watching Verily leave. 'I used to have a crush on Rose.'

'When?'

'In school. Rose never looked at me twice. I thought she was a bit of a toffee-nosed-snob for not dating any of the blokes in town, until that weedy bookkeeper showed up.'

'Verily's father?'

'Yeah. He wasn't a bad bloke, for someone with hands softer than a woman's, but he was bloody good with figures. Talking about figures, I was going through the books with the accountant in Darwin this trip.'

'And?'

'We'll have enough to expand, son. We'll get a loan to get an extra truck, especially for things like this derailment. Shame we can't find another driver to hotbed in the trucks, we'd make a killing.'

Alex instantly thought of Verily and wondered what it would take to transfer her licenses over from the States? 'How bad is the derailment?'

'It should be back online tomorrow, but it'll be going express to Darwin to catch-up to its schedule. Which leaves plenty for us truckies to pick up the missed freight along the highway,' Neville said, rubbing his hands together. 'You'd better get that truck bed of yours ready, coz it'll be home for the next few months if this keeps up.'

'But I've got the season…' Alex had the mangos to look

after and his beer to bottle.

'We're not talking about bloody softball, are we?' Neville thumbed back to the kitchen's screen door. 'That pretty little thing in there hasn't whispered in your ear about that bloody game, has she? Easy for her, that girl must've made a fortune being paid to play a silly game. I heard she scored some major sponsorships and I'm sure there was an insurance payout for that accident she was in, too. Sportspeople insure themselves for stuff like that. Christ, Dolly Parton insured her boobs, you know.'

'That's none of our business.'

'What I'm saying is, we have our own business which takes priority, son. We're not like Molly with her mortgage-free property, when I've got debts to pay on that truck.'

'Why expand and get further into debt?'

'Why not?' Neville said. 'The time is right to cement this partnership using what we'll make from this derailment. We'll invest it back into this new truck. You must've saved some money working for me, or did you piss it up against the pub's wall?'

'I rarely go near the pub.' Why would he when he was working on his own brewery.

Again, Neville thumbed back toward the kitchen door. 'Weren't you planning to show off that pretty little girl at the pub tonight?'

'Stop it.' Alex leaned over the table glaring at his father and almost growled with lowered tone, 'Don't talk about Verily like that.'

Neville sat back. 'What's got into you?'

'Verily is a good friend who's been hurt.'

'We all deal with pain.'

'Verily was at the top of her game and had everything taken from her, Dad. Everything she knew was gone overnight.' His heart hurt for her. 'Show some empathy for the woman who's suffered a lot.'

'Huh.' Neville crossed his legs at the ankles, and stared at his work boots. 'Molly said it crushed that kid and she lost her a step-sister.'

'She was Verily's best friend and she died right beside her. Verily was lucky to have survived.' Alex had seen the horrific internet images of a pileup on the freeway. The team bus had tumbled off the side of the overpass, slamming roof first onto a crammed car park. Unfortunately, emergency services were so busy with the massive freeway pile-up with its countless other victims, they couldn't get to that bus until it was too late. Many, like Verily's step-sister, would have survived if only they'd received help sooner. Only a few survived, and thankfully Verily was one of them.

'Well, aren't I the insensitive bastard, huh?' Neville scrubbed his fingernails through his salt and pepper hair. 'Anyway, I'll need your signature and what you've got in the bank for a deposit.'

Alex was saving those funds for a multi-batching brewery with stainless steel fermenters that would hold ten hectolitres per tank and a bottling plant.

Also, he couldn't be away from the mangos for too long.

The wort mash he'd made with rosellas was due to be bottled and he didn't want to miss that window or it'd spoil.

He was chasing that perfect unique Sour IPA and this Rosella brew may very well be his answer.

No, he couldn't afford to go into partnership with his dad, not when he had his own goals.

Although, the money he'd earn on the road would help him reach his own end game sooner.

'Um, can I think about it first, Dad?' Why couldn't he just say no.

'No sweat. Later in the week we'll talk to the accountant. We'll have a cuppa with him between loads, down at Darwin wharf.'

'Sure, Dad.' Yet, unsure as the burden of guilt pressed across his shoulders.

'Can't wait for you to dig in and we become partners. We'll own this section of highway, you'll see.' Neville rummaged through his esky and pulled out an icy beer. 'Here, drink up, son. I bought a slab that'll put hairs on your chest, not that crap they call craft beer them lawyers drink with their lattes.'

'Nothing wrong with craft beer, there's an art to it.' Alex's shoulders slunk. How much of a stupid kid was he? Too scared to show his dad what he'd done at school because most of the time his dad never bothered to listen. It was always Neville's way or the highway in his macho-man's world. Why was it so hard to say no to the old man now?

THIRTEEN

Verily lay in bed flicking through one of Molly's magazines, unable to sleep, when there was a tap on her window. 'Ah!'

'I'm not that ugly, am I?' Alex said, grinning at her through the open window.

'What are you doing?' She complained, her panicked heartbeat pounding in her chest. 'And what's wrong with using the door, or the phone?'

'Why ring, when I can walk towards the light shining from your room?'

'Have you done this before, lurk outside a lady's room, perve?'

'You wish. I can't sleep and I've been getting stuff ready.'

'I heard. Don't you have an early start?' She glanced at her clock showing it was a little after eleven.

'Yeah, in a few hours, but I need your help.'

'Me? Are you bringing in more cattle?' She really didn't know much else when it came to farming stuff.

'No. Can you come down to the shed, I don't want to wake Molly?'

'Sure, meet you around the back.' Did she have time to change and hide her scars?

Why, when she was just one of the guys to Alex. So, in her boxer shorts and singlet, she met Alex waiting with a lit torch by the kitchen's screen door.

'Do I need a water bottle and a hat for this adventure?' She asked, trying to keep the back-door's squeak to a minimum.

'You don't get sunburnt in the dark.' He chuckled, shaking his head. 'Come on, daylight's almost here.'

She slipped on her thongs and headed down the orchard's track beside Alex. A curlew eerily wailed in the distance, and an owl called to his mate, who echoed its reply. There was an almighty crash from the trees just above her head, she jumped to his side grabbing his shirt. 'What was that?'

'That...' Alex put his arm around her shoulders and shone his torch to expose a furry creature blinking back at them from within the tree branches. '...Is a possum.'

'Aww, they're so cute.'

'There's quolls around here too. They're even cuter, but don't touch, they're like a wild cat with claws. Remember, we don't live in a petting zoo.'

'I guess swinging off tree-pythons while playing Tarzan in our manicured jungle would be out of the question then?' Pity, she'd love to curl into his warm chest to listen to the rumble of his laugh. 'I've never seen so many stars.' They were so close and clear like a sea of diamonds caught in some invisible black net in the sky.

'The moon's dulling the shine a bit. It reminds me of camping where we sit back to watch the Outback TV and its choice of two channels.'

'Which are?'

'Watching the flames dance in the campfire or the stars and satellites crossing the sky.'

'That'd be nice.'

'Maybe I can take you camping sometime, while you're still here?'

'Only if you have time.'

'Which I'm short of at the moment.' Inside the packing shed, he flicked on the small yellow light on his workbench where he kept his paperwork. 'As you're aware, I'm doing the run from Elsie Creek Railway Station to Darwin Harbour with Dad. He's got contracts coming at him so fast he can't keep up to make the ships.'

That sounded pretty formal for an informal guy? 'Is this all because of this derailment?'

'Cattlemen are a suspicious mob and it'll take a while before they trust the train this muster.'

'That's a good thing, for you and your father's business, right?'

'For making money, you bet. If you had your truck licence, I'd hire you to come along and we'd hotbed it.'

'We'd what?'

'Take turns driving. One would sleep in the cab while the other drove.'

'You'd let me?'

'Of course, I would. It's obvious you can drive; you

drove my truck better than most men I know and they've been doing it their whole lives.'

'Thank you.' About to float into a pile of self-pride, when one thought paused her private parade… 'Let me guess, you want me to do something for you?'

His grin spread while his blue eyes captured the lamp's light, the combination made her stomach slowly spin she had to look away and started fiddling with the bottom edge of her singlet.

'I don't know how long I'll be away.'

'I'm only here until the Rosella Festival.' His frown matched hers as her feminine fantasies got shelved at the thought of leaving. 'You need someone to watch the orchard.' *Crap! Just a mate.*

'Could you, please?'

'I'll have to check my diary so I don't overbook myself.' She had nothing else to do, and even if she wanted to, she found it hard to say no to Alex. With a shrug she said, 'Sure, what do I do?'

'It's simple. The irrigation is all on timers and I check the systems on Sunday. Molly knows where the bore shed is and I showed you what to do at the windmill. It's just the same. If you get stuck, call me. I have complete faith you'll do it easily enough, but there's one more thing?'

'Don't drink the beer while you're away.'

'That'd be good. Think you could bottle it too?'

'What?' How big was his worklist?

'It's the same as we did before with my past few batches, except you'll be doing it on your own. My latest batch of wort is in the fermenter and it'll be ready for straining and bottling on Monday. Unfortunately, I'll be in Darwin then, and if it doesn't get into the bottles, it'll spoil. It's the Rosella Beer.'

'Are you sure you want to trust me with your beer?'

'I haven't got a choice.'

The prick! 'Thanks for your outstanding level of confidence in me.'

'I didn't mean it like that. If I didn't think you were capable, I wouldn't ask, and I am asking. I'll pay you in—'

'Beer, yeah, I got that part. I swear half your brewery is stockpiling in the house.'

'So, you'll do it?'

She hesitated, tempted to let him sweat it out or maybe even make him beg. Since when did she want to play games with people's lives, especially when it was one of the guy's dream goals? 'It'd be a shame to let that brew go to waste after all that effort Molly and I put into handpicking those rosellas for you.' *Duh, just admit it, I can't say no to the guy.* 'Okay, what do I do?'

'Thank you,' he said with such obvious relief he reached over and hugged her.

She was swallowed by his aroma. Her knees softened in his embrace, skin prickling from his touch. Then it was over, far too soon.

'Anyway…' He stepped back, clearing his throat and pointing to the sheets he had on his clipboard. 'I wrote you a list of instructions for the watering.'

'You're organised.'

'Gotta be, I don't have time to waste when I'm working three jobs.'

While she was on holiday, bored. Since when did she become so selfish? 'Any other instructions?'

'I've made these laminated sheets I keep on this clipboard, they're my brewer's guide sheets made simple.'

He liked things simple and stress-free, she admired that about him. She stepped in closer and peered at the instructions. 'So, I have to wash the bottles in hot water then bake them in the oven. I can't cook.'

'It's simple. All you have to do is sterilize, pour, cap, and stack. I hope the capping tool isn't too hard for your shoulder.'

'I'm okay.' She wasn't useless. Sure, her shoulder was an issue, but after today's effort with the cattle, she was determined to not let her injuries take over her life. 'Are you moving the cattle on Sunday out the back?' Did she almost sound like a local? 'Are you sure I'm capable to look after that many cows?

'You'll be fine, you can sit there all day tomorrow and watch them for us.'

It was like he'd read her mind. 'I might do that. I'll pinch one of Molly's umbrellas, drag out what beer of yours I can drink, and set up a vantage spot to play shepherd.'

'Sounds perfect. I reckon I'd enjoy doing that too, but I'll be stuck on the road swilling roadhouse coffee.'

'It sounds like you don't want to go.'

Alex sighed, sliding hands into the back pockets of his jeans, he looked around the work shed that was his office. 'I'd rather stay here. But the money will give me a boost for my microbrewery.' His eyes shone as if envisioning his future as he pointed to the interior corrugated walls. 'I'd take out a long-term lease on this place, and I'd put my steel fermenting tanks over there. I'd have a proper bottling station in that far corner, with plenty of space leftover for washing and packing mangos and a decent storage area for bottled beer.'

She could see him doing it too and was jealous she couldn't picture her own future with the same excitement.

'I don't want big, but...'

'Boutique.'

He frowned at her.

'I was only kidding.'

'It's not you, it's my dad. He calls craft beer crap beer that lawyers drink with their lattes.'

'Can lattes and beer mix? Hey, can you make a coffee flavoured beer with chocolate? Can you imagine?'

Alex chuckled. 'They have caffeinated chocolate beer already on the market, but that imagination of yours is cute,' he said, messing up her hair.

'Watch-it, I spent hours achieving this coiffured look.' Which she never did, shoving it back from her face.

'Yeah, I can see that.' He brushed a stray strand free from her cheek, his eyes roaming over her face as his fingers gently stroked her hair. 'I like this messy look on you, it suits you with your bedroom eyes.'

She liked how he touched her hair, but, no one had ever said that about her eyes before. 'Sleepy eyes, you mean.'

'Nah, I've seen them when you're focused, it's a good

look.' He looked at her like he could see right through her. A look that flipped back the rusty trap-door that was the gateway to her soul.

'Yeah, right.' She dropped her head.

With fingertips, he lifted her chin. 'Take the compliment, princess.'

She was so close, seeing the clarity of his ice-diamond-blue eyes she could barely breathe as her pulse ka-thumped slowly in her ears like sludge. 'Thank you.'

He stared at her for a moment as if reading whatever lies her eyes were telling him. 'You've gotta know, I appreciate everything you're doing for me. I mean that. If I could, I'd pay you with more than beer.'

'Remember me when you're famous.' Would he remember her after her holiday use-by-date?

'You're the most famous person I know.'

'I'm no one,' she whispered, still captivated under his stare.

'You're a someone to me.' He leaned closer and his lips barely brushed hers. Softly, her upper lip, then her bottom lip as his warm lips caressed hers. She leaned into him—just as he pulled back.

She blinked up at him, licking her lips, staring at him with a numb brain as the pleasure flitted from her heart through to her limbs, to the tingling tips of her fingers. Was that real? Was that a tease of her daydreams, the ones that usually ended in disaster?

'Are you okay?' His forehead barely rested against hers as he watched her with hooded, darkening eyes.

'Ah, huh.' Her breath ragged and her cheeks tingled with heat.

His kiss was breathtakingly different. It took a moment for her eyes to focus through the haze, like it'd been an elixir that made the broken and scarred parts of her seem beautiful once more.

Did she dare risk their friendship to become the briefest of lovers, for one moment in the dark?

But her desire had been awakened, and she'd learned to enjoy the short affairs of bliss before her tour was over. 'Ah, huh.'

'Good,' he murmured, licking his lips as his gaze fell to her mouth, 'because I'm going to kiss you again—okay?'

And he waited.

She too, held her breath, waiting.

Her lips were tingly, but the way he looked at her shredded the layers of loneliness she'd been under for so long. She could only nod, trapped by that deliciously lazy smile of his, wanting to retaste the press of his lips against hers.

'Ah huh.' Again, she nodded. His strong heartbeat pounded under her palm, mirroring the rhythm of her own. How dare she say no to him now.

'For once, I don't mind you not speaking,' he whispered, sealing his lips against hers like she was his oxygen and he'd run out of air.

'Hey—'

'Shh, I'm kissing you, and I've been wanting to kiss you for a very long time.' He grinned with his lips against hers. Pulling her into his broad chest, his fingers gripped the back of her neck as if taking control and the kiss deepened. It claimed her, twisted her insides and melted her all over in one deep mouth-watering moment. She'd never been kissed like that before and could only follow his lead, pouring all of her into him in return.

'You're killing me,' he grunted against her mouth as a gravelly moan travelled through his chest. Lips still locked together, he pushed her against the wall of the shed, their bodies pressed and aligned. Their clothing irritated her, and all she wanted was to feel his skin against hers. Pushing up his shirt he tossed it aside, breaking contact only for a moment until his mouth re-meshed hungrily against hers.

Threading her fingers through his thick hair, chest to chest, their tongues stroking as the heat intensified. A sizzling, electric sensation crackled through her, unleashing a moan as his palm glided across her skin, her shoulder, her scars, her breasts.

No one had touched her since the accident, and she wanted this.

No—she *needed* this.

To feel desired and not some broken toy that people whispered about as they passed her in the stadium corridors. None of it mattered, just him, and she lifted her singlet. He pushed it over her shoulders, and it dropped at their feet as he again, captured her lips with his.

How did one man put so much power in a kiss that sent a curveball rolling slide through her universe…

At midnight he kissed her, controlled and claimed her with his mouth, his tongue, his touch, his aroma, and his heat.

All of him was drugging her. She forgot all her past pain and all her fears of the future, where everything mattered in this moment. It was the taste of home on his lips, the shelter of his hands powered by the strength of his heartbeat.

Had she found her paradise beneath billions of stars, with only the whispering wildlife as their witnesses?

FOURTEEN

Verily sat with Molly in the shade of the empty grandstand and watched the Dusty Dingoes practising on the parched oval. The surrounding scrublands had been charred black by the local fire brigade's burning-off regime to combat bushfires where spirals of black smoke still dotted the distant horizon. It'd been months since it had rained and the place looked desolate, especially with no Alex for Verily to perve on.

Molly filed her fingernails beneath the shade of the houndstooth patterned umbrella that matched her dress. 'Will Alex be back in time for the game?'

'I think so.' He'd been on the road for over a month, just like Neville had predicted. Only showing up to his cottage to have sex, sleep, change, check over the orchard and his beer, have some more scorching wall trembling sex, then out the door and gone.

They spent more time talking on the phone than they saw of each other, mostly to discuss his projects she was caretaking for him on the farm. When she did see him, they didn't talk because his kisses were like scorching flame throwers filled with desire. Even now, touching her lips, she thirsted for their touch and taste. She knew she shouldn't, but they were—all of him was addictive.

It wasn't going to last.

After all, he was a known player, and she was only here on holiday. And they both knew it.

Returning her focus to the field, she narrowed in on her own special project, Speedy.

'Agnes isn't impressed that Alex isn't here. She'll be unbearable if he doesn't make it for the game. Can you catch?' Molly asked.

'Nope. Never, I've always been on the other end.'

'How is Speedy doing?'

'Okay, I guess. I wish Agnes would coach Speedy's pitching too. Why does she insist on only focusing on the batting? There's so much more to the game than just swinging a bat.' So said the world's lousiest softball batter.

'Well, you would know, hon,' Molly said, nudging her in the ribs. 'You could offer suggestions?'

'And risk losing my ability to breathe?'

'Does Agnes scare you that much?'

'Um…' Verily looked across the softball field to the Dusty Dingoes' coach. There were no words to describe the colourful Agnes.

'CATCH THAT YOU HAIRY WOMBATS!' Agnes bashed the softball to the outfield sending Bella's handfed flock of birds into the sky. Tess and her sparkly hot pants twinkled in the sun while she too filed her nails like Molly. Karen was shouting at her tribe of children to stop fighting in the playground. Lucy, Jenny, and Kat were busily talking using their gloves as personal fans, while the jillaroo sisters, Mandy and Mindy, played soccer with a softball.

'OI, PAY ATTENTION, YA FEATHERLESS FRUITBATS!' Agnes screamed out in her fluorescent pink boardshorts. Her black-and-white striped football socks blended with her black thongs, while the stained once-white t-shirt poked out beneath a tiny kid's hoodie. Her signature yellow duck-bill sun-visor highlighted the monobrow as her thick shiny plait trailed past her bum longer than a Clydesdale's tail.

'Is Alex the team's backbone?' Verily asked Molly.

'What do you mean, hon?'

'Who is the longest player you have?'

'Um… Alex. He's been playing since he was five and used to play in the outfield. He was the only one keen enough to run around, and we needed the numbers that year.'

'So, because Alex isn't here, they're all like that.' Verily pointed to the team that wasn't behaving like a team at all.

'I never noticed. It's rare for Alex to not be here.'

'Alex hits the ball and gets them involved. He's like Agnes's assistant coach.'

'More like a slave. Agnes likes bossing Alex around to carry the heavy things. Hey, you're not doing too much for Alex with your shoulder, are you, young lady?'

'I'm okay.' She was over sitting around with nothing to do. Helping out Alex wasn't strenuous, and she enjoyed the laid-back pace of the place.

She even had her own routine. In the mornings she ran around the farm's perimeter, past the pink bougainvillea and frangipanis by the front driveway. She'd follow the fire break down to the native bushland where candle-clumps of orange bottlebrushes contrasted with the yellow wattles and grey leafed banksias. Wallabies roamed the low valley edging the paddocks beneath the still windmill at sunrise, where the land shone under the heavy dew.

She walked the rows of the flourishing orchard tossing a softball in her glove while swatting the odd fly and dodging low hanging webs. She even had a tree with a tyre set up for herself in the far corner. A patch of paradise in the shade, immersed in the thick honeyed scent coming from the blossoming mango trees. 'I like the orchard at the moment, even if their flowers aren't pretty, but it's kinda pretty.'

'Wait until you see the mangos, they hang like ornaments on a Christmas tree and their aroma is divine.'

'Can't wait. Hey, I finally spotted the quolls today.'

'The wildlife is coming in for water, the back dam starts looking like a bird sanctuary for a bit. Careful, don't swim in that dam and don't go near it if there are no birds there.'

'Why? The place is full of birds.'

'When they're not there, it means a croc's moved in.'

'A crocodile?' She'd been warned about them in the area. She'd even seen some sunbaking on the side of river crossings on her daytrip out with Alex. But she didn't think they'd get this close to home. 'Would they come this far out from the river?'

'It happens this time of year, they're looking for water,' said Molly. 'We haven't had one since the new fences got put in over…must be ten years now.'

'New, huh?'

Molly rolled her eyes. 'Just keep an eye on the fences, okay? If you see any long dragging marks and the bottom of a fence pushed up, tell me, that's usually a sign.'

'Right, so it's quite safe to run the fence line.' Promising herself to be more vigilant when it came to running the perimeter checking the fences.

'Of course, it is. Hey, how many quolls did you see, hon?'

'I think it's a small family with their cute white spots and long tails, climbing the mango trees.' The mango orchard may seem manicured but it was home to many creatures, with native lands surrounding them.

Soft grey brolgas blended with colourful rainbow lorikeets, emerald doves, or the permanently paired pygmy geese waded on the edges of the large dam where she'd stop to admire their squawking parade to stretch after her run.

It had become a daily ritual. She'd run back and over breakfast, she'd search online for the name of a new bird species or plant she'd discovered around the farm. The quolls were her greatest discovery to date. No, she did not want to see any crocodiles in a hurry.

'Quolls are cute, aren't they? They're an endangered species, so don't play with them. I must let the ranger know they're breeding again. How many were there?'

'Half a dozen.' She'd spent ages watching them, even now smiling at the memory.

'That's great.'

'Are we getting more cattle in?'

'The musters are slowing down now the trees are fruiting. They used to say, the bigger the mangos get—the less cattle there are to collect.'

Verily giggled. 'They have the strangest sayings in this town.'

'But you liked the cattle, didn't you?'

'I did.' She'd now babysat three separate herds from the overflow of the train. Alex would call and she'd scoot down in the quad and play gatekeeper for other drivers in smaller trucks and stockmen who came to unload the cattle. She'd flushed troughs, checked fences, and helped Speedy unload the feed hay, all before they practised her pitching by the windmill while babysitting the cattle until sunset. She liked watching them, until Alex or his father, Neville, arrived in their road trains to haul them to Darwin harbour.

The people she'd dealt with on the farm all knew her as Molly's niece or Alex's girlfriend. Wow, she had a boyfriend!

Or did she?

They didn't date, not that there was anywhere to go, except the pub. They shared numerous daily phone calls and were friends more than anything else.

She was used to relationships being casual because she'd always left when the season was over. So this was no different, especially when she already had a ticket booked and paid for.

'We should go shovel cowpats from the paddock and put it on my dragon fruit,' said Molly.

Verily laughed at her aunt. 'Really? Gee that sounds like fun. Not.'

'It's the only time I do manual labour. I like my dragon fruit.'

'I've never eaten it.'

'Well, this year will be special then, not that I eat it either, hon. It does wonders for the complexion.'

The coach, Agnes, let loose with a shrill whistle that made them all stop and stare, again sending the flock of galahs screeching for freedom. 'THAT'S IT YOU MOB, PRACTISE IS OVER. AND, CAN SOMEONE TELL PRINCESS ALEX HE'D BETTER BE HERE FOR THE GAME THIS WEEKEND OR FIND ANOTHER CATCHER.'

She swung her bat over her shoulder like a caveman's club, with whistle swinging around her neck and with her flip-flopping thongs crunching on the dead grass, Agnes left.

'Huh? So that's it? Where's the pep talk on placements for the team, or the strategy for self-practise until gameday,' Verily said.

'Erm, what?' Molly asked.

Speedy came tearing over and jumped the short boundary fence to sit beside Verily. 'What a waste of bloody time that was.' She ripped off her softball glove and threw it on the brittle grey grass. 'Agnes wouldn't even let me bowl.'

'Pitch,' corrected Verily. 'Don't treat your glove like that!'

'Sorry.' Speedy scooped it up off the ground. 'I'm just so—'

'I get it.' Verily squinted over to the carpark that was nothing more than dust from the others leaving. 'Stuff it.' She got up and jumped the small fence with ease. Yes, her sneaky morning fitness routine was getting her back into shape. 'Come on, grab the bucket of balls. Molly, you don't mind waiting?'

'No, hon. Why, what are you going to do?'

'Can you play catch?'

Molly flexed her arm saying, 'I'm not a good thrower, got that dodgy elbow.'

'Neither am I. This is why I've enlisted the super coach, I have,' said Speedy.

'I'm no super coach.' Not when Verily was used to just being a player. She may be doing this for Alex and Speedy, but she was also doing this for herself. What if she could coach Speedy to throw a strike?

'Come on, Speedy, let's go stand on the pitcher's plate. Molly, can you put the bucket on the home plate and just stand there looking glamorous as always.' Verily hooked her good arm through Speedy's and guided the girl back to the centre of the diamond.

A few white cockatoos stood out among the tiny zebra finches that remained scavenging seeds on the outfield. The rest of the place was deserted as the sunset's-red rays stretched across the horizon.

'I'll be a bloody target,' called out Molly, putting the bucket on the white plastic home plate that contrasted against the dirt. She then leaned against her folded umbrella using it like a walking stick.

'I can't chuck that far, remember,' said Speedy.

'Pitch. Yes, you can, and you'll do it today. I'm not doing the drive for nothing,' Verily said sternly, standing behind Speedy on the pitcher's plate. 'Stand here and I'll shadow you. Okay, I'm not gay, but I'll be getting really close to you.' Practically hugging the girl, she tried to get the manikin into position.

'I know you're not. My cousin really likes you, but you know Alex is commitment-phobic, he is. Never lasts with a woman unless he wants something.'

No way! She fit his profile of female perfectly with a plane ticket back to the US as well as doing an awful lot of work for Alex, for beer she didn't drink. Why? To fight her boredom?

Her heart twinged that it wasn't more than just a holiday fling. Everything, her whole life was all for one season, and she was trained to never get attached. So why was she letting Alex get under her skin like this?

'We're here to focus on you, Speedy.' Verily straightened Speedy's head and grabbed the wrist that held the softball. 'We'll swing and throw, and we're not going home until you hit that bucket by Molly. Okay?'

'You betcha, boss, I will,' Speedy said, sharing a huge grin.

'Don't bounce, try channelling all that jittery energy to the ball. Here we go, solid base with your footing, and let's swing the arm.' From behind Speedy, while holding her wrist, Verily rolled Speedy's right arm in a swinging motion, hoping this worked. Verily pitched with her left, but she had to try something to show Speedy the correct swinging action and the perfect point to release the ball. 'Let go, now.'

Like normal, Speedy let go of the ball a second too late.

It dribbled out of her hand in an upswing motion and plonked a metre away from their feet. 'Sorry.'

'Don't be. We're here to work on it. Just think of your arm like a slingshot, now let's try that again.'

And they did. With the next few throws the ball landed further and further away from Speedy.

Ball after ball.

Bucket after bucket.

In the last of the dying light, the softball hit the purple bucket that sat in the middle of the home plate. Molly pointed the brolly she'd been swinging like a bat in the air and shouted, 'STRIKE ONE and I'm out!'

'*I did it. I did it.*' Speedy jumped in the air with arms above her head. 'Did you see it? Did you see?' She skipped to the home plate and hugged Molly.

'I saw it, Speedy,' Molly squealed, also jumping up and down like a teenager.

Verily picked up the bucket of balls from the pitcher's mound and made her way to the happy couple dancing on the home plate. 'So, I guess it's home time.'

'Thank you, coach.' Speedy rushed up and hugged Verily.

'Careful.' Verily flinched, protective over her shoulder.

'Bugger, sorry about the shoulder, but I did it. Did you see me?'

'Well done, Speedy. Now you know the swing to use, keep practising and you'll get faster and stronger.' Just like she was practising what she preached and could feel the difference in herself these past few weeks. 'Find me tomorrow and we'll work on it some more. I might ask Alex to borrow his catcher's gear.'

'His gear will be on his back veranda, hon, it's his dressing-room,' said Molly.

Verily was well aware the guy would strip himself and her off at the back door before carrying her inside. It was rare to be clothed inside his place, and she never entered through the front door.

She'd never been in a relationship like it, but then again, she wasn't having a relationship; it was just a friendly holiday fling. Nothing more.

'I'll be there I will. You're the best. Seriously, you're the best. I'm gonna hate it when my cousin breaks your heart. See ya tomorrow,' Speedy said, skipping off with her bucket of balls to her waiting ute.

'What did she mean by that?' How? Her heart wouldn't break when she was prepared to never get too close, because she was always leaving.

'No idea, hon, the kid's on her own planet, but she's so happy, it's contagious.' Molly hooked her arm through Verily's. 'We should go have a quiet meal in the pub to celebrate your coaching brilliance.'

Molly had always been there to celebrate her major victories in the past, in many countries. Was this moment worthy of a celebration? 'The pub?'

'You haven't been there yet. Besides, I don't feel like cooking and your cooking skills are—' Molly screwed her nose up.

'Brilliant when it comes to two-minute noodles and

toast.' They both laughed.

'Let's have a nice, quiet meal in the Pub's lounge, that way we both get away from doing the dishes.'

'I could handle that.' Molly was right, Verily deserved to celebrate this small milestone. As a left-handed pitcher, Verily had helped the right-handed Speedy pitch. It'd been her biggest hurdle in coaching anyone… until now.

FIFTEEN

Alex, while on the phone with Verily, walked around his truck parked on the far side of the deserted highway. He needed the break to stretch his legs, grateful to finally find a phone signal. 'So, I hear congratulations are in order.'

'For what?'

'For Speedy pitching all the way to the home plate.'

'Did Speedy call you?'

'Nine times.' He smiled at her laugh. 'I'm so proud you did it.'

'I've never been able to before.'

'Why not?'

'I'm a left-handed pitcher —'

'And Speedy's a right. Well, you did it. You should consider coaching full time.'

'I'm not interfering with Agnes when I'm only here until the Festival.'

He hated hearing that. 'What about coaching clinics? Didn't you say you and your sister were doing something like that?'

'Where would I start? I'm a player used to taking directions from the coach or the catcher.'

'And you're superb at that too.' She followed all of his instructions brilliantly.

'I'm not a people person. I don't want to put up with parents and fielding questions and all that stuff.'

'Why?'

'Because all I wanted to do was play. I never got involved in the politics.'

What kind of politics would there be in the game of softball? 'Is that because you never stayed in one place for more than a season, you were never there long enough to get involved?'

He heard her sharp intake of breath followed by a heavy silence.

Had he said the wrong thing, that only made him swallow down the scratchy lump in his throat.

They weren't permanent. Did he want it to be? Did she?

After a long pause, Verily asked, 'Do you think you'll make it to the next game?'

Nice change of topic, princess. She was good at that, but it was better than her customary shrug. 'I'd like to, but I think Dad has me booked.' He sighed as he leaned against the truck he'd been living in this past month. He missed the farm, the mango orchard, brewing his beer in the shed, and crawling into his bed at night after a home-cooked meal. Most of all he missed Verily.

'Have you ever missed a game before?'

'Usually one a season,' he said, 'when we're at the height of the musters, but I try not to.'

'It's work, you take it when you get it.'

'Except Dad wants me to invest it straight back into the business, to get another truck.'

'So, who'll drive that?'

'I asked him that same question, as well as why go into more debt when we still owe on Dad's new beast. I met with the accountant the other day and, I dunno, it makes little sense.'

'What? The numbers?'

'Hey, numbers aren't my thing. My issue is, why would Dad risk it?'

'Like why would you risk brewing your beer? Have you talked to Neville about your plans?'

'No.' Yet, he'd happily shared all of them with Verily. It was so good to finally share with someone and not be judged. Although her smartarse comments kept him on his toes, along with her brutal honesty that made him think. Most of all he liked seeing her messy hair spread across the pillow on his bed, knowing he'd done that to her, along with that dreamy look in her eyes. Especially first thing in the morning when she'd wake up and look at him.

'Is Neville doing this to set you up for your future as a partner?'

'I wish I could say yes, but honestly, I want…' *phone sex.* But, talking about his dad was killing the mood. 'We're not that close as father and son.' They weren't even friends.

'If Neville knew you weren't interested, what would he do?'

'He'd hate me forever for letting him down.'

'It's your life, not his. I'm lucky my father had always

supported me.'

'I'm hoping Dad and I can sit down soon. I don't want him signing my wages over to the bank, I want it for me.' He hadn't seen his dad, except to receive instructions over the phone for the next load.

If only he had the guts to say it to his dad's face that he didn't want to be in the family business when they really weren't a family. There was no father-son relationship because he never really saw his father after his mother died.

He'd learned more from Molly's family, or working at other places while on the job.

When he did see his dad, Neville was either too tired and cranky from being on the long road hauls to talk, or he was too busy talking about his travels to even listen or ask what Alex was doing. Alex had learned to never bother with his old man, knowing it wouldn't be long before he was gone again.

Just like Verily.

He stumbled a little, sagging against the side of the truck. At least Verily listened, and talked, and kissed with so much power he'd never enjoyed kissing a woman as much as he did with her. All he wanted to do was kiss her and keep kissing her until they were breathless and naked. Then he'd do it all over again.

'It might be better to tell him sooner, rather than later,' said Verily. 'I know what it's like to have your dreams ripped out from under you, Alex. It's devastating. The guy deserves to know — and soon.'

Damn. She'd done it again, made him see it from

another point of view. His heart dropped for the pain Verily had to endure by herself.

A ute tooted its horn and slowed down to park behind his truck.

Alex recognised it and shut his eyes tight, pressing the heel of his palm to his forehead. 'Oh, that's just great.'

'What? Did I say the wrong thing?' Verily asked, over the phone.

'No, not you, never. It's Tim.' He watched Tim get out of his ute, giving him a wave.

'Tim from the Station?' Verily asked.

Alex waved back at Tim it wasn't like he could hide in the crowd on the side of the road. 'Yep, from Rigby Downs.'

'You haven't told him about Sherice yet, have you?'

He winced. 'Ah no.'

'Are you scared of confrontations, Alex?'

'Are you?'

Verily's laugh answered his question. 'I played in a highly competitive sport where sledging was a daily thing, battling against top-class batters who would aim for me at the plate. What do you think?'

'Yeah, you're a tough cookie who's cute,' *and the most unbelievably sexiest, sassiest female ever.* 'I've gotta go, Tim's here.' So much for phone sex.

'Say hi, to the guy.'

'I will. Talk soon, babe.' He stared at the silent phone in his hand. Damn, he missed her.

'Talking to the little lady?' Tim asked.

Alex grinned, yes, she was his girl—for as long as he

could keep her in the country. 'Verily says G'day. So, how's tricks?' The two men shook hands and stood in the shade of the massive truck on the side of the deserted highway with only a view of the spindly low-lying scrub.

'The muster is over for me, so I'm on my way to Darwin. Hey, thanks for shuffling my herd to town so fast.'

'It's what mates do.' Guilt had played a big factor in prioritizing Tim's herd first among the many he'd hauled to Darwin harbour in time to catch their ships. 'Are you going for a break in the big smoke?'

'They still burning off in Darwin, huh?'

'Yeah, Palmerston is nothing but a constant sea of smoke when you hit Darwin's outer limits. Are you going shopping?'

'I'm finally buying that engagement ring I promised Sherice.'

'Is that why she doesn't wear a ring?'

'I didn't think you were the type of bloke to notice a woman's jewellery, mate?'

Bloody hell. He shrugged just like Verily.

'I couldn't get the one Sherice wanted last muster, but I have enough to do it now. I'll buy both wedding and engagement rings while I'm there.'

'Ah, listen, mate...' Alex inhaled deeply and realised Verily was right, he hated confrontations. 'You're gonna hate me.'

'Why? We go way back.'

'That's why this is so hard... I didn't know you were seeing Sherice.'

'I've been out west and I don't get to Elsie Creek that much, I've been going straight to Katherine to see Sherice. You, you've been doing whatever you do.'

'Thing is…' Alex licked his lips, preparing to sip some nasty medicine, and blurted out, 'I've been seeing Sherice too when I did our Katherine run.'

The smile fell from Tim's face as he stepped back, thumbing up the brim of his sweat-stained Akubra. 'You what?'

'As soon as I found out you two were together, I stopped seeing her and I've been kicking myself ever since. Mate, I'm sorry, I didn't know. I've been trying to find the right time to tell you, which is now, because I haven't and won't touch her ever again.'

'Bull! When did this happen?'

'First time was last year at a carpark party after a softball game.'

'So, it's true what they say, you're just the team's man-bag.'

'Oi, I've got a lady.'

'Were you screwing Sherice and Verily at the same time?'

'No, I don't cheat. Sherice told me she was single and wasn't wearing an engagement ring.'

'Because I've been busting my guts trying to buy her one. *You bastard.*'

'Fine, punch me in the head, mate, get it out of your system. Just know I hate myself for what I've done to you. I hate Sherice for putting me in this position coz it's been eating me up for not telling you sooner.'

'Why didn't you?'

'The first time I've seen you in a year was that day at Rigby Downs when you met Verily, and Sherice was there.'

'You could've called me.'

'And say this crap over the phone? No, I needed to say it to your face, so you can take your swing at me.'

'*Farrrk!*' Tim punched the truck's side panel and stepped back from Alex, wiping his mouth.

'I deserve a smack in the mouth, I do,' said Alex, 'but I swear I didn't know.'

'Who else knows about this?'

'Sherice, and Verily. You know I don't blab around the bush-blocks, and I trust Verily too.' He trusted Verily enough to manage his entire operation while he was away.

'Why does Verily know?'

'I don't keep secrets from Verily. Look mate, that time you met Verily, we weren't together. I was using her as a shield to get away from Sherice, that's why I had to explain it to Verily.' He could tell her everything and wished she was here right now because he hated dealing with crap like this.

'What? You're not with Verily?'

'It's complicated.'

'You don't do complicated. Everything's a simple yes or no with you.'

And that's how well they knew each other. 'You're right, Verily is only here as long as her holiday lasts, but we're not talking about Verily, we're talking about...' He inhaled deeply, not even wanting to say the woman's name who'd caused all of this. 'I'm sorry, Tim. Hate me forever, but you had to know before you married her and spent a fortune on a ring. If Sherice has done it with me, who else has she got visiting when you're not around.'

'*Bull...*' Red in the face, Tim ripped off his Akubra and slapped it against his jeans. 'You'd better not be making up this crap.'

'If you think I'm that cruel a bastard to bullshit you like this, then we aren't mates.'

Tim stepped in close and shouted in Alex's face, '*You slept with my future wife!*'

'Who told me she was single!'

'How many other taken women are you screwing?'

'There is only one woman who has ever slept in my bed back home and that's Verily. That's it.'

'Bull! Everyone knows truckies have got their bunks with them and they sleep their way around the country.''

'Oi.'

'You just said you did *my fiancée* on your Katherine run. You lied to me about Verily being your girlfriend.'

'I never said she was, you just assumed.'

'You're just like your bloody old man, who's got his women scattered all over the joint. No wonder he never goes home. Like father like son, ya like bloody wombats, you eat, you root, you leave.'

'Who says that old-fashioned jargon?'

'My mother.'

'Right, so we're taking dating tips from a woman in her seventies, huh?'

'You never commit to anything. Not to the one woman and certainly not to the one job. The only reason you're with Verily is for the free room and board when she deserves better.'

'That is not true!' Tim was right about him changing careers, but he had plans now.

'Must be a step up from sleeping with her aunt.'

'*Enough!*' Alex grabbed Tim by the shirt and slammed him against the side of his truck as a protective hatred surged through his veins. 'Molly is like a second mother to me. You've been there when we camped at her house as kids. Don't you ever dare say another bad thing about that woman, or her niece! I get you're ropable, and so am I, but it's Sherice we should be angry at, not those who I consider family. Do we understand each other?'

'Bloody hell.' Tim hung his head down. 'Sorry, mate, I shouldn't have said that about Molly.'

'Too bloody right.'

'Okay, okay.' Tim put his hands up and Alex stepped back, taking deep breaths. 'I'm sorry about what I said about Molly.'

'Me too.' Alex wiped his mouth, trying to calm his temper. 'I truly am sorry, mate, I swear I had no idea you were with Sherice.'

Tim straightened his shirt and looked up with pain etched across his face. 'What do I do?'

Alex wanted to shrug like Verily. Instead, he shoved his hands into his jeans pockets. 'I dunno, but I do know you deserve better than Sherice.'

Tim scuffed the heel of his boot on the edge of where the black bitumen met the red dirt. He hooked his thumbs in the belt loops of his jeans as another road train approached, blaring its air horn. The pair nodded to the driver as it thundered past, then they leaned their backs against the truck.

The passing road train became nothing more than a dot lost on the hazy horizon as a whistling kite glided above them in the cloudless sky.

Tim removed his Akubra and smoothed down his hair, putting his hat back on, he sighed with deflating shoulders.

'I'm sorry I had to be the bearer of bad news,' said Alex. 'Or would you have preferred I kept my mouth shut? I've never done this before and I hope to Christ I never have to do it again.'

'Um… Yeah, nah, I'd want to know.'

'That's what Verily said.'

'Huh. She's a great girl you've got there—if you can keep her. But then that'd suit you with your fear of commitment.'

'Oi?' Alex frowned.

'Just being honest here, mate.'

Alex nodded as he sighed. Tim was right, Alex hadn't committed to much in his past because he didn't want to get hurt. Not like how Tim looked now.

Yet, Alex missed her. He totally and completely missed Verily more than anyone or anything else in his life. Had he fallen in love with her?

'I'll, um…' Tim pushed off the truck and started walking down the road.

'Where are you going?'

'Katherine.'

'Your ute's parked back there.' Alex thumbed over his shoulder.

Tim stopped and stared at the deserted highway then back at his vehicle. 'Ah, yeah.'

'Are you okay to drive?'

'It'll do me good, clear my head.'

'Look, mate...' Alex approached and put a hand on Tim's shoulder. 'If you need anything at all, you call me.'

'Thanks.' With his eyes shaded by the wide brim of his Akubra, Tim gave a curt nod to Alex, then started for his ute. Suddenly he stopped and said, 'I had to do this once.'

'Do what?'

'Remember Crackers?'

'The fireworks junkie? The Ringer who enjoyed colouring our outback night skies with an endless personal stash of firecrackers.'

'That's him.'

'Didn't he head out west after a messy break-up?'

'Yep. It was me who told him his ex-missus was playing buckle-bunny with some guy at the rodeo in his horse float. Crackers gave me a bloody nose and wouldn't speak to me for a year.'

'And now?'

'I was the best man at his wedding to his new lady. He's got two kids and lives on a farm on the West Coast. He calls once a month and visits every year for Territory Day to stock up his firecracker stash.'

'Hey, you have my number.'

'Yeah, well, you're never bloody home, are you?' Tim tapped his hat's brim with a nod and headed for his ute.

Alex watched Tim drive away until the dust settled beneath the highway's heat waves shimmering above the black tar.

Tim was right, Alex was hardly home these days, and he hated it.

SIXTEEN

Molly and Verily sat on the deserted bleachers, with only one minibus as the extra car in the carpark, other than that the place looked uninhabited.

'You're not wrong about people not showing up to games,' Verily said, resting her sneakers on the short fence line to watch the lack of action on the sports field.

'It's expected. We're at the height of the musters, hon,' said Molly. 'It's a shame Alex couldn't make it. He sounds so down being stuck on the road. I keep telling Neville that his boy is a homebody, but that man won't listen.'

'Is that why Alex won't tell his father about the mangos and his beer?'

'Where you've been doing a fabulous job managing the orchard. Make sure you keep the water up it keeps the flesh juicier in the fruit.'

'How do you know all these things?'

'When you grow up under the roof of a second-generation mango farmer, you pick up a thing or two.'

'Why don't you like working in the orchard?'

'I never have. Oh, but your mother loved it. She'd walk up and down the rows with your grandfather, inspecting the fruit. He tried to teach me, but I never had my heart set on mangos, so he gave me an acre to do what I wanted.'

'And?'

'I planted peanuts one year, that was okay. I grew sunflowers, which the galahs destroyed. I tried Chinese vegetables and various fruit trees, until the magpie geese massacred them, not to mention the stampede of wallabies, so I gave up. That was until a customer gave me some dragon fruit and told me all about its anti-ageing properties. It does wonders for my crow's feet, and from that one plant...'

'Grew many. Do you ever eat any?'

'Yes, with ice cream, sometimes. The mango trees closest to the house are hand planted by your grandfather and great-grandfather. They're the grafting stock used for the Kensington Pride mangos, that's the popular market variety everyone gets. For us, the family, we have the strawberry mango blend your grandfather created. Now those mangos are superb. Nothing beats sitting under those trees in the orchard in summer, eating fresh juicy mangos. Just the acid is a bother.'

'Acid?'

'When you pick them. Speedy knows the best way to do it, ask her for tips. I wonder if Alex has bought the detergent for the mango wash, yet?'

'I have no idea.'

'Oh, look, Speedy's bowling.'

'Pitching.'

'Sorry, must have cricket on my mind.'

'*Come on, Speedy, you can do it!*' called out Verily from the stands. 'This is the quietest game I've ever been to. Why aren't they supporting each other?'

'Because they're all used to seeing Speedy never pitching the distance to the home plate.'

'She will.' Verily leaned forward, almost praying that Speedy could do it.

Speedy jittered on the spot and with a wide swing, she typically let go of the ball too late. '*Bugger.*' It arched high into the air and plonked on the dirt two feet from where she stood.

'It's okay, Speedy. Deep breath, you'll do this,' called out Verily.

'OI! WHO BROUGHT MIGHTY-MOUSE'S MEGAPHONE TO THE GRANDSTANDS?' hollered Agnes from the bench where the team kept their gear.

'They're not playing chess,' snapped back Verily. 'Although you're the kind of queen who'd kill the king to advance to your own mutinous board—or do you prefer water-boarding in the Dry?'

'You didn't?' Molly snort-laughed at Verily.

'TIME OUT!' Agnes demanded from the umpire. With her long plait swinging like a donkey's tail, her thongs flip-flopped across the dead grass. Red, black, and white footy socks slipped to her ankles exposing her hairy, lily-white legs shaded by her lime green board shorts. Topped off by a brown t-shirt, a black and blue chequered flannelette shirt, and her yellow duck's bill sun visor.

'Is Agnes coming over here?' Verily asked Molly while looking around at the empty stands.

'Well, no one else is sitting over here, hon.'

'WHO THE FRICKIN' HECK ARE YOU?' Agnes

demanded, standing directly in front of Verily with only the small fence dividing them.

'Why are you wasting your time on me when you should be focusing on your team?' Verily asked.

'COZ SOME SMARTMOUTH CAN'T SHUT UP ON THE BENCHES.'

'I'm on the bleachers. You're the one who's sitting on the bench, not me.'

'DON'T SPROUT THE TECHNICALITIES OF TEAM TALK TO ME! I'M THE COACH. SO, YOU EITHER SIT THERE AND KEEP THAT TRAP SHUT OR NICK OFF.'

'I'm just supporting the team.'

'NOT IN MY TIME, LAMINGTON-LEGS. THAT KID DON'T NEED LIP FROM YOU TWO HAS-BEEN GLAMAZONS.'

'Well, I never.' Molly sat up and slammed her umbrella shut. 'We know when we're not wanted.' She picked up her bag and esky and headed for her car. 'Consider me off the Softball Committee and the Rosella Festival Committee too.'

''BOUT BLOODY TIME YOU STOPPED INTERFERING, YOU OVER SHINY CHRISTMAS BEETLE. YOU'RE WORSE THAN THEM DRUNKEN LORIKEETS WHO DON'T KNOW WHEN TO STOP DRINKING FROM THE BOTTLEBRUSHES.'

Verily scowled as she stepped toward Agnes. '*Hey*, I don't care who you are, but you do not speak to my aunt like that.'

'WHAT ARE YOU GONNA DO? HIT AN OLD WOMAN?'

'If that's what you call yourself. Wouldn't want to snap a nail getting hooked in that monobrow of yours.'

'*Ooh.*' The team chorused in the background.

Agnes scowled over her shoulder and the team were instantly silenced.

'Can we get on with the game so we can all go home?' Called out the umpire from behind the home plate.

'We're leaving. Come along, Verily,' said Molly, beckoning from the edge of the carpark.

'I'VE GOT YOUR NUMBER, BABY-BIATCH.' Agnes pointed her short stubby finger at Verily.

'Well, call me anytime. I'm not shy. I'll bring the sparkles and we'll make bridles from your plait as the start of your cult to capture unicorns, shall we?'

'OOHHH BURN. TAKE YOU A DECADE TO COME UP WITH THAT DID IT, POISONOUS PETAL?'

'Well it was your therapist who gave me tips to taunt. He said he'll be late for your next appointment; he's trying to see if you and Medusa are related. It seems you both share that same fear of facing your own mirror, but in your case, it's well-founded.'

'LIKE YOU'RE SOME HIPPY PSYCHIC WHO GOT THEIR QUALIFICATIONS OUT OF A WEET BIX BOX.'

Verily laughed. 'I like that one. I must remember it.'

Agnes flinched as if bitch slapped and blinked fast at Verily.

'*Come along, Verily,*' called Molly from the carpark.

'Thanks for the sledging match, monobrow, that was fun. We should do it again sometime. If you need me, I'll be down on my luck.' Verily laughed, picked up the water coolers and followed Molly to the car.

'AND DON'T YOU COME BACK YOU DATELESS BUCKLE-BUNNY, YOU'RE RIDIN' IN THE WRONG RODEO.'

'Go swallow some nuts and get an allergy,' shouted back Verily over her shoulder. 'Keep at it, Speedy, you can do it.'

Speedy waved with a huge smile on her face.

'GO DUSTY DINGOES,' Verily cried out as she climbed into Molly's SUV, laughing.

Molly stared at Verily from the driver's seat. Both teams and even the children in the playground had stopped to watch, all while Speedy kept smiling and waving from the pitcher's plate.

'What was that all about?' Molly stared at her as she started the engine.

Verily laughed to herself. 'Agnes isn't my coach. I was just the holidaying heckler in the grandstands. I've never been able to do that before. Huh, being retired is fun.'

'I'm never bringing you back.'

'I don't think Agnes wants me back.' She laughed as Molly put the car into gear, then sobered up some. 'I'm sorry, Molly, you shouldn't quit the committee because of me. You've put so much effort into the Rosella Festival and the team.'

'No, it's time. With no Alex playing and you not playing, there's no family out there.'

The guilt hit Verily hard across her shoulders and

tightened her chest. 'I'm sorry.'

'It's fine. Besides, that was the best thing I've ever seen. It'll be all over town before they finish the game, you wait and see. You really stirred her up, hon. About time someone gave it to Agnes.' Molly led their laughter that filled the car as they left the team behind. It was the first time Verily had ever left a game early. Maybe there were other things out there besides the game.

SEVENTEEN

'How come you have no lawn, Molly?' Verily asked her aunt seated on the cane chairs under the cool veranda where they watched the shade shift across the mango orchard.

'Your grandfather always said it was a waste of water and time.' Molly cradled her wine glass in her lap and glanced at her watch. 'In the wet season, you can see the grass grow so fast mowing becomes a weekly chore. Not for just around the house but the entire orchard too. You get sick of it, you'll see.'

'Will I?'

'You're not thinking of running off anywhere?'

'I only came here for a holiday. I have a return ticket.'

'This is your home too. There are four bedrooms in this house, feel free to choose one, except mine, of course.'

'But this is your house. I should be paying you for board or something.'

'The place pays for itself from the Trust that collects the agistment fees, the orchard lease, and the shed's rent. Your grandfather set us up well. My husband carried that on from my father, so I wouldn't have to work if I didn't want to, but I love my shop and the people who visit. So, no. I will not be taking any board money from you, not when you're helping out here all the time doing the laundry and the mangos.'

'But, I'm just…' *Holidaying.*

'In case you hadn't realised it, hon, you've been managing the farm.'

Was she really? 'I'm only helping Alex, and you.'

'Sure, but you seem to be enjoying yourself.'

She did like it, and had settled into a routine of sorts, but she was also used to leaving. 'I'm just following instructions because I don't know what I'm doing.' It's what she did, follow other people's plans.

'Hey, I've lived here all my life and I'm still clueless about what I'm doing. But what I have learned is that you can make it as simple or as complicated as you want. Didn't you ever dream of doing something else besides softball?'

'It's all I know.'

'Stop saying that!' Molly leaned closer, pointing her finger at Verily. 'You didn't get a world-class education to just know how to throw a ball, young lady. I want you to use that knowledge to manage our Trust. It's ours. Yours and mine, for our family's future and I know you'll be careful with it, too. You've been doing it for yourself for years, so consider this as an expansion on your skill set. I won't take no for an answer, especially when your father said you could do it with your eyes closed.'

Ugh! Her dad had a lot to answer for.

'Go on, I dare you to admit you like it here.'

'I have enjoyed working around here. It's peaceful.' It was well away from all the stresses she used to put herself under to perform in a game.

'It is, and that peace is only found when your home.'

Was she? 'How did my gameday bag get here?'

Molly's eyebrows raised and she took a big gulp on her wine. 'Did I forget to mention that?'

Verily stared at her aunt trying to be coy.

'You were so upset after the accident—not that anyone could blame you—and your father and his family were grieving over Kylie's passing… they sent it here.'

'Why?'

'Did you miss it?'

'No. Not until I found mum's bats and balls, and my baby glove.'

'I forgot they were in that cupboard, with the scrapbooks.'

'Ah-huh.' Poker would not be a game suited to her aunt. 'Why did you put my gameday bag under the bed?'

'Because it was too heavy for me to put it in the attic and that's your room unless you want to pick another. All those trophies and medals you've won are all in the attic too.'

'How come?'

'You were on the road all the time and your father sent them here for safe-keeping.'

'We never had the room, travelling.'

'I know. I'd bring a load back in my suitcase whenever I visited you, because this is your home, Verily. I'm hoping that, maybe, you'll use the gear you have in that big chunky bag of yours again.'

'I'm retired.'

'Sure, as a professional softball player, but you're too

young to retire from life, young lady,' Molly said, looking at her watch again. 'They should've finished their game by now. I wonder how they went.'

'I hope Speedy's pitch made it to the plate at least.'

Not even a few seconds later, stirring up the dust, Speedy's ute drove into the yard and parked under the trees. Speedy jumped out of her seat with a big smile on her face. *'I did it. I did it.'*

'You struck out?' Verily called out, hopeful.

'No, but I made the home plate, and they hit my ball and it flew so high, it did.'

Another car pulled in, followed by three utes, a very fine-looking vintage red beast of a ute, and a combi-van. Verily recognised the cars belonging to the other members of the Dusty Dingoes, all wearing their gameday uniform which was just a t-shirt they wore over their shorts or jeans.

'What's going on?' Molly called out, getting up from her seat.

'We thought we'd bring the after-game carpark party to you, Molly,' said Jenny the bush nurse. 'How ya feelin' Verily?'

'Fine, thanks.' She knew Jenny from the smallest country hospital she'd ever visited, getting her painkillers she rarely touched anymore.

'When we saw Speedy pitch to the plate, we had to ask and wanted to meet the secret super coach. Hi, I'm Bella, we haven't officially met.'

'Speedy, you didn't,' said Verily as she shook hands with the bird-feeding-fielder.

'I didn't tell them, I swear. I only said I was getting help, I did.'

'Speedy didn't have a choice,' said Tess in her shiny black short-shorts. 'Speedy swore she couldn't tell us so she showed us on her mobile. Olympics, huh?'

'Oh, man.' Verily hid her face in her hands.

'Can't keep secrets in this town. I'm surprised we got away with it this long,' said Molly, giggling behind her wine glass. 'Did we win?'

'We got hammered, as usual,' replied Bella.

'Coz Speedy pitched so well, they hit the ball all over the place,' said Tess, 'We're so used to just standing out there getting a suntan, we weren't ready to do any fielding.'

'That's why we're here. Hi, I'm Karen, I left all my kids at home with my husband for this.'

'For what?' Verily asked, shaking Karen's hand.

'To ask you to coach us.'

'You have a coach, Agnes, who is a great batting coach,' said Verily. 'She's volunteering to help you guys, and that has to count for something, so I will not step on Agnes's toes, especially when I'm only here on holidays.'

'Pft,' muttered Molly, cocking her manicured eyebrow at Verily. 'Stop saying that.'

'I have the ticket to prove it, Aunty.' Rolling her eyes at her aunt, she then faced Speedy. 'So how was your pitching, Speedy?'

Speedy's face lit up brighter than a bank of spotlights shining down a dusty outback track. 'I had one strike at the last pitch of the game, I did. Didn't I?' She said looking to the other girls.

'You should've seen it. Speedy's jumping up and down, and we're all hugging her like she'd won the premiership. The coach and the other team left us while we're still in the middle of the diamond hugging Speedy,' explained Tess, with the other girls laughing. 'We want you to help us like you did with Speedy.'

'I'm not interfering with Agnes,' said Verily. 'I can't bat, and Agnes is good on that side.'

'But you can pitch, and you can field, I've seen you do it all over the world,' said Molly.

'Me too. Alex and I watched you, we did, on YouTube at that world championship where you broke the world record, twice!' Speedy said. 'Can I have your autograph later, can I?'

'So, can you help us?' Bella asked.

'Why? I mean, why do you play when you know you'll lose,' Verily asked all of them. The team had a ten-year losing streak, so why were they putting themselves through this?

Mandy, the jillaroo, stepped forward, removed her Akubra and nodded at her sister beside her. 'We're not expecting to be some grand champions, we do it for the girls, for the town and our mother played.'

'Same-same to what they said,' said Bella.

'I'm an outsider, so I do it to make new friends and be a part of this town,' said Jenny.

'Ditto,' said Kat, half-raising her hand in the air. 'I also promised my family I'd get more involved with the town, now it's home for us and not just a summer holiday.'

Verily's eyes widened at Kat, did she have something similar with another woman in this town? Did she dare make friends when she was so used to leaving them behind?

'Besides dragging Lucy with me to get over her shyness and outta the kitchens,' said Karen, hooking her arm through the timid Lucy's, 'I do it for a break away from my children or I'm up to my armpits in nappies and toddler talk. I need this, and these women,' said Karen, putting her other arm around Jenny the bush nurse—the link was strong.

'I play because it doesn't involve sewing or glue and glitter and other craft stuff, like my craft-obsessed-mother and grandmother,' said Tess with her short-shorts, putting her arm around Speedy. 'Plus, I get a tan while I hang out with my friends who don't judge me.'

Verily saw the team spirit in the women of all shapes, sizes, and ages, that stood before her. She had to admire their courage for showing up to games knowing they would lose, just like Agnes who showed up to coach them too. They had nothing to lose.

So, what did Verily have to lose that she hadn't already lost herself?

EIGHTEEN

Alex jumped out of the truck with its many trailers snaked around the cottage surrounded by mango trees. Exhausted, he dragged his duffel with him to the back veranda and dumped it at the washing machine. He opened his fridge, grabbed a bottle of water and took a deep mouthful while eyeing off his beer.

'Hello, ladies.' He grabbed a labelless bottle and checked out the brew number scribbled on the lid in Verily's handwriting. He was looking forward to this one, it was the Rosella beer.

Should he wait and share this moment with Verily?

What if it was revolting?

Perhaps he should try it now, then he'd have time to prepare her for the worst and let her down gently.

Alex popped the bottle's cap and listened for the crisp hiss of escaping gas. He grabbed his favourite chilled tasting glass from the top shelf of his beer-fridge and poured.

With the glass up to the sunlight, he inspected the pale ale's clarity and colour. Small bubbles ran in lines to the frothy head that was clean and white. He sniffed, taking in the blend of yeast, hops and spices with the slight tarty hint of a fruity aroma. He then sipped the crisp flavour, swishing it around for his pallet to savour.

Was it too sour or too sweet?

He swallowed, licked his lips, and nodded at the glass. 'Not bad. Not bad.' *It was bloody good!*

Now he wanted to celebrate with Verily, to hear her opinion on the new brew.

He stepped off the edge of his veranda and checked out his orchard. The tyre in the tree he'd hung for Speedy stood still with no softballs in the net.

In the shed, his quad was gone, but his ute rested beneath a layer of dust in the same spot he'd parked it. The shed floor was clean and his workbenches were spotless with his boxes of beer neatly stacked to the side. Verily had done a good job with this workspace, which he always took pride in.

The Rosella brew rested in the many crates Verily had bottled, he inspected each one while sipping from his glass.

This batch had been a new recipe, chasing that unique flavour. Or he'd be like everyone else brewing their beer in the backyard.

He wanted quality and full flavour, had he cracked it with this beer? Had he finally perfected the ultimate Sour IPA?

Alex needed another opinion and went to Molly's house. It was quiet and there were no lights on in the kitchen. 'Verily?' He called out through the kitchen's screen door. 'Molly?'

No answer.

He was suddenly anxious to find the woman he hadn't stopped thinking about.Every chance he'd call her for conversation and when he wasn't talking to Verily, he was thinking of all the things he wanted to discuss with her.

He'd never been like this with anyone and had to know that what he was feeling was real, that this wasn't a figment of a lonely imagination from being on the road too long away from home.

Following the track back to the shed, he looked over his orchard, its leaves a rich glossy deep green with the growing fruit thick along the branches. He'd have to prepare poles soon, to prop the branches from the weight of all the fruit. Verily had done a brilliant job.

Where was she?

WHACK!

Alex frowned at the sound that reminded him of a stockwhip cracking in the distance, followed by women shouting.

'What the—?' Were Verily and Molly partying? Or did they score another herd to babysit?

Leaving his tasting glass by his laundry sink, he stalked through the orchard chasing down the sound.

Laughter floated through the bountiful clusters of green fruit that dotted the dense foliage covering sturdy branches of the orchard. Sunshine greeted him as he emerged from their canopies to meet the fence that led to the back paddocks. The slow turning windmill blades caught the sun, and beneath its solid steel structure were half a dozen assorted parked cars, utes, a combi-van, Molly's SUV, and his quad.

'No way.' He stopped and thumbed up the brim of his Akubra.

In the middle of the dusty paddock lay a softball

diamond stretched out before the windmill. Molly, with her bright red striped umbrella, stood behind the home plate playing umpire with his team sorted in different field positions. Each woman had a beer or wine glass with them and were laughing as they played.

And they were properly playing.

There was no bird-feeding, no suntan slathering, no soccer kicking, just a definite focus on the game while having fun.

Then he saw *her* and the rest of the world vanished.

His heart expanded making it hard to breathe, so tempted to hurdle the fence and grab her for another one of those sizzling kisses. Wearing a softball glove and calling out instructions as the coach. Her hair was shining, her smile was wide, and she was the most absolutely stunning woman he'd ever seen.

He knew then, just by looking at her … He was in love with Verily. And believed it with every cell in his body.

He'd never been in love, to know if this was love, but it felt good—and painful—and complicated when he always wanted simple. But what made it complicated was that he didn't know if Verily felt the same about him, and she was leaving. Too. Bloody. Soon.

In awe of the moment, as the irritation of not being certain how she felt about him squeezed his ribs, Alex leaned against the fence and watched Verily coach the team where she stood beside Speedy on the pitcher's mound. His younger cousin wound her arm and let it rip. His eyes widened as he followed the pitch where the softball actually made the distance to the plate, and with speed.

Super-mum Karen was batting, and she slammed it out and over the diamond and straight in his direction.

'MINE.' Alex hoisted himself over the fence, with his boots kicking up the dust he ran through the short pasture with an eye on the ball. It arched straight for him and he caught it against his chest with two hands. Safe. 'YOU'RE OUT!' He pointed the softball at Karen.

Speedy led the charge of his teammates as he strolled to meet them in the middle. He'd never seen them so excited, not like this.

'Did you see it? Did you see me pitch, Alex?' Speedy cried out, hugging him like a kid.

'I did, you've improved a lot.'

'I got a strike too.'

'Three strikes?'

'Not yet, but soon. Verily reckons I will. She believes in me, she does.'

'Good girl, Speedy,' he replied, putting an arm around his little cousin's shoulders. 'What's going on here?'

'We've been having coaching sessions out here, so we don't upset Agnes,' said Tess in long leggings.

'Where're the hot pants, Tess?'

'Verily's been teaching me how to slide in this paddock and I'm not that keen on gravel rash from stealing bases.'

'You're all still practising in town, aren't you?' Alex asked in between the customary sisterly kisses from his teammates.

Mandy nodded and her sister Mindy answered, 'Yeah,

for the batting practise. Then we come here for the pitching and fielding practise.'

'No birdseed, Bella?'

'Nah, not here, this is Verily's turf.'

'I see.' Technically it was, but he had plans for this area next Dry.

'Are you going to be at the next game, to see me pitch in Jabiru, Alex? Are you gonna?' Speedy asked. 'Or we gonna have Agnes play catch. She's scary to pitch to.'

He imagined it would be scary pitching to Agnes. 'I'm planning on playing.'

'Verily and Molly aren't. Can you talk them into it?' said Tess with the rest of the team shaking their heads.

'Why not?'

'Well,' Speedy said, 'Verily and Agnes got into a slagging match—'

'Heckling match,' corrected Karen.

'Yeah, that,' said Speedy with a grin. 'Then Molly quit the Rosella Festival Committee, she did. So then we came here and had our first carpark paddock party.'

'All of this happened while I was away?' He wasn't gone that long, was he?

'Welcome home, Alex,' said Molly, warmly hugging him.

'Thanks, great to be back, but I wasn't expecting this.' Alex nodded to the softball diamond, complete with a chalk outline and plastic padded plates in the paddock. 'Whose idea was this?'

'Verily's. Not that the team gave her much of a choice,

but it's been great fun,' replied Molly, smiling at the diamond.

From the back of the group Verily collected balls and mats, calling out, 'Let's call it a day, ladies.'

'Alex, can you please talk Molly and Verily into coming to our game?' Bella asked for the other women as they said their farewells, leaving Verily to load up the quad and Molly pack her SUV.

'Hey, Molly, what's this about you not going to the game?' How come no one had told him about this?

'Are you going to the game?'

'I'm here, aren't I. Why didn't you tell me on the phone you'd quit the Committee? You love the Festival.'

'That's my business. But I have to brag, Verily has been brilliant. She's placed all the girls' in proper fielding positions based on the strengths they didn't even know they had.'

'Verily would've known from watching them from the bleachers.' He'd asked her to search for that from their very first game. *Good girl*—but was she his girl?

'Verily has even been throwing a few times to show the girls how to field and pass to each other.'

'Really? She isn't hurting herself?' An intense wave of protectiveness burned up inside. He didn't want Verily hurt. Not again, not when she'd come so far in such a short time.

'She's fine, we're all taking care of our secret coach,' said Molly with a wry grin and a glint in her eye.

'Secret, eh?'

'Well, I'd better wash up and start dinner to celebrate your return. I imagine you'll be hungry.'

'Always for your cooking.'

'Welcome home, hon.' Again, Molly reached up and hugged him.

'Thanks, but we haven't finished this discussion.'

'We'll talk over dinner where you can regale us with your fabulous adventures on the road.' Molly got into her SUV and drove off.

'So, the secret coach is it?' He faced Verily, itching to hold her, but he also didn't want to scare her off. She looked like a cornered wild bird, ready to fly away loading up the bike. 'And in my quad?'

'You told me I could use it anytime.'

'I did,' he said, approaching her with care. 'How's the arm?'

'Fine, I know my limits. How are you?'

'In shock.'

'Why?'

'At all of this.' He waved at the softball field in the middle of nowhere. 'How come you never told me about this over the phone?'

She shrugged.

He frowned. 'You dare to shrug when I've travelled for days on the lonely road...'

'Oh please, you were just down the track.'

He chuckled. 'Listen to you, picking up the local lingo.'

Again, she shrugged but grinned, her eyes shining as he took a step closer. 'How was the trip?'

'Boring.' He stood in front of her, inhaling her aroma while brushing her soft hair away from her beautiful face. 'I missed you.' That was the truth, the temptation of those soft lips calling to him was irresistible to not kiss. He ached to kiss her again and deeply, so he did.

The windmill creaked above them. The breeze blew at the diamond's chalk lines in the dust as the sun lowered on the horizon. His entire world was in this one moment. Her touch, her flavour, the feel of her skin, and that sexy hum she made as their kiss deepened. He wrapped his arms around her, bringing her closer to his chest, needing her closer. Her body pliant and perfect for him as she melted into him, crushing against her soft warm lips he swallowed her flavour deep into his lungs. He may be standing and kissing her, but it almost brought him to his knees.

'Now that was what I wanted to come home to.' He gasped for air ready to dive deep for more. He wanted to devour all of her and bury himself deep inside her as his ultimate home-coming-prize.

'Welcome back,' she murmured with glazed, dreamy eyes.

Smoothing down her wind tousled hair free from her face, admiring the way the world reflected in her bedroom-eyes, tenderly brushing her swollen lips with this thumb. 'Why did I ever leave you in the first place?' He couldn't say it. He wanted to say it. To tell her how much he loved her, but would it scare her off?

Somehow, she'd crawled into his head and found a home in his heart. He didn't want to let her go. She belonged there, with him.

So instead of telling her, scared of her reply, he kissed her, refusing to think of who would be leaving who first.

NINETEEN

eneath the shade of the mango tree in the heart of the orchard, Verily plucked a softball from the string bag hanging off the branch and tossed it into her glove. The ball's stitching contrasted against the smooth leather with fingers spreading as her palm took its all too familiar grip. She scratched her sneaker in the dirt for the perfect solid base and stared down at her target—the tyre hanging from the tree.

The breeze stilled and the tyre taunted her with its open mouth. She inhaled, swung her arm in a windmill action and let the ball fly straight through the tyre's gap to get caught in the net.

She grinned, satisfied, rolled her shoulder and pulled out another ball from the string bag.

'What do we have here?' Alex asked, with his black Akubra tilted back on his head. Leaning his broad shoulder against the tree, he hooked his thumbs through the belt loops of his jeans.

'Alex!' *Sprung.* 'I, ah, didn't hear the truck?'

'It's at my dad's waiting for a service when he comes into town. What are you doing?' He pushed off the tree and approached.

She clasped her hands behind her back feeling like a

kid. 'Nothing.'

Alex chuckled as he stood in front of her. 'You're really cute, you know that.' Kissing her forehead, he reached around her body and gently tugged the softball free from her hand. 'You're pitching?'

She shrugged.

He frowned.

'It's a habit.'

'What is? The pitching or your shrugging? I ask a question you answer, it's called a conversation, not sign language.'

'I do sign.'

'Do you?'

'Not sign-sign, but the signalling between pitcher to catcher.'

'You should teach me.' He tossed the softball like a one-handed juggler as he inspected the tree with the hanging tyre. 'How long has this been going on?'

'Um… a few weeks.' She lowered her head, toeing the soft soil with her shoe. 'Ever since I started coaching Speedy.'

'Why don't you use the tyre I set up for Speedy at my place?'

'That's Speedy's.'

He pointed the softball at her. 'You didn't want to get busted.'

She shrugged.

He frowned. 'How is the shoulder?'

'Good.'

'How fast have you been throwing?' He tossed the ball

at her and as a reflex she caught it in her glove.

'Not that fast, I've been finding my limits.'

He stood in front of her and with gentle fingers, he kneaded her shoulder region, like he'd done many times. It almost melted her on the spot. 'I'd noticed the muscle tone on your shoulder last night.' He kissed her shoulder making her giggle and squirm as he nuzzled into her neck. 'Well, come on then.' He reached over to the tree and collected her string bag of softballs and led her by the hand.

'Where are we going?'

'I need practise catching, and with Speedy now pitching properly, I may have to catch a ball or two.'

'I don't catch.'

'Didn't you say a pitcher is only as good as their catcher?'

'I did.'

'So, my catcher's stuff is at my place where you can pitch and teach me those signals.' He slipped his arm over her shoulders as they strolled through the orchard. 'You've done a good job with this place, the trees are in excellent condition.'

'I'm just following your instructions.' Following instructions had never been a problem for her, it was giving instructions that was harder.

'You're not overdoing the pitching, are you?'

'No, it's not like a game.'

'Why? What happens in a game?'

'I throw everything. Here, it's just me.'

'And me now.'

'Tell no one.'

'Why not? I'd love to play a game with you pitching. I'm proud of you, and you should be too.'

'I haven't been doing this to play, I've been doing this for myself, to just see what I can do. You have to see this from Speedy's side too. She's your team's pitcher and I won't take that away from her. Not when she's tried so hard.' Not like she'd done to so many others in her past when she'd been recruited to play.

'She's very excited.'

'I know, and I'm retired.'

'Is there some rule written to say you can't play again?'

'Not professionally.'

'Why? Do other clubs have ownership over you?' Alex said, frowning.

'No. Contracts were terminated and they compensated me for the accident.'

'My dad said you'd be insured and have sponsors from your sport.'

'I did, but I'm not rich like superstars of football with their multi-million-dollar contracts. Softballers don't earn that kind of money, we do it for the love of the game. My dad was my agent, and together we carefully invested what I'd earned because without a pitching arm or a game to attend I have no other income.'

'Do you really talk to your dad about finances?'

'He is an accountant and I talk to him about most things.' She'd never discussed finances with anyone but her father.

'I wish I was like that with my dad, to talk to him about

my future, well anything beyond truck-talk.'

'You can.'

'You've met my dad. He talks, I listen, and then he drives away.'

'You haven't met mine.'

'When?'

'What?'

'When can I meet him?'

'My father lives in the States.'

'Have you told him about me?'

'What's to tell?' She couldn't shrug because he had his arm around her.

He stopped and faced her with a frown flitting across his brow. 'You're very casual about all this—about *us*.'

What *us*? 'I'm used to being casual. I moved around, always committed to my sport first, following the seasons. Remember, I'm only here on a winter holiday.' She'd suffered plenty of heartbreaks leaving places and people in the past, that she'd learned to never get attached to anyone.

Yet, she was finding it harder to keep that distance from Alex, especially when he looked at her like this. And when he kissed her, nothing else mattered because her world was all him.

It scared her that he had so much power over her.

He tenderly tucked a tendril of hair behind her ear. 'Why are you returning to the States?'

Emotion clogged her throat at the thought of leaving him behind, so she shrugged.

He frowned.

'I have a ticket.'

'What do you have to go back to?'

'My father's courier business.'

'Why? When you have this place with Molly.' He swallowed hard and said, 'and me?'

'I can't stay here and work for beer, and I'm not taking over the orchard either. I'm not qualified or experienced like you—this is your dream.'

He winced, and croaked out, 'What if I was to say I'd share?'

'You share now, Alex. This is your vision you've been working on for years before I showed up. Even though this is winter, it's like a summer-holiday job for me that relieves some of the pressure you're under, trying to juggle everything. You know, I was so jealous of you when we first met, and I still am in a way.'

'Of me? Behave.' He scoffed at her in jest.

'It's true. At first, I was jealous at how close you and Molly were and still are. You're like a mother and son team, and you know more about my family history than me.'

'I was lucky that your family helped me when my mother died.'

'They gave you a home too and you fit here. I'm also jealous because you know exactly what you want for your future.'

'Hey, hold up. You have no reason to be jealous. I'm still not sure if I'm going ahead with this, or if this mango crop will make me any money, or if it's worth the risk. It'd be easier to take my dad's partnership.'

'Don't you think it's time you told him yes or no?' she said bluntly, pointing at him. 'Don't you think it's time you stepped out from behind your catcher's mask and commit to yourself first and take that swing? Because you know —'

'Know what? That I have this fear of commitment that everyone keeps telling me about? You'd see it as ridiculous when you're my opposite on that one being one of the most committed people I know. You committed yourself to a sport that made you a world champion.'

So, it was true—Alex did fear commitment. Why was she wasting her time? 'I loved a sport that was my first commitment. But it was all just a bunch of goals I broke down to smaller goals that started from one game to the next, to the next season, to the next nationals. You have a goal that goes much further. They may seem like a bunch of small pieces at the moment, but how I see it is all your bases are loaded and you need one big hit outta the ball park that'll lead the rest of the plays toward that home plate, safe; where you'll be sure to score big-time.'

'And you're jealous because I'm juggling all of this, working three jobs? Or that I haven't let anyone taste my beer but you.' He looked at her with a confused expression.

She'd come to learn a lot about the guy who had been teaching her, too. 'That's your perfectionism talking, which is brilliant, but it's also your procrastination against making that commitment to yourself and your own future first.'

He stepped back with eyes widening and she knew she'd hit a nerve.

'I'm jealous because I can hear that passion when you

speak about your future,' she admitted. 'There's this amazing shine in your eyes where you're just envisioning where this brewery is going. I can see, taste, and smell your entire future, it's everywhere I look in this place. It's in the trees, the beer we drink, the plans you see for the shed and it's even in the soil in the back paddocks. You might not have the courage to tell your dad what you're doing for your future, but it's there ready to grab. And yet I can't tell my father what I want when I still don't know what I want—when all I know is, I only came to stay for a winter season, your dry season, and that's all I have as a goal—a stupid plane ticket.'

'What do you want beyond this season?'

'I. Don't. Know.' Her bottom lip trembled as fear bubbled up inside, overwhelming her as tears blurred her vision. 'All my life I've had people, coaches, and softball schedules to follow, now I have nothing.' She was so lost.

'Hey, I'm so sorry. I didn't mean to panic you.' He held her to his chest as he rubbed her back soothing her.

The breeze rustled the leaves in the orchard as the scent of green mangos filled the air. A few honks from geese in their V formation flew overhead casting shadows amongst the break in the trees. There they remained, with him holding her until she could breathe easily once again.

'Sorry, it just, um, I didn't know it was building up like this. Sorry.' Verily wiped at her stupid tears, or was that perspiration from the warm weather?

'Don't ever be sorry with me.'

The way he looked at her calmed her down and made her feel like the centre of his world. Somehow, he'd become the centre of her world too. He was her last and first thought when he was away, she'd never experienced this kind of heightened happiness with anyone except with Alex.

It also scared the absolute crap out of her!

'Do you still want to play catch with me?' She asked with a wince after her dummy-spit.

'I'd love to.' He kissed her nose, hooked his arm around her neck and they recommenced their stroll through the orchard to his cottage.

Rummaging through his gameday bag on the back veranda, Alex grabbed his catcher's mitt. 'If you're pitching to me, I'm definitely suiting up.' He grabbed his protective chest and legs pads, slipping them on. With helmet in hand, he strolled out into the vacant carpark area of his cottage that had so much room without the truck.

Verily stood at the pitcher's end tugging at her t-shirt that was sticky from the weather. The season was changing from the mild winter weather she'd adored these past few months. Clouds gathered on the horizon and a slight breeze wove its way around the fruit trees, carrying a rich earthy scent. Would she still be here when they harvested the mangos?

Did she want to be?

Alex tossed the ball to Verily as he got into position equal to the distance from the pitcher's plate to home plate. 'I'm ready.'

'I'll start slow.'

'I bloody well hope so.'

She grinned at him as she casually tossed the ball.

It landed with a slap in the middle of his glove and he threw it back. 'Why not come to the game with me tomorrow? It's in Jabiru and you haven't been there. I can show you some spots in Kakadu National Park that are worth seeing, and I did promise you a camping trip, something about outback TV?'

Were there any faults to this guy? Even after all she'd said and shouldn't have said to him, he was still willing to put up with more of her baggage. She'd never met a man like it. 'Molly isn't going and I'm supporting Molly. Ready?'

'What do I do?'

'I'll nod at you to tell you I'm ready, you nod back and wait steady with the glove and then I'll pitch. All I do is aim for your catcher's mitt that's in your strike zone. It's you who sets the target for my aim that's usually based on the weak spots of the opposing batter's swing.'

'Do you know how scary it is to be your target when I know how fast you throw?'

'I *used* to throw.'

'It's still fast compared to what I usually catch.'

She grinned at him. Alex always made her feel better and so effortlessly too, with just a simple look. 'You've got protective padding on, don't be a wimp.'

'Think I need more,' he muttered, squatting into position with his glove up.

Verily nodded.

Alex nodded back with his glove steady as her target. Within five seconds she let rip a slow ball that still slammed hard into his glove.

As a pitcher, she loved that sound.

'Are you mad at Agnes too?' He asked, throwing the ball back to her, which she caught securely with her glove.

'No. Agnes just doesn't like me.'

'Agnes doesn't like anyone.'

'I get that impression.' Again, she got into position, scratched at the soil for her perfect place, the soles grinding the flat spot on the dirt. She faced her target and nodded at Alex.

His glove stood square and he nodded back.

She inhaled deeply, held it, and swung her arm. Stepping forward, she powered through her throw and unleashed the ball. It slung from her palm, hurtled across the gravel and slammed into his glove. 'Good catch.'

'Good bowl.'

'Pitch. This isn't cricket.'

He winked at her from beneath his helmet and his smile shone as he tossed the ball back to her.

Guilt again rested on her shoulders for what she'd said to him, and yet, her stomach spun with warmth and desire from his smile.

'Agnes isn't snaky at you,' said Alex, 'we're just sideline casualties in the feud between Molly and Agnes.'

'Weren't they friends, once?' Again, she lined up the ball, gave the nod, he replied, and she pitched a curveball straight into his glove.

'I remember Agnes used to hang out with Molly on the veranda when I was a kid. They shared a lot of fun times back then.' He tossed the ball back. 'You're making this too easy for me when we know Speedy doesn't throw straight.'

'Do you want me to make you work for it?'

'I need the practise.'

'Okay, I'll do some sidewinders with extra spin.'

'What about teaching me the signals? Why do catchers have to signal?'

'Catchers have the box seat on the field.'

'We do?'

She titled her head, screwing her nose at him. 'Hello, how many years have you been playing catcher?'

'Remember, my darling softball princess, I haven't had to catch anything because Speedy's pitches never made the plate. So, please explain.'

'Huh. I've never had to coach a catcher before.'

'Well, I'm privileged. So, go on.'

She mirrored his grin, how could she not?

'In a game, all eyes are on you,' she explained. 'As the pitcher, I'm aiming for you and everyone watches you to either catch, or the batter connects with the pitch for a hit. You can see if someone is making a steal for the second or third base and can easily signal to the pitcher to throw it to the other fielders. The field of play does not stop until the umpire calls *time*. In your position, you'd know the batters, so it's you who calls the shots. If you want a curveball, left, right, or low, I'll throw it that way, and we rarely throw the same pitch twice in a row because they'll expect it.'

'Do you honestly believe Speedy is at that level?'

'No. I've just been training her to aim straight but I have faith she will one day.' Would she be here to see it? 'So, I'll mix it up for you.'

'As long as you don't overdo it.'

'You can rub my shoulder later.'

'Done, and I'll rub down the rest of the body that comes with that shoulder too.'

She felt the heated blush prick at her cheeks and pitched to the right making him reach wide, just missing his outstretched fingertips.

'Wasn't expecting that,' he said, running after the ball and tossing it back, 'but I'll be ready now.' He gave her the nod and she threw it at his chest making him jump high like a frog. 'You're enjoying this.'

She couldn't stop laughing. 'I am. Are you?'

'Yeah, it's your laugh that makes it all the better.'

'Aww…' The guy was perfect—and with her. Why?

For the convenience of living and working in the same place? Or just for the ease of a simple summer romance–in winter? She'd had plenty of seasonal romances, but none quite like this.

She threw a low ball that travelled inches off the ground and he fumbled to catch it.

'You're really putting me through my paces now, aren't you?'

'You wanted that, didn't you?' Why was it so hard to know what she wanted? Was it because others had always approached her with an offer first?

'I did.' He threw the ball back at her and she caught it with ease.

'It doesn't mean I should punish you.'

'Thank you, but I'm tough, I can handle it.'

'Well, okay then.' She tried to not smile as she nodded at him, ready to pitch. He nodded back and she let one rip. It slapped loudly into his mitt. 'Huh.' That was a pain-free throw with power.

'Damn, that stung. You must've put muscle behind that one.' Alex shook his hand from his mitt. 'You're not throwing your shoulder out, are you?'

She stretched her shoulder and arm muscles across her body. 'No, nothing. It's good, it's freeing it up, but there's no way it'd hold for a whole game.' In a game she would give it her everything and throw through the pain for the win, but who was she playing for now? What was her prize?

'Please, don't overdo it.' Alex tossed the softball back and got himself into the catcher's position.

Verily was so used to talking to her catchers with ease, it was always pitcher to catcher, throw, catch, repeat. She'd learned it was a partnership that had to be built—to win.

Besides her dad, she'd never done it with another guy and certainly not in the middle of a mango orchard. Yet it felt so right being with Alex.

How long would this perfect bubble of bliss last?

'Hey, what happened between Molly and Agnes?' Surprising herself she'd dared ask when she didn't usually bother with the details. So why ask now? Did she dare dream for more time in this place, to be with Alex?

'Molly won the jam competition five years in a row at the Rosella Festival. Then Agnes won it. The thing was,' said Alex, flipping up his helmet's face-shield, 'Agnes and Molly made that batch of jam together, in Molly's house. Molly had no idea Agnes had entered because it's all done anonymously with blind tasting by the judges.'

'So, it was Molly's jam and Agnes got the credit?'

'Yep.'

'No wonder Molly calls Agnes a cheat, which is kind of weird when I've noticed how rigid Agnes is with the rules during a game.'

'According to Molly, Agnes twisted the rules in the jam judging to win.'

'Who knew jam making could be such a serious sport.'

'It is, so is the scone and sponge cook-off and all the other bake-off's they have.'

'Do you enter any of them?'

'I only cook for one—make that two.' He smiled at her through the helmet's visor. He was a great cook who'd regularly claim breakfast in bed as his specialty.

A skill she wasn't going to complain about.

'Ever since Agnes won that jam competition, Molly not only stopped playing softball, she also refused to enter any of the town's competitions. She focuses on running the Festival and supporting the team as the secretary for both.'

'Where she's no longer doing either,' said Verily. 'Who will run it now Molly isn't?'

'Without Molly, there won't be a Rosella Festival, which raises funds to maintain the sportsground, paying for all of our town's future sporting events.'

'So, no festival, no softball team.'

Alex nodded and tossed the ball back to her.

'Isn't there a committee to help run things?' Verily

asked.

'The committee relies on Molly. I've had phone calls all morning from the other committee members, pleading with me to try and talk sense into her.'

'Glad it's you and not me. I don't have your talent at phone-call-fielding. I don't have the patience or the skill, but you're a natural at it.'

'Eh?' He paused to scratch beneath his helmet. 'I've never noticed.'

'You do. I saw how the team talked to you yesterday, they go to you first, like a middle-man, before they speak to Agnes. You're like their approachable mediator.'

'Thanks, I'll take that as a compliment, even if I see it as my way of dodging confrontation. But I'm open to suggestions about Molly.'

'Molly won't do it because of what happened between Agnes and me.' She rolled her shoulder feeling that guilt bearing down on her. 'I should never have done it.'

'Why did you stir up Agnes?'

'She said some nasty things about Molly and I bit back, it became a sledging match. I've never been able to do it before, being on the field I have to behave to play. Now I'm retired I can let fly—and it was fun, Molly and I laughed about it afterwards.'

'You should come with me to Jabiru and play heckler in the stands again.'

'I'll be a dickhead, carrying on by myself.' She was used to the noise of the crowd behind their team, parents cheering on their children, but not with this town's team. 'It's like they're playing lawn bowls, not softball.'

'Karen's bringing her kids. Mind you, she's always dragging her tribe behind her. Reckon in a couple of years the Dusty Dingoes will be an all-male Kimble crew. It's how my mum sucked me into the sport.'

'Maybe I should give them some drums and whistles to scream from the sidelines, that'd stir up Agnes.'

'That's the spirit. You should go and see if Kat's kid has got some spare tutus.'

'Now that could be fun.' She grinned at the idea. 'I'd really like to see how the team performs with their new positions and to see Speedy make her first strike.' She'd enjoyed helping the girls, but she'd done that playing alongside them in the paddock as a player, not as a coach. It was Speedy who'd started it. For Verily to teach a right-hander to pitch when she was a leftie had been her biggest challenge. Once she'd worked that out, the rest came so easily it wasn't coaching, it was just hanging out with new friends.

'I'm counting on Speedy striking out,' he said.

'I know.' Then Speedy would become a part of his picking team. Verily was already Alex's employee, working on the property. So what did she have to gain, besides more beer to store in the spare room and the work experience?

'Let's make this a simple yes or no... Do you like camping?'

'Yes. I enjoyed it when I got the chance, but I've never owned any camping equipment.' Just a bag still packed in the closet, and her gameday bag that was the monster she kept under her bed.

'I do, and all you'll need is a change of clothes—well, clothes will be optional after dark,' he said, his eyes darkening as they crawled over her. 'We'll sleep in my swag under the stars in Kakadu, well away from the tourists. Yes or no?'

'Sounds like fun, yes.' Being with Alex usually ended in a new adventure that didn't involve softball and she liked that about him. She pitched the ball and he caught it with ease.

Again, raising his helmet's face cage, he gave her his lazy grin. Her stomach went giddy like it had trapped a dust-stirring willy-willy making her want to spin and smile at the sky. What was wrong with her?

'This is fun,' Alex said. 'Can you show me those signals?'

'Really?' She hadn't shown him anything, because she usually learned from Alex.

'Absolutely. I need to be ready for that game tomorrow and maybe we can convince Molly to come?'

'She won't. She's taken bookings at the hair salon to make sure she couldn't be talked into it.'

'Cunning wench.'

'We can't force her to do something she doesn't want to.'

'Believe me, Molly loves the Festival, she's just being stubborn. Are you stubborn? Simple, yes or no?'

'Yes.' She said and threw the ball at him with force.

It slammed hard against his leather glove and he shook his hand as if it stung. 'Remind me to never argue with you when you're holding a softball.'

Their laughter echoed in the orchard with the whack of

leather to glove as they practised together.

With the little time they had left, she may as well enjoy this moment of perfection before the season ended. It's what she was used to—or did she dare try and change today?

TWENTY

Side by side, the pair of prime movers stood next to the tiny house on the hill where a rusty hills hoist stood like a stripped skeleton out the back. The place was barren with no trees for shade and it was just a haunted shell of what was Alex's childhood home.

Alex parked his ute under the shade cast by the pair of large trucks where his dad, Neville, had one of the large cabs tilted forward and was busily servicing the truck's engine.

It'd been months since both trucks had parked in the yard together, but they'd passed each other plenty of times on the highways. This was the closest Alex had been to his father to talk.

'G'day, Dad, how was the trip?' It was the same sentence he always greeted his father with.

'Good,' replied Neville, wiping his greasy hands on a rag, he then checked his phone's screen.

'When do you head back out?' It was the second sentence Alex always asked, which reminded him to never get attached, because his dad never stuck around.

What the—was this what it was like for Verily? She'd been so casually non-committal about their relationship, he'd never had a girlfriend like it, who wasn't demanding of his time.

He was also here because of Verily.

Not just because of how much she meant to him, but what she had said, too. It had only backed-up Tim's comments about his fear of commitment to one person and to the one job. It had forced him to think hard.

If Alex wanted to commit fully to his future, it was time to grow up, be the man and take that first step. Today.

He cleared his throat and said, 'Dad—'

'How was Jabiru, you win any games yet?'

It surprised him that his dad bothered to ask, or was it the usual small talk? 'It was close this time.'

'Bull?'

'Speedy's getting strikes now. She hasn't struck anyone out, yet, but she's getting there and so is the team. You should've seen it, Verily was on the sidelines with all of Karen's kids banging toy drums and whistles like a personal cheer squad overdosed on sugar, all of them wearing war paint and tutus.' He chuckled at the memory of Agnes sulking while Verily called out from the sidelines when they were fielding. Then Agnes did all the shouting when the team batted. It was like his team had two coaches who didn't talk to each other.

'You were gone awhile? Wasn't the game on Saturday?'

'I went camping and showed Verily around Kakadu.' He'd loved every second of their long lazy drive, sharing comfortable silences or endless conversations while exploring deserted roads. They discovered lush billabongs brimming with barramundi and wallowing wild water buffalo. They hiked along rocky trails to swim in secluded tropical waterfalls where he'd made love to her in the clearest of waters. He adored the shine to her smile as he watched her stare at the flames when he taught her how to cook their dinner over a campfire. Then held her in his swag as they lay under an infinite sea of stars, only to gaze deep into her dreamy bedroom eyes when she first woke up and smiled at him. It was pure heaven. He didn't want to come back.

'Did Molly go?' Neville asked.

'No, Molly had work to do.'

'Like you should've done hauling another load back to Darwin.'

'Dad, I've been on the road for a month straight. I wanted a weekend off.'

'To play with the girlfriend?'

'Yeah.' Alex couldn't wipe the smile off his face if he tried and didn't want to—not when he loved Verily.

Shame he didn't have the guts to tell her, scared she'd reject him and get on that damned plane.

Sadly, he was used to people leaving him behind.

'Now Molly's got her niece there, you don't need to keep an eye on the place anymore, you can move back in here.'

Damn. It'd been his excuse to move into the Picker's cottage when he took on the orchard's lease.

'How long is Verily staying?'

Alex wished it was forever, but like Verily had said about Molly—you can't make a person do what they don't want to. Verily had to find her reasons to want to stay. If he could help her with that, he would and fast, because the countdown was spinning. 'Verily's got a ticket to fly back after the Rosella Festival.'

'I'm surprised to hear that.'

'Why?'

'I'd thought she'd stick around for the mango picking. I heard in the pub last night, that young Verily's been managing the place fine. I notice those trees are looking good, Molly's got a good crop coming on this year.'

'I know.' Alex smiled wide with pride filling his chest. 'She's been doing a great job.' He'd enjoyed teaching her too.

'What about the cottage you're renting, you could be putting that money back into our business?'

'That's why I'm here.'

'For your paycheque?'

'That… and to talk to you.'

'Your money got transferred to your account, the accountant did all that this morning. You've spoken with the accountant?'

'Yeah.'

'That accountant show you the plan, it's good, huh?'

'Um, yeah, it's okay.' But it wasn't what Alex wanted to do with his life.

'I've got the contracts here to sign for the bank loans. We'll use what you have in the bank and I'll re-mortgage this house—'

'Dad, I don't want to do it.'

'Do what?'

'Get into debt like this.'

'No one does, son. You've gotta spend more to get more

by investing in our future.'

'Your future. You're the one who pushed me into driving trucks, telling me I had the job for as long as I remembered. As a kid, sure I may have wanted that, to be like you, and when I finally got to work with you, I gave it my everything for a few years. Mostly, the reason I did it was just to try and spend time with you because you were never home. It's the only thing you'd talk about, and I did it just so you'd be proud of me.' Alex hesitated, wiping over his mouth trying to find the right words. 'This is not what I want for my future anymore. I want to do something else.'

'Since when? Not since that Verily came to town.'

'I've been planning this for years, but you never stopped to ask and listen to what I had to say.'

His father scowled at him, chucked his greasy rag to the side and put his hands on his hips like a gunslinger ready to draw, complete with narrowing eyes as the sun hung high in the sky. 'All right, I'm listening.'

Alex took a deep breath and kept his place in this showdown. 'I took the lease to manage the crop for Molly's mangos this year.'

His father's lip curled as he took a menacing step closer. 'What the bloody hell for?'

'To pay for my other project.'

'Yeah, what's that?'

'I want to run a microbrewery.'

'Where? In the middle of Molly's bloody mango farm?'

'Yes. It's the perfect buffer zone and… it's home.'

'Wait a second, this is your home.' Neville nodded to

the house on the hill. 'Not Molly's place.'

'This hasn't been a home since Mum died. I don't know why you bother keeping it when you and I are never here.' Whenever his dad drove away Alex stayed at Molly's, and his dad had been away a lot.

'Are you telling me you don't want to drive?'

'I'll still haul around the stations for the musters for as long as you can keep paying me wages. Just understand that there will be times I will say no.' Like he was saying no now, for the first time in his life.

'Like when?'

'The Rosella Festival.'

'I've got a great trip lined up for you to go to Adelaide, and then we've got the mango season.'

'I know, it'll also be my first mango season as a primary producer.'

'I see.' Neville tilted his head with that same scowling expression that used to shut Alex up as a kid.

But Alex had to try and make his father see the bigger picture. 'Look, Dad, I don't want a life on the road like you. I'm not like you, I like being home—at Molly's.'

'What about this house? Why don't you call it home?'

'Do you?' Alex pointed to the place and couldn't remember the last time he'd stepped inside. 'You could sell the place and pay off all your debts.'

'And where would I live when I retire?'

'Wherever you want to, Dad. I can offer you a hot shower and a home-cooked meal with plenty of space for you to park in-between hauls. It'll be the same, just like you've done my entire life where you're only passing through. Admit it, we're not that close.'

'But… You're always changing bloody jobs; you don't know what you want?'

'I changed jobs to get experience before I was allowed to work with you. I also did it until I found what I was looking for and I have found it—right next door, where it's been my entire life.'

'You know nothing about mangos.'

'I've been on the picking crew for that orchard since I was a kid when Mum was alive and I'd work alongside her and the crew for pocket money. Verily's grandfather taught me while he paid me to spray or brush-cut the weeds around the block after school. I'd mend their fences, do his irrigation, collect the eggs, fix trellises or paint that house. I've seen what all the past managers did with that place while sitting on Molly's veranda doing my homework. I also learned at Ag-school, and I got good grades.' Pity his father never bothered to read any of his school reports.

'Mangos are seasonal.'

'So is hauling for the musters, which I'll continue to do until the brewery is up and running enough to be my full-time operation. I understand it'll be a bunch of baby steps to reach my goals because I am not jumping into this blindly. I've been studying hard to gain my qualifications as a brewmaster.'

'You're a what?'

'A brewmaster and I've got the tickets to prove it.'

'Since when?'

'Last year. I've even visited other breweries while on

the road these past few years, to see how they run their operations. This isn't a hobby for me anymore, Dad.' He may have perfected his unique brand of beer with the rosella brew, but was he ready to go public with it?

Again, Verily was right, he'd been giving in to his procrastination caused by his fear of commitment, but he wasn't going to let it win. Not today.

'All on Molly's property?' Neville asked with squinty eyes.

'I'm starting small and hoping to lock in a long-term lease.'

'Sleeping with her niece would ensure that.'

The heat fired-up so fast in his veins his hands curled into fists. 'This has nothing to do with Verily.' Yet, it had everything to do with Verily—should he make her a permanent partner?

'So, you're sleeping with the girl for cheaper rent.'

'That's bullshit.'

'Well, that's what it looks like from here.'

Christ, he hoped Verily didn't think that. 'It's not true.'

'Why go to all that effort starting something up, when you can walk into this business?'

'It's not what I want.'

'Could you do that here?'

'You don't have the infrastructure. There's no shed, no bore or rainwater tanks, no three-phase power or machinery.' It was nothing but a house on a hill.

'And with Molly's?'

'I'll have the lease to manage the agistment yards, the

orchard and sheds. That'll be the income to support the micro-brewery. I want to trial a special tropical barley and hops crop next year as ingredients for a new beer. I can do this while living in the picker's cottage.'

'And the house Molly's in?'

'That's Molly's home.'

'Molly was always sitting pretty in that place, handed to her on a golden platter by their father.'

Alex frowned, Molly worked long hours in her salon which, of course, his father was never around to see. 'Weren't you trying to do the same for me, or is this partnership for you?'

Neville took a step back as if flinching.

'Either way, Dad, I don't want it and you're free to do what you want. Sell this house and both trucks to buy a brand new one for yourself. I'm sorry if I've disappointed you, but it's the truth.' There, it was out. He shoved his hands into his jeans pockets and waited.

Neville's light blue eyes stared at him with lips tightening into a thin line.

A whistling kite glided on an air pocket casting shadows across the parched earth. Sunburnt weed heads swayed on the slowest of breezes as heat waves rose toward the searing afternoon sun.

'So, your mind's all made up then?'

Like Verily had never said no to him, Alex had never said no to his father—until today.

It was one of the hardest things he'd ever had to do.

Already he could read the failure and hurt spreading

across Neville's face, ageing the old man, just for daring to say… 'No. I will not be going into partnership with you.'

Neville exhaled as if the wind had been sucker punched right out of him.

Alex didn't dare give in now. 'The money I've earned driving for you these past few months is going to my future. I'll still do the hauls you've booked me in for, but only until the Festival. After that, call me if you need any local trips or if you need a hand and if I'm available, I'll gladly help you out.' That's if his dad ever spoke to him again.

With nothing more to be said, Alex nodded to his old man and headed to his ute. Neville would need time to think.

Gripping sweaty palms against his ute's steering wheel, Alex glanced into the rear-view mirror at his dad, shadowed by the massive trucks. Had he just thrown away his whole future on a risk?

A large honk drew his attention to the four large groups of magpie geese gliding in extended V formations. Their shadows stretched across the sunburnt land, reminding him of Verily, flying away far too soon.

He still hadn't found the guts or the perfect time to tell her he loved her, scared if he did, he'd stuff it up and she'd fly away from him sooner. What sort of future would he have then without her?

TWENTY-ONE

Alex parked his ute beside his cottage. At the back door, he shucked off his boots and dropped his hat on the hook by the beer fridge, his guts churning over the conversation he'd just had with his father.

He'd always hated confrontations. His last one had been when he'd broken Tim's heart, and he'd just done the same to his dad.

Now he had to wait for the outcome. Neville would either split a gasket—or slink away quietly.

Yeah right, like that ever happened.

It was done. No more hiding his lease on this property. He wanted to be here for the harvest that would start soon after the Festival. With luck, Speedy would be running the picking teams and he could manage the packing sheds, like he'd done many summers for others, but this year it'd be for himself.

On his veranda, he tore off his shirt, jeans, socks and jocks, and chucked them straight into the washing machine by the back door. He tore the towel off the clothesline stretched across the back veranda and headed inside for the shower to wash off the muck from the day.

Earlier, he'd spent most of his day working on the

orchard, inspecting the trees, propping limbs heavy with fruit and checking over the irrigation. It was in great condition. He was proud of what Verily had achieved, they'd made a great team.

Time on the road had allowed him to plan his goals, and the endless conversations he'd shared with Verily that had made him think more. Driving these past eight weeks, Alex had also cemented his contacts and increased his network. It wasn't just about driving for his dad, he'd been doing it to set himself up for this harvest. With buyers lined up, he was already planning the next season, including his micro-brewery's work plan.

If Speedy struck-out a player, he'd be in a healthy position to buy his first set of vats and set up the shed, debt-free. He could then put in the groundwork for growing hops and a specialised barley strain from the Philippines that could handle the tropical heat.

But was his brand of beer worth it?

Would people buy it?

Was it good enough for strangers to want to drink?

In the shower, he hung his head under the jets and let the hot water massage his scalp, neck, and shoulders. A hand rubbed over his arm. 'Are you back from town, already?' He smiled, wiped the water from his eyes and looked up, expecting to see Verily. '*What the—*'

'Hey, sugar, mind if I join you?' Sherice said, taking off her shirt.

Alex hid his naked body behind the shower curtain. 'Sherice? What are you doing in here?'

'The back door was open. Hey, why do you live here and not up at the main house? I got told you lived with the hairdresser, in her house. Want me to scrub your back while you explain?'

'If you'd found out where I lived, then you'd know I'm with Verily, who you met back at Tim's Station.'

'Come on, you and the gym-junkie-wannabe aren't serious. I thought it was a joke myself because, sugar, you're the guy who doesn't do serious—you do simple.'

Was he that bloody predictable?

'Put your shirt back on and get out of here, you're not welcome in this house.' He turned off the tap, wrapped the towel around his waist and then held out her shirt. 'You're doing this on purpose because I told Tim about you.'

'Why did you do that?' She frowned, snatching back her shirt.

'Tim's a mate who deserved to know what he was marrying.'

'I have a wedding dress I can't wear because of you.'

'No, you did this to yourself. You screwed around on Tim, who would've given you everything.'

'I know. He's nice, but you're more—'

'Rack-off, I'm not touching you again. I'm with Verily. You're not even in her league and I'm not letting you ruin a good thing for me. Now, *get out.*'

'But we had so much fun—'

'Nick off and go find some other moron to put up with your bull, because you're only good enough for a drunken shag in a dusty carpark, nothing more.'

'*You arsehole.*' She swung back and slapped him across the face.

He didn't even flinch. 'If you were a bloke, I would've decked you for that. Now GET OUT.' He pointed to the door, stuck in his second confrontation of the day.

* * *

Verily walked through the orchard to the Picker's cottage with Alex's mail. Another car was parked in his yard and she assumed he had visitors. She strolled around to the back veranda just as the screen door opened and out walked the shiny Sherice.

'Oh, hi, sugar. Just get back from the gym, did we?' Sherice slid on her shirt and buttoned it up to hide her lace bra.

'Verily?' Alex burst out the door wearing nothing but a towel and snatched a pair of jeans off the clothesline. 'Baby, this is not what it looks like.'

Sherice laughed. Touching up her lipstick with a manicured nail, she stared down at Verily. 'Oh, it is, believe me, this is *exactly* what it looks like.' She then blew a kiss to Alex who was putting on his jeans, his towel fell to the ground and his naked arse flashed itself to the world. 'Thanks for the good time, sugar. You have my number,' she said, slapping him on the rump.

'*Rack off, Sherice,*' he called out, struggling to slip on his jeans.

In that split second the entire world shattered like glass and it was if Verily was the only one left standing on the other side of a broken mirror. The parcel and mail she'd collected, fell from her fingers to stir the dust at her feet.

Speechless, she turned back to Molly's house. With eyes watering, she stumbled down the path, clutching her stomach as nausea washed over her. It was hard to breathe, to walk, to think.

'*Verily*, it's not like that,' called out Alex behind her.

But she couldn't look back.

She should have known it was too perfect to last.

Was Alex a liar, cheating with Sherice all along? *Poor Tim.*

That bastard! What else did Alex lie about? He'd lied to his friend, Tim, about them being a couple that day at the station when they weren't. Then there was all the deceit of managing a stupid mango farm behind his father's back.

What about the lies Alex told himself, hiding his beer in the shed with grand plans of a brewery, when he wouldn't even let anyone else taste it? He was like an unpublished author, writing an epic story, only to put it in the cupboard so no one would read it.

Another ute pulled into the yard, cutting her off. It was Neville.

'Um, Alex is down at the cottage.' Unable to face Alex's father, she pointed behind her with a shaky arm. Her whole body trembled with shock at what she'd seen, mixed with rage at herself for daring to think she could stay. She didn't belong here.

Neville slammed his driver's door shut. '*I'm here to talk to you!*'

'Me?'

'It's your fault my son won't join our family business. You and Molly have been filling his head full of bulldust about being a bloody farmer and not driving trucks.'

It wasn't the first time she'd been blamed by someone who didn't make the team. It's also why she never got involved with anyone or the politics in places because she normally only stayed for a season.

It was definitely time to leave.

'You're the reason Alex won't work for me,' Neville shouted, waving his finger at her. 'Because of you, he's throwing his whole life away on some stupid project to brew fancy beer. He should never have gotten involved with you.'

She should've known better to get involved with Alex in the first place.

'You're right, Neville. Blame me for daring to let your son live his own life his way. But it's okay, my holidays are nearly over and just like you, I too will be driving away and leaving all the drama behind me for someone else to deal with.'

She hated the unwanted tears spilling down her face, but she'd also learned to never be scared to face the firing line in the game—ever! So, she glared at the old man as if daring him to take a swing.

Neville blinked at her and stepped back from her stare… but for only a second. He then inhaled deeply, puffed out his chest and shouted, '*Who the hell are you are to judge me?*'

'Ditto—Dickhead!'

'DAD! *Don't you DARE talk to Verily that way, this is not*

her fault.' Alex ran up with t-shirt in hand. At least he had his boots on and had bothered to button up his jeans.

Sherice's car tooted and she waved out the window, letting the dust roll behind her vehicle, turning at the front gates and headed down the main road back to town.

Bitch! 'Your father, your drama, your life,' she pointed to the driveway and Neville and said, 'I'm out. Game over.' Verily couldn't even look at Alex without her chest squeezing so tight it hurt to breathe.

'Verily, no. Let me explain—'

'You'll be bloody explaining yourself to me first.' Neville grabbed Alex's arm to stop him.

Verily tried to walk away with some dignity, but as the tears fell, her pace quickened and she ran. Blood pounded in her ears, the tears wouldn't stop and her legs were like lead, but she kept running. She just had to get away from all this drama.

How could her happiness have burst in the blink of an eye?

She should never have come to Elsie Creek to heal, when the place only magnified her heartbreak.

TWENTY-TWO

'Verily?' Alex searched through Molly's house, checking behind doors, under beds, he'd even searched the attic.

The screen door creaked shut and Molly dumped her shopping bags onto the kitchen counter. 'Are you two playing hide and seek?'

'Did you see Verily on the road coming back from town?' He'd scoured the trees in the orchard searching for her.

'No, hon, but I saw your dad hightailing it past me. Stroppy thing didn't even wave.'

'*Where is she*?' He raked fingers through his hair, overwhelmed by this crappy confrontational day. When all he wanted to do was talk to Verily.

'Alex, what's wrong?' Molly grabbed him by the wrists and pulled him down to meet her at eye level like she'd done when he was a boy. 'Tell me?'

'I told Dad I didn't want to be a partner, and he's blaming Verily for it.' He explained what Verily must have seen with Sherice and how she'd been blamed by his father. 'I can't find her to explain. Verily said its game over, I don't want her to go, Molly, but I found her bags in the cupboard, packed like she's ready to go.'

'Neither do I. I've told her this is her home, but that girl has never unpacked.'

'She's been here for months, surely she would've unpacked her bag at some point.'

'She never has. For years when I visited her, she never did.'

'Why not?'

'We both have to remember that girl has always been on the move, she shifted every season with her father since she was eleven.'

'Why?'

'For the sport. Did you know that for years as a little girl she never played, too scared about being judged? It reminds me of what you're like with your beer, not letting others taste it, just like Verily used to always practise her pitch and never play. She's quite shy, you know.'

'Verily is shy about her achievements in softball, when she should be proud. But she's not shy when it comes to trying new things and meeting people.' Alex just wished he knew where to find her.

'I agree. When her father finally convinced her to try-out for her school team, Verily pitched and went straight to senior level. I remember, I got the phone call. Not long after that, she got offered her first scholarship and that's when it all started.'

'Did her dad drag her around the world like mine dragged me around the country?'

'It was Verily's choice, if she didn't get her grades, her father wouldn't let her play. So Verily always had good grades and graduated college.'

'In what?'

'I'm surprised you haven't asked her.'

'It hasn't come up.'

'Verily is a certified financial investment planner. She's a clever cookie on that side of things, with interest rates and stuff. You do know her father was an accountant?'

'Yes. So, you're saying Verily knows numbers.' He was lousy at numbers.

'Verily majored in finance, economics and all the boring stuff to do with business. You should've seen what she did for my books in the hair salon and our Trust for this place.'

'Why didn't she tell me?'

'Because Verily is used to not getting involved. She only did the financial investment thingy for her father and herself. It was the only thing they talked about besides softball. I practically had to force her to help me, but I'm so glad I did.'

'I want Verily to get involved. It's why I've included her in everything.'

'Me too. Did Verily tell you any of her plans? She keeps telling me she has none.'

'She had mentioned setting up a coaching clinic with her stepsister and helping in her dad's courier business driving for him in the off-season.' The courier business Verily could go back to, but was that what she wanted? 'She said she only planned to stay for a season and we live by seasons, the dry season, the wet season.'

'Mango season, softball season.'

A roaring V8 engine belonging to a large ute grabbed

their attention as it skidded to a halt in the yard. Once the cloud of red dust fell it revealed the ute's massive bull-bar with a set of buffalo horns taped across the bonnet and a bank of spotlights across the roof.

'Agnes, what are you doing here?' Molly demanded without any welcoming to her tone.

Agnes slammed the car door and stalked toward the house with her black thongs flip-flopping clouds of dust with each step. 'YA BLOODY COULDN'T HELP YOURSELF, COULD YOU, MOLLY? I KNOW YOU AND YOUR NUTCRACKIN' NIECE HAVE BEEN INTERFERING.'

Alex blocked her path, pulling himself up to full height and glared down at his coach. 'Never come into this yard and speak like that to my family,' he snarled through gritted teeth. 'Do. You. Understand?' He was over people shouting at him and his family. Twice in one day, first his father, now this. When would these confrontations ever end?

Agnes stretched her neck so far back her yellow duckbill sun-visor fell off and her thick black plait nearly touched the dirt.

Molly crossed her arms over her chest and remained on the veranda. 'What do you want Agnes?'

'Ah, ah...'

'Alex, let Agnes speak.'

Alex stepped back but kept himself between the two women. He'd never gotten between them before, but Molly was his family. She'd always been there for him, more than his father ever had. Even Agnes had been there, in her own way. 'Agnes, you need to apologise to Molly.'

'WHAT FOR?'

'So, Molly can get back to doing what she loves.'

'WHAT'S THAT, BESIDES MAKING MY LIFE A BLINKIN' MISERY?'

'Running the Rosella Festival. Everyone knows that without Molly, there is no Festival, and with no funds raised to play softball, you'll be out of a team to torture.'

'WHAT DOES IT MATTER? I'M NOT NEEDED COZ THAT VERILY'S BEEN COACHING THE TEAM BEHIND MY BACK.'

'How did you find out?' Molly asked.

'YOU CAN SEE IT. THEY'RE FIELDIN' IN PROPER PLACES. SPEEDY'S BLOODY PITCHING TO THE HOME PLATE. THEY'RE EVEN SPEAKIN' THE BLINKIN' LINGO.' Agnes then pointed to Alex. 'I SAW THOSE HAND SIGNALS BETWEEN YOU AND YOUR GIRL WHILE SHE WAS SITTIN' ON THE FENCELINE WITH KAREN'S MOB OF KIDS. BASHIN' DRUMS AND BLOWIN' HORNS LIKE A BUNCH OF BLOTTO BOGANS ON A FOOTY-FINAL BARBIE-BINGE.'

Alex grinned. 'Verily did that for the atmosphere.'

'It's how they play in the States,' said Molly.

'WE'RE IN THE OUTBACK, NOT NEW-BLOODY-YORK. THIS IS MAD HATTER'S CENTRAL WITH A PICK-A-LILY LANE OF RED DIRT OUT FRONT. I KNOW SHE'S COACHING, ISN'T SHE?'

'Stop shouting Agnes and turn your bloody hearing aid on,' snapped Molly. She stepped off the veranda, patting Alex's arm who stepped back so she could face Agnes.

'I didn't know you wore a hearing aid, Agnes?' Not that he could tell under that long horsetail of hers.

'My hair keeps knockin' 'em off,' mumbled Agnes, flipping her plait over her shoulder like a long, thick tree python.

'Get it cut.'

'Can't.'

'Why not?'

'The only hairdresser in town hates me.'

Molly grinned, sharing a half-shrug with Alex before she faced Agnes. 'You're right, Agnes, Verily has been coaching the Dusty Dingoes in fielding and pitching only, because she can't bat like you and doesn't want to interfere with that side of things.'

'I knew it! Behind my bloody back too.'

'The only reason she wanted no one to say anything is because she respects you, Agnes,' said Alex.

'*She does*?' Agnes and Molly said together, with noses screwed up at him.

'It's true. Verily respects how you volunteer to coach, for sticking by the team when we're always losing, and your respect for the rules.' Verily saw so much from being an outsider, it'd made him see things so much clearer. So how was he going to get her to see his side of the story?

Agnes's stance softened. 'She's gotta be the only one who bloody does in this town.'

'Pft, I'll say,' said Molly with a sneer.

'We get why you coach, too,' said Alex.

'Because she likes to be a demanding control freak,' said

Molly.

'Oi, Molly.' Alex put a hand on Molly's slim shoulder to stop her taunting the coach like a sulky teenager. 'Agnes does it for the same reasons you do, it's because you both care for the team and this town. Agnes, Verily didn't coach the team to takeover—'

'She bloody well has, miss fancy world champion.'

'Be very careful what you say about Verily,' warned Alex, frowning down at Agnes.

'How do you know who my niece is?'

'I try my damnedest to ignore you, Molly, but what you do say, I remember,' said Agnes. 'I was here when you got the call from Verily telling you she'd got offered a spot on the flamin' Australian Junior Olympics Team. I also know all about the dinky-di-drama that girl went through to play in the World Championships for the States in the Netherlands.'

'What drama?' Alex asked.

'It was brutal. Two countries, one girl, and Verily was stuck in the middle of all this immense pressure when all she wanted to do was play,' replied Molly.

'Bah,' scoffed Agnes, 'to be that bloody popular.'

'Verily was only fourteen,' said Molly with hands on hips, wearing a ferocious scowl. 'That was the year you stole my jam and made it your own.'

'Okay then...' Alex sidestepped away from the women who snarled at each other like wild quolls posturing before a fight.

Agnes said to Molly, 'I only entered that frickin' competition to prove to the town it was your jam.'

Molly barked back, 'What are you babbling on about?'

'All those other women were spouting off about you paying them judges to win all the time.'

'I did not. It was all anonymous.'

'I know, so I entered to prove to them it was your jam.'

'Why didn't you say it was my jam when you won.'

'I tried, but you were too busy accusing me of cheating, and then all the other over-dressed women called me a cheat too, when I didn't cheat.'

'Poppycock,' said Molly with chin high and lips pursed tight.

Agnes stood square with hands on hips and her chin raised to match Molly's. 'It was me who brought out all of the ingredients with me from town. I even helped you pick them damned rosellas that I also cooked with you. I made the labels, added the ingredients, and stirred that batch while you were on the flamin' phone talking to Verily. Then you blinkin' rang around trying to organise tickets so you could see her play, bitchin' bout time zones, visas and the foreign exchange rate on the Aussie dollar.'

'Is that true, Molly?' Alex asked.

Agnes waved her hand in the air as she wound up for air, like a propeller on an airboat. 'I'd bet ya a bunch of bloody blue-balls it's true!'

Alex cringed, while Molly remained tight-lipped with arms crossed.

Agnes continued, 'By the time Molly got off that flamin' phone with her tickets booked for the Netherlands, I'd finished bottling the jam, washed the equipment and was putting the lids and labels on the lot. You, Molly, were on the phone the whole bloomin' time making plans while I'd made that entire jam batch in your kitchen.'

'Molly?' Alex asked the woman he loved like a second mother, who was fidgeting with her necklace.

'It's still my recipe, hon.'

'You bloody well told me it was your grandmother's,' said Agnes.

'That I've tweaked and made my own.'

'And accordin' to them flamin' rules I never cheated by entering that jam batch, neither. No matter how much you lot whined and carried on like a spoiled bunch of fly-blown bananas, them judges never called me a cheater. Only you did and the rest of 'em over-fluffed emus followed.'

'Agnes, did you really enter to prove to the town that Molly wasn't paying the judges to win?' Alex asked.

'I did.' Agnes nodded.

'Huh?' Molly put her hand on her hip and stepped back. Both women remained staring at each other but the anger had dispersed.

'Right, it's obvious you two have a lot to sort out. Molly, where would Verily hide?' Alex had delayed long enough on finding the one person who mattered the most.

'Try the back paddock, hon. Verily likes sitting under the windmill. She's made a deck up there.'

'What deck? When?'

'You've been away. I'd never realised what a great spot it is until Verily made her perch, the team helped her build it. We'd sit there drinking cocktails, babysitting the cows or watch the sunset after practise on our very own softball diamond.' Molly squinted at Agnes, who screwed up her nose.

'Do I need to stay and chaperone?' Alex asked the two women. 'I don't want you killing each other until the Rosella Festival is over because there are far too many people relying on the both of you.' Which also meant losing all hope of his deal with Speedy ever eventuating. No festival. No game. No deal.

But as his stomach fell at the thought of losing his dream, a stronger ice-cold surge of fear burst through him, scaring him more. It was the fear of losing Verily.

'Ladies, this feud has gone on long enough. Sort it out today for the sake of the team and the entire town.'

'How would you know?' Agnes scoffed.

'Because, not only has the team been ringing me, but the entire committee has been hassling me to resolve this situation—which is you two,' he said, pointing at the pair. 'The rest of us are just casualties of your feud and if you don't work it out, today, there won't have a Festival or annual race meet. There won't be a softball team and you can forget all about the footy team in this town playing again. And if that happens, we all know that sports oval will become nothing more than a relic and an overflow for cattle waiting for the train. Am I making my point clear?'

And the beautiful Verily was right. Again.

He'd been fielding phone calls all day, like a conflict mediator. After the day he'd had, Alex realised he wasn't afraid of confrontations, he wasn't afraid of commitment or failure; he was afraid of taking risks and being responsible for those risks.

He faced the two women before him who'd practically cared for him like a mother and an estranged aunt. They'd always been there for him as a kid, supporting him, always ready to protect him, but they'd never let him take responsibility for his actions.

It was time to cut those apron strings and take responsibility for himself.

He'd been doing that by managing this farm and successfully driving for his father, too. He just never took the credit for it, like Verily, who shied away from her outstanding achievements when she had every reason to be proud.

The two women stared at Alex then at each other with raised eyebrows. He hoped they got the message.

'Sort it out between yourselves, ladies, because I'm not your middle man anymore, not when I've got another urgent issue that is my one and only priority.' Alex ran for the shed leaving Agnes and Molly behind. He needed to find Verily to explain everything before it was too late.

TWENTY-THREE

Verily sat beneath the still windmill, staring at the scenery that unfolded endlessly to meet the thick grey clouds building on the distant horizon. Humidity clung to the air, creating a tropical atmosphere, making her clothes stick to her perspiring skin. In a few weeks, the heat and flies would make sitting out here unbearable. In a few months, it'd be nothing more than a skyline of electrical storms and monsoonal rains. How amazing would it be to see these arid paddocks of gold, go green?

She heard the quad before she saw it, spying Alex steering through the open gates, past the painted softball diamond to park beneath the windmill.

'Is this where we get to play the balcony scene from Romeo and Juliet, coz you don't have enough hair to play Rapunzel,' he called up from his seat.

'Go away.'

'Nope, not getting rid of me that easily, princess.' From the back of the bike, Alex tucked a wide box under his arm and climbed up the windmill's ladder, onto the platform. 'I'm here to talk to you.' He shuffled next to her, blocking any chance of escape. 'Wow, this is a great spot. Who put this wood up here?'

She shrugged.

'This isn't that spare board from the side of the shed, is it?'

Again, she shrugged.

'Look, what you saw with Sherice, it wasn't like that.'

'You were getting dressed and so was she.' She didn't want to know the details.

'Didn't you hear me shouting at her to get out? Nothing happened. She did that because I told Tim about her and she was stuck with a wedding dress she can't wear.'

'So, Sherice thought she'd come and tell you with *her shirt off?*'

'She did that purposely to upset you. That thing came inside, without an invitation, and caught me in the shower where I tried to hide from her behind the shower-curtain. You know I leave my wardrobe hanging on the back line. I never fold it away.'

That part was true. The guy used his back veranda as his dressing room. She'd never judge him, or anyone, on their laundry habits when she kept her entire wardrobe in a suitcase.

'I was kicking Sherice out when you arrived, I swear it. I can do an oath or I'll swallow truth serum or take one of those lie-detecting tests because nothing happened. You know how I feel about that cow and what she did to Tim. That thing put me in a position where I almost lost a good mate, and you know how hard it was for me tell him.'

'Like how easy it was to lie to him about us?'

'I told Tim it wasn't true. I said sorry to him about that,

and I'm also sorry about my Dad, who had no right to blame you. I told him I was working on these plans long before I met you.'

'Like I was part of your plans to coach Speedy so you could get a cheap deal for the mango harvest. Not to mention what I did for you while you were away, all cheap labour paid in beer.'

'Now you're just looking for excuses to hate me and this place,' he said. 'You're like my father, looking for someone else to blame instead of me and him because our relationship sucks. Dad and I are not a father and son team and he knows it. But we're nothing like him, Verily, you and me, we've got a good thing going on.'

'Neville was right too,' she murmured, as a tear trickled down her cheek. 'We should have just stayed friends.'

'We are friends.' He grabbed her hand and said, 'You're my best friend, Verily. I thought I'd been friend-zoned by you in the beginning, but the level of friendship we share has only gotten deeper. It's been one of the easiest relationships for me.'

She narrowed her eyes at him in and said in a low tone, 'Are you saying I'm easy?'

'Christ, no. Quite the opposite. I'm saying you're easy to get along with, to be with, to just hang-out with while babysitting a herd of cattle, having a beer on sunset, or just sharing bench space in the shed, bottling our beer. Being with you, as my partner, takes this relationship between us as lovers and friends to a whole new level. Beyond levels, like soulmate levels.'

'Soulmates?'

'I love you, Verily Rose Wayfaren.'

She gasped, leaning away from him like he'd said he had some incurable disease he'd caught from her.

'I'm completely and totally in love with you. You're all I think about when I'm not near you.'

'B-but—'

'Dad was right.'

'Which part? That we should've stayed friends.'

'No, I mean, yes.' He wiped a hand over his face as if reprogramming his thoughts, then looked up with such emotion heard in his words. 'You are the main reason I said no to him today because I hate being away from you. Did you know, my most perfect moment is waking up to you in the mornings, to see your sexy bedroom eyes and that messy bed-hair spread over the pillow beside me? I've been trying to find the right moment to tell you, scared if I do, you'll fly away on me like a migrating bird following the season.' He pointed to the V formation of the honking black and white magpie geese stretching across the skyline. There were dozens of flocks made by hundreds of birds.

'I've never seen so many geese.' Her neck craned back at the amazing skyline filled with black and white long-necked birds.

'Magpie Geese. It's a major sign the season is changing when those birds show up. It's also a sign that the Mango Season has started—which explains why everyone is suddenly angry today. And, no, Verily, our season isn't over, it's only just beginning. I don't want you flying away from me or this place when it's home. Our home—but it's not!'

'You're not making sense,' she said, fiddling with her fingers in her lap.

He grabbed her hand, and with the other, his fingertip lifted her chin making her face him. 'Dad got angry with me over the house next door because I told him it hasn't been home to me for a long time. It lost its life the day my mother died, so I get why your father left this place with you after your mother died. I also know that if you were to leave this place, it wouldn't be a home for me either.'

'You love it here.'

'I think you do too.'

'How?'

'You were jealous of my connection to this place, you said it was a place where I belonged. Sure, I believe that too, but I love you more and want us to create our own history here. I want everything in my future to involve you. I may have been planning all of this long before you showed up, but I never committed to it, I've always been testing it.'

'Do you have a fear of commitment?'

'No. Not anymore. I know where it came from though.'

'Where?'

'My father. He was the only family I had left. And so, every time he drove away from me in that truck, it reinforced my inner shields to never let anyone get close. I don't want that, not with you. Relationships are all about compromising and commitment, it's not a simple yes or no answer, but I will give up everything and go with you when you leave.'

'I said it before and I'll say it again, you love this place.'

'And I'll never get tired of saying I love you more,' Alex

said, and she gasped with the need to flee, but he wouldn't let her hands go. 'I want to be with you permanently, as a couple. So, how about we trial it? Let's see if we can have a working partnership. We're doing it now, managing this place as it is.'

'But I…'

'I know you're learning about life away from softball, so you also need to realise you're doing exceptionally well with everything here on this farm—except when it comes to cooking. But hey, I don't mind cooking and I can't wait until you get your truck licence.'

'Who said I was?' Especially if she was leaving.

'That's what this is. I've been waiting for it to come in the mail, as a surprise for you.' He passed her the package she'd carried from the house. 'It's a booklet to tell us what we can do about transferring your licences from the States. Our town's Sergeant said he'd help too.'

'Why?'

'Because you like driving.'

She did. 'But…'

'Don't worry, there's plenty of time to practise all wet season to get you up to speed for the next muster—if you stay. It's something to consider for the future. You were going back to the States to drive for your dad anyway, so why not do it here? I'll gladly share my truck bunk with you any day.'

She blinked at him unsure, yet wondered at the possibilities. But to drive alone on a remote road in a truck taller than a house and longer than most suburban streets?

'Here, open this box.'

'What is it?'

'It's part of your new uniform.'

'My what?' She lifted the box lid and gasped. 'A hat and boots?' The boots were the standard elasticised work boots nearly everyone in the area wore.

'You're first Akubra. I pinched your National's gameday hat to make sure it was the best fit. I remembered how cute you looked in that oversized cowboy hat at Tim's station, so I hope this will suit.' He placed the pale-coloured, wide-brimmed Akubra that fit snugly onto her scalp. 'It suits you. You look like a local, now.'

'I'm not a local.'

'Yeah, you are,' he said, lacing his fingers through hers. 'You were born in this town. You might have been away for a while, but you're home now.'

'What if I don't stay?'

'I'll follow you wherever you want to go. I can get a job anywhere as a truckie, heck, I'll even wash dishes in a truck stop if I have to.'

'Why?'

'Because I have no future without you and with you gone, I wouldn't want to stay here. I'd be like my dad coming home to an empty house that has no heart. You are my heart in this place where we've been managing this farm together as a true partnership. This partnership came so naturally, so effortlessly, it's been brilliant, I never doubted you for a second in leaving this place in your hands.'

'How would you know? We've only just met.'

'You're still looking for excuses, eh?' He shook his head, then pointed to the orchard below them. 'You came here when those mango trees were barren after I'd given them a hard pruning and stripped them back to nothing. You helped water that orchard, tip prune and fertilise it. You've watched over it, giving me regular updates and photos of the blossoms, where your smile was the prettiest. I could hear how happy you were. I was jealous of you then, to see your smile, frustrated I wasn't here to share it with you. Verily, you've invested your time and energy into this place and you deserve to be a part of the harvest you helped create.'

'I just…'

'It's like our relationship, this place has plenty of room to grow, and it will grow and get better as it changes with the seasons. You've helped me manage a mango farm, and in case you don't realise it, you're a fourth-generation mango farmer.'

'I am?' She stared over at the lush orchard where the shade deepened as the sun set. She hadn't truly realised her connection to this land until now.

'I've never doubted your ability to look after this place and it's flourished under your touch. I mean, come on, you created your own private softball field. Most people would go for a tennis court, but you are my softball princess sitting in her tower beneath a windmill, watching over her kingdom.' He leaned over, kissed her cheek and grinned.

'That's pretty lame.' She burst out a small giggle.

'I'm no pretty poet.' Nuzzling into her, he made her smile, then gently wiped away her tears with his thumb, barely resting his forehead against hers, he gazed deep into her eyes. 'You may have been a star to some; but to me your shine will never dull. And you also told me a catcher is nothing without the pitcher and Verily, you're perfect to me in every single way.'

She forgot to breathe.

'You believe me, don't you?'

She shrugged.

'Are you kidding me with that shrug shit?' He sat back, frowning at her. 'How about we break this down to you answering one question? It's a simple yes or no answer.'

'Depends on that question.'

'Do you love me?'

She inhaled sharply, biting her lip as she stared at her hands.

Again, he raised her chin and made her face him. 'Besides my mum, I've told no one I loved them until today. Have you ever told anyone you loved them as a partner?'

'No.'

'It's the scariest thing in the world, isn't it?'

'Yes,' she whispered.

'I know you're in love with me. If you weren't, you wouldn't have been so upset over what you *think* may have happened with Sherice.'

Her frown came back and his palms whipped up in surrender. 'I swear nothing happened.'

Alex was right. Not even an hour ago her heart was breaking, and it had been more painful than anything she'd ever experienced. Had she found a new best friend? A perfect catcher? Had she really found a home?

She stared at the diamond in the dust below her, then looked up at Alex with a shrug, but beat his frown by admitting, 'Yes, I love you.'

'I'll let that shrug slide. Come 'ere, I want to kiss and makeup.' He pulled her to his chest accidentally knocking off her hat.

'My hat!' she said, catching it on the fly.

'You need to break it in, like these boots. There's a trick to it.'

'Probably, like breaking in a new softball glove.'

'Hey, how about we drag that suitcase of yours to the cottage and unpack it by the back door? I reckon your underwear will look good hanging off my clothesline. It'll stop unwanted visitors for sure.'

'W-w-what?'

'Let's trial it. You and me, unpack your bags in the cottage. You haven't stayed there yet, besides the sexy-sleepovers, but you used to live in there as a baby. So why not try it? You said that room in the house was like a shrine to your mother, so we'll drag that case of yours down to the cottage and actually unpack it for once.'

She faltered, feeling her heart pounding inside her chest, her mouth suddenly dry. Swallowing, the words creaked out. 'Seriously, unpack?'

'Yep. I reckon I'll hide that empty suitcase in Molly's attic until the Festival, then you'll be the one to decide if we stay or go. That should give me enough time to pack and book airfares, Molly's a whizz at that—'

It was her turn to grab his hands and face him. 'We... go where... when... what?'

'I'm not losing you, Verily, but I'm not going to pressure

you to stay and do something you don't want to do, like my father did with me. I know I have a lot to learn about commitment, and I'm going to prove to you how committed I am to us by taking responsibility. So, from here on out everything I do is for *us*.'

'Huh?' She wanted to shrug too, but that was all she could muster.

'So, if you decide to use your ticket and take that plane trip, I'll use the money I've saved to get a seat next to you. I'll have enough to live off for a bit and I'll work anywhere. I'm pretty good at getting casual work.'

'I've heard.'

'But it doesn't mean I'll be casual with you. Look, I'll admit I was someone who believed in never, well now I want forever! So, I'm committing to you first above everything else, Verily. I'm booked to drive for Dad until the Festival, so I reckon I'll make that my goal, like you with your ticket.'

'B-b-but what about the orchard? Your bet with Speedy? Your beer?'

'This mango crop isn't mine, it's yours.'

'No, it's not.'

'Fine, it's *ours*. For us. What we make out of it, we'll use for our future together. Whether it's following you to go hang out in Spain for the summer softball season. Although, I'd like to do a snowy winter once. Doesn't your dad live near Canada, that place would have some snow, right?'

'It does.'

'That'd be cool.'

'It's freezing.' While here she sat in the heat, heading

into another summer.

Alex hooked his arm around her shoulders as they sat facing the sunset beneath the still windmill where its shade spread across the softball diamond laying in the dust. 'I'm giving you the choice to ask and answer your own question on what you want, Verily. Do we stay, yes or no? I know it'll take time for you to answer that.'

It was a question she'd been obsessing over all winter.

Alex pointed to the wave of incoming geese dotting the orange sky. 'Those migrating magpie geese mate for life, and there are some geese who miss the migration if their life-mate stays. You would've seen them around the dam.'

'I have.'

'It's like a bird sanctuary in one way, although they make a mess of the mangos.'

'Will they destroy the orchard?'

'They're still too young for that lot to bother, I'd like to wait until the fruit is at least the size of softballs.'

'So the mango season has officially started?'

'It won't be long now. I'd say the fruit-picking can start soon after the festival for us.'

'If Speedy strikes out, you'll—'

'That deal doesn't matter to me anymore,' he said with such clear conviction.

'But—'

'I realised how scared I felt losing you, that your happiness is more important to me, Verily. Not some deal. You.'

'I'd still like Speedy to do it.'

'Me too, not for my bet but as the reward you both have put into her pitching.'

'Really?'

'You've both been working hard for that strike.'

Didn't she know it.

For a moment they watched the hundreds of large geese glide above them with wide black wings, their webbed feet tucked under their white underbellies, echoing distorted honks like an out of tune orchestra.

The season was definitely changing.

Alex gave her shoulders a squeeze and said, 'So far, you've committed your life to a sport and I've just been getting by, but to me, you are my lifemate, like those geese. Your entire life, you've always let people take charge of your decisions with their contract offers and playing seasons and set training schedules. So, here's my deal, I'm going to leave the choice entirely up to you—'

Again, she gasped, sitting with a straight back and slack jaw staring at him.

'—if we stay it's forever or we go, together. I will follow you, so don't even think about leaving me behind, especially now you've admitted you love me.' He shared his lazy grin and her stomach flipped. 'Oi, you said you loved me. You. Love. Me!' He leaned in for a kiss but she stopped him by pressing her palm to his chest.

'You can't expect me to make that choice for the both of us.'

'I can, I will, I am, and you have until the Festival to make your decision.'

TWENTY-FOUR

'Yoo-hoo, Verily,' called out Molly, walking into the packing shed with a bunch of flowers and a bottle of wine.

Verily parked the small hand trolley holding a crate of bottles that jingled as it rested against the concrete floor. 'Hey, how was work?'

'Normal. I got these for you.'

'Wow, thanks. How do you get flowers, out here? And, what's the occasion?' Verily inhaled the fragrant, colourful arrangement and came eye to eye with a card in the middle. 'Molly, this card says these flowers are for you.' She held out the card. 'Who's Riley? He says he wants to have dinner with you.'

Molly snatched back the card, tore it up and threw the scattered pieces into the bin. 'No one.'

'You're giving me second-hand flowers?'

'I thought they'd look pretty in the cottage.'

'And the wine?'

'Mine. It'll make a nice change from beer. What are you doing, hon?'

'Bringing down all my beer wages.'

'That's a lot of beer.'

'I know.' She had crates of it stored in the house. Besides giving her body a workout hauling them into the shed, it gave her something to do while she tried to work out her future. With Alex on the road, her thoughts just wouldn't stop.

'Was all that beer in the spare room?'

'Yep.'

'Good thing they didn't explode, you'd have flooded the house.' Molly walked over to the crates and lifted out a labelless bottle. 'Alex's first batches were so bad they'd explode daily. He had to cover them with tarps to try and contain the shattered glass. You'd swear we were in a war zone, because there is no way to disguise the sound of exploding glass.'

'Guess not. So why are you giving me your second-hand flowers from Riley? Don't you want to do dinner?' Alex had bought her flowers when he arrived in the truck, even putting a frangipani flower in her hair while they walked through the orchard together. He was doing his best to get her to stay, but he hadn't asked again. They just went through the days with no future talk at all.

It had also been the first time in years, where she didn't have to get her clothes out of her suitcase. Alex didn't own a cupboard, but he'd helped her unpack and made room for her clothes to live alongside his on his clothesline. He even hid her suitcase from her, only to return with champagne to celebrate the occasion on the back veranda watching their clothes swing side by side on the clothesline. It was a sweet and private ceremony that suited their uniting perfectly as a couple.

The man loved parts of her no one would ever know,

yet it was a love without trying that had the bonus of being best friends.

Even though she'd finally unpacked her suitcase, the question was still bubbling away in the background like the boxes of beer that were stacked on the concrete floor before her — what was her final decision? Stay, or go?

'What are you going to do with all that beer?' Molly asked.

'No idea. Alex could sell it.' All that effort he'd spent on perfecting his beer would be wasted on her. It reminded her of her father, who'd sacrificed his chances on a lucrative accounting career just to help her achieve her goals in a sport.

'Is Alex licensed to sell beer?'

'He hasn't let anyone taste it, except me.'

'Are those the bad batches?'

'We emptied out all the inferior batches as soon as he worked out the Rosella beer's recipe.' Alex had perfected the recipe for his unique IPA, a dream he'd been chasing, long before he'd met her. That celebratory moment was shared within this shed seated on overturned crates staring at his stockpile. Alex had dragged his barbecue to the shed's open doorways, where he'd taught her how to barbecue spicy chicken wings he'd marinated. There they drank his icy Rosella beer that not only tempered the heat of the wings but brought out the palette of the beer in ways she'd never known were possible.

They'd played beer snobs, sitting in the shed where their laughter echoed through the mango orchard. Even now, the memory still made her smile.

Molly pointed at the crates. 'So that's all homemade Rosella beer?'

'That stack is.' There were hundreds of bottles, thousands of dollars worth, stockpiled in the shed silently fermenting in the shade.

Alex hadn't brewed anything since their conversation on the windmill. It was like all projects had stopped, except the watering of the mangos, fattening on the trees.

Clip-Clop. Clip-Clop. Clip-Clop. It came from the front drive.

'Are the neighbours going for a horse ride?' Verily asked, searching for the noise only to hear the sound of a sickening crow or a strangled hen.

'Oh no, it's Cecil and his chook,' cried out Molly.

'Why is the water buffalo this far from town?' Verily watched its wide heavy-hoofed waddle as it headed down the driveway, sniffed the air and walked straight past Molly's house. He had yellow childlike chalk flowers drawn on his sides that matched the ribbons wrapped around his horns and tail.

'Cecil's after my flowers.'

'You mean to tell me that a great big colour-coordinated water buffalo followed that bunch of flowers you brought from town?'

'No, the dragon fruit must be flowering. Quick, take these and cut that beast off.' Molly thrust the bunch of flowers into Verily's hand.

'I can't feed a water buffalo flowers! I don't know anything about feeding a buffalo.'

'Cecil will follow the flowers.'

'Aren't flowers poisonous?'

'It's daisies. Besides, Cecil is harmless, the children feed him their school lunches and draw all over him.'

That explained the chalk drawings covering his black coat. 'Why would he still be hungry after soggy sandwiches to then munch on more flowers?'

'Cecil likes flowers. '

'Obviously, if it's part of his wardrobe. I can't believe we're discussing the wardrobe of a buffalo.'

Molly glared at her with wide eyes. 'Listen carefully, Verily, Cecil eats flowers, he's a vegetarian and doesn't bite anyone. He's quite tame and everyone knows it.'

'So why don't you feed him? You seem to be quite educated on the likes and dislikes of the town's buffalo.' Her eyes widened at the huge animal casually strolling through the yard with a red hen on its back and ribbons waving from his tail.

'You run faster.'

'I'm not dressed for running,' Verily replied, dressed in the boots Alex gave her and her shorts. She wore them because they were a gift from Alex. Besides, she was ruining her sneakers doing yard work.

'Pft, you run the firebreaks daily. You'll easily outrun that black lump.'

'You mean, you want me to play dodge with a set of buffalo horns? Don't ask me to play chicken with that hen — I've heard it attacks people.' Verily pointed at the red hen, posing like a short dumpy general in charge, standing on the back of a short-legged buffalo, waddling its big butt as it headed down the side-track.

Verily then realised what it was doing. 'Oh no, he really is going for the dragon fruit. How does he know where to go?'

'Cut him off or he'll destroy them. I'll shut the front gate. NOW, young lady.'

'Okay, okay. Good thing they're a second-hand bunch of flowers.' Verily jogged to the front of the water buffalo. 'Here, buffalo, buffalo,' Verily said with arm outstretched, holding the colourful flower arrangement towards the massive beast. 'It's ignoring me.'

'His name is Cecil,' hollered Molly.

'Who'd call a buffalo Cecil? '

But the big black beast stopped.

It raised its black head. Its ears flickered beside horns wider than a set of handlebars a burly tattooed biker surely would struggle to keep a grip on.

'Hi, Cecil. These are for you.' She shook the bunch of flowers unsure this would work.

Its big, black, moist nose sniffed the air towards the lane that led to the dragon fruit, then towards her bunch of flowers. With a snort and a slow heavy thump of his hoofs into the soft soil, Cecil turned around as she stepped back. It took everything inside her to not drop the flowers and climb the nearest tree, but she stepped back and the buffalo moved closer, sniffing at the flowers. 'It's working, what do I do now?'

'Walk him out of the yard, I'll close the gates,' Molly shouted, wrestling with the metal railing. 'Great time for Alex to be on the bloody road, I could do with his muscle about now.'

'He could be dealing with the Cecil factor too…' Slowly, Verily walked the buffalo through the gate and out to the main dirt road. 'Now what?'

'Chuck it to the side of the road, and help me close this gate. I'll call Esther and she can come and take him home.'

Verily threw the bunch of flowers like a one-way boomerang and they twirled head over stem. Petals flew in an explosion of colour and the buffalo chased after them like a dog playing fetch.

The two women tugged, pushed and pulled on the rusty gate until it swung free from the vine's tangles releasing an ear-piercing scream, it sent the red hen flying off the broad set of buffalo shoulders. Cecil jumped like a sloppy boulder size lump of jelly and bolted in fright.

The two gates slammed together with a clang and a rattle of the chain and Molly snapped them in place. 'There, that'll hold that flower-reaper until Esther comes and gets him.'

'Cecil's gone.' Verily pointed to the thundering, heavy hoofed, galloping beast, kicking up a small puff of powdery red dust, with the red hen flying above trying to catch up.

'He'll be back.'

'Where are you going?'

'To call Esther, then you and me, we're on guard duty tonight.'

'Guard duty, for what?'

'My dragon fruit!'

That's when Verily lost it.

She couldn't stop laughing. With hands on knees, the happy tears spilled as she laughed so loud it echoed through the orchard. 'You had me sacrifice myself with a bunch of flowers for another set of flowers?'

'My dragon fruit are special.'

'I thought we did it because the mango leaves are poisonous to stock.'

'Cecil knows not to eat them. Esther trained him well.'

'Not well enough to have him wandering the streets.' Verily leaned against the front fence and watched Cecil the water buffalo, who'd stopped running to stand in the middle of the road. 'This is the first time I've seen this gate shut.'

'These days, the only time we shut it is to keep Cecil out.'

'So, this is an annual event?' Verily was still giggling at herding a buffalo out of the yard with a bunch of flowers.

'If Cecil's here, my fruit is flowering.'

'We've had an entire orchard blossoming.'

'Dragon fruit are special, you'll see. Come along Verily, we have a date defending dragon fruit.'

* * *

'I can't believe we're doing all of this for cosmetic purposes.' Verily giggled behind her champagne glass as she bit into a plump, juicy strawberry dipped in chocolate.

'At least we're doing it in style,' said Molly, picking at the tray of delicacies sitting beside the iced champagne bucket on their small table.

'That's true.' Verily leaned back in her deck chair that was sitting on the back tray of Alex's ute. They'd watched the last of the sun surrender to the night, marvelling as the sky came alive with a sea of stars in the middle of the short trellises that made up the field of dragon fruit. The long cactus limbs looked like pythons under the glow of the flickering flames from the tiki-torches they had set around the perimeter.

'What do we do if something big does come in, or Cecil makes another visit?' The water buffalo had been carted away by a low car-trailer, where Verily had officially met Esther, who wasn't wearing a ball gown this time, just a sarong and work boots. The eighty-something-spritely woman had hugged her buffalo like it was a lost dog.

Cecil really was tame, and Verily had finally found the courage to pat him, but she was still unsure about sitting in the dark defending fruit!

'So, what is the plan of attack, or is that defence?' Verily asked her aunt.

'You'll blind them with Alex's spotlights and I'll bang on my pots and pans.' Molly pointed to the box of pots on the side.

'I thought you were cooking dinner with those.'

'Me, no. We have enough fabulous party flavours to get us through tonight's festivities.'

'We should just put up a string line with something noisy like a tripwire, not sit out here all night.'

'What's wrong with sitting out here?'

'Nothing. It's just not what I'd expected to do tonight. Where are the flowers we're meant to be protecting?' It was just a mash of green cactus limbs that looked like something out of a bad horror movie.

'You wait and see.' Molly sniffed the air. 'Can you smell it?' She dug around in her bag and pulled out a pair of headlamps. 'Put these on.'

Verily slipped the night light over her head as she inhaled deeply. 'Yum, what is that smell?' It was a floral fragrance that had such a rich intoxicating aroma. 'It's delicious.'

'It's the dragon fruit flower. Look, they're starting. Come along Verily, we have work to do.' Molly climbed down from the ute's back tray and stopped at the nearest set of spiky stems.

Verily followed to stand beside her aunt where they stared at the end of a clump of green ugly mass of cactus tendrils that looked like octopus legs leading from a large pot on a pole. There, a flower bigger than her whole hand started to open. Right before her very eyes. 'No way. I've never…'

'It's beautiful, isn't it?' Molly smiled as if she was looking at a newborn baby through the windows of a labour ward. 'You should be taping this to send to Alex. Only the few get to see this.'

'Ah, yeah.' What would Alex say about this? Had he seen it before? She pulled out her phone and started the video as more clusters of flowers all around her, opened to the night, releasing their rich fragrance into the air.

'You'll need these.' Molly handed her a huge soft blush-brush and a round dish that could be used for rouge powder.

'Are we going to wear makeup? Who'd see it out here

in the dark?'

'We're hand pollinating the orchard.'

'Don't bees do that?' The orchard was full of native bees. Thankfully, according to Alex, they didn't sting like the European honey bees.

'Dragon fruit are a night flower. They'll die on sunrise and we only have tonight, hon.' With champagne glass in hand, and a rare moment of wearing work boots and overalls, with hair in a bandana and in makeup and jewellery, Molly looked like a poster image of a WWII factory worker. She was far too glamorous to be working amongst the cacti, in the dark.

'Don't they have night bugs to do this?'

'We're just giving Mother Nature a hand. Trust me, it's easy, hon. You delicately use the brush to gather the left-over pollen from the petals into the dish, then dab it ever so gently onto the female stigma, like so.' Molly demonstrated and soon they were separated in the patch working from the centre out.

The music from Alex's ute played in the background as part of the night time magic. While all around them, large white petalled flowers opened before her, releasing their thick fragrant yellow pollen. With the softest of makeup brushes they hand pollinated the crop until long after midnight.

The two women sat on their deck chairs, the tiki torch flames had long snuffed out, as the sunrise stretched like a wave of pink ribbons slowly shifting on the distant horizon.

'Did you have much planned for today?' Molly asked, sipping on her coffee.

'No, I'll sleep for a bit.'

'Me too, but I had fun, did you?'

'This was amazing. I've never done anything like it.' Verily cradled her warm cup, still admiring the heady aroma slowly dimming as the beautiful flowers among the green cactus limbs started to close. 'It's a shame those flowers and this fragrance only open for one day.'

'Night you mean. Shame you won't be here to see what you've done.'

'Sorry?'

'The fruit is so pretty and pink. They'll be ready to pick in twenty-eight days. I must book out that day in my calendar.' Molly rustled around in her handbag and pulled out her mobile phone and tapped notes on the screen. 'I know you and Alex are waiting for the Festival to make up your mind if you stay or go, and well, you know I want you to stay.'

'For me or for Alex.'

'Both of you. That boy is like a son to me. Yes, call me selfish, I don't want Alex or you to leave, but he is a grown man free to go like you are. What's that saying about the birds leaving the flock?' Molly pointed to the flash of bright red from the tiny finches that stood out amongst the green tendrils of the cacti. They were soon joined by the bright azure blue of kingfishers in their spectacular aerodynamic displays for the insects hovering around the closing flowers.

'Nest.'

'Oh yes, but you just got here and now—'

'I only ever intended to have a holiday.'

'I know. I want you to stay, hoping you'd settle in and you have. You've made friends, you're coaching—'

'I'm not coaching, Agnes is. I'm just a retired player

helping.'

'Why did you come here?'

'I'd promised you I would visit one day.'

'You could've gone anywhere, why here?'

'I'm not sure. Dad suggested it...' He'd done it to get her off the couch she'd been moping on ever since she'd been let out of hospital. Back then, all she had were physio appointments and some new series to binge on Netflix, stuck in a house in suburbia.

She'd never imagined she'd be doing something like this. Staring out over the bright white clusters of flowers almost reflecting the pink splashes of colour widening across the outback sky.

'You never say you miss it,' Molly said.

'Sorry?'

'You don't say you miss the sport or the States,' said Molly. 'You say it's all you knew, and that's okay too.'

'It is all I knew.'

'You need to accept that chapter of your life has ended, which will allow you to start the next one. Hon, what you see as your flaws, like the scars on your shoulder, but what they show us is where you've been in your journey as a sign of your courage where you'd dared to live in this world.' Molly then pointed toward the field of dragon fruit. 'Look at these flowers that have only one night to live, they're so beautiful and fragrant. Yet, they only shine in the dark for a fleeting twelve hours of existence, but it's just a chapter. It's not the end, but a new beginning. The fruit they produce has seeds that will eventually create a whole field of fabulous flowers we only get to see under the stars.'

'It was pretty special.'

'Do you miss Alex?'

'Yes, of course I do.'

'Me too, but I'm used to him leaving for short trips. It might do him good to go on an extended trip, even if he is a person who likes being home. I'll miss the both of you very much.'

'You've said he's a homebody?' Verily said with a shrug, it was a foreign concept to her.

'Alex always has been a homebody, it's his nature to stay close to enjoy the comforts of home. Not that he's materialistic either.'

No, Alex liked simplicity. He didn't fuss over furniture, when the guy kept his clothes on the back clothesline because he didn't own a cupboard. Yet, his bed, even the linen and pillows were surprisingly top class in quality and comfort. 'How do you know, Alex is this…'

'Homebody? I recognise it because I'm the same. I like being home, where we can enjoy adventures within our own backyard. As much as I enjoyed my annual trips abroad to meet you in the world, I always missed my home. But I love it more when I return to just sit and sip wine, staring at the orchard from my favourite chair on the back veranda. You can always travel, but you need a place to return to, that's why they call it a holiday because it's always good to go home.'

'I don't know what a home is, only softball.' She was scared it would all be taken away from her, just like the game. Gone.

Had she somehow flipped roles with Alex—who was now fearlessly committing to them as a couple, while she was scared to commit to her own unchartered future?

'Let me tell you something, hon…' Molly put her hand on Verily's hand and with the other, she pointed to Verily's heart. 'Your true path to home is only found in the centre of your own diamond, my darling, and it's only you who can truly make that shine.'

TWENTY-FIVE

In the tiny town of Elsie Creek, streamers and banners lined the road and adorned the shops proclaiming the Rosella Festival. Cars, trucks, ag-bikes and utes filed past, heading for the town's sportsground as the grandstand filled with people.

The carpark was lined with rows of tents and marquees where many wandered through, tasting the local jams, fruits, inspecting arts and crafts displayed for a chance to win best in the show. Handmade jewellery, metalwork, woodwork, second-hand books, pot plants, and food were on sale. There was something for everyone.

Alex grabbed his customary sausage-sanger from the cave man, Jimmy, a mechanic by day and the town's barbecue king by night.

Scoffing his sandwich, smeared with sauce, Alex waved at his fellow team-mate, Kat, selling her handmade scented candles and tutus, that every kid seemed to be wearing on the day. Kat's Aunty Bea worked beside her in the stall, busily face-painting the line of children holding large pink wads of fairy floss.

On the other side he waved at Lucy, his shy team mate the girls dragged along each week to practice. Her softball uniform was hidden under her apron as she busily served assorted tea and cakes with her boss, Nancy who ran the train-station's tea house.

But where was the rest of his team? More importantly, where was Verily?

Alex continued to weave his way through the many stalls, amazed at the turnout for this small-town fete.

Molly had done a great thing, calling a truce with Agnes to work together on today's events.

'Molly?' He spotted her umbrella and did a double-look at her hair, now black reminding him of a roaring-twenties style. He was used to Molly changing her hairstyle and colour, but her warm smile never changed.

'Welcome back, we were worried you were going to miss this.' She hugged him warmly as part of his homecoming.

'I got a bit delayed, but I wasn't going to miss this.' Was it his last? 'Have you seen Verily and the rest of the team? We're playing in a minute.' If this was going to be his last Festival and his last game, he wanted to make it count.

'You'll find them all at Verily's tent.'

'Where?'

'That tent where the men are,' she said with a smile, shading herself under the yellow umbrella.

'They didn't do a kissing booth, did they? Hope not, she's my girl.' Possessiveness gripped as he frowned at the long line of men waiting their turn to stand under the shade of the tent. He wanted to be the only man kissing his lady for the rest of their natural lives together.

Molly laughed at him, hooking her arm through his.

'Well, best you go find out and rescue your lady and team then. Excuse me, VIP coming through.' Molly pushed her way past the men who grumbled about them jumping the cue. 'Don't be like that you mob, he's part of our team.'

'What's going on?' Alex's eyes adjusted to the tent's shade where a long table was stretched in the middle. Beer glasses were on the table in sets of five groups and his teammates were pouring small amounts of beer into glasses, then placing them before a large number.

Alex recognised the number; it was a batch number.

They were *his* batch numbers.

Too stunned to move, he watched the men from his town, sip his beer from proper beer glasses. This was the front-bar crew of blokes who didn't do glasses; they sculled from cans or bottles.

Yet here they sipped like snobs at a Sunday picnic at the Lords' cricket ground. They then scribbled on a piece of paper, shifted to the left along the table to taste another waiting brew, then shuffle along to try another. His teammates poured and washed glasses while grabbing bottles from five separate eskies displaying the batch numbers to represent the five different brews.

They were his batch numbers and his brew.

And there was only one person who had access to his stash with an intimate knowledge of his beer. 'She didn't.'

'Verily did such a good job at organising this, don't you think?' Molly smiled, leaning on her closed umbrella like a walking stick.

With arms crossed over his chest, Alex watched the

table. Where Speedy and his teammates were busily pouring his beer into glasses that the men eagerly drank. They then added their comments on their sheets they handed to Verily at the corner of the table by the exit. 'What are you doing?'

'Ah, hi. You found us?' Verily said with a half shrug, hiding her hands behind her back.

She looked cute when she did that. Even if it was a shrug.

'Care to explain all of this?' Alex thumbed over at the town's men tasting his beer. They passed pieces of paper and pencils back to Verily as they walked away, only to stand at the end of the line and wait for another turn.

'We're getting feedback,' said Verily, sliding the comments into a cardboard box.

'We're what?' He liked that she always said *we* as part of the team, discussing everything as an equal partnership. 'We never discussed this. Why are they tasting our beer?'

'Um, because you're a winner.'

'Am I?'

She shrugged.

He frowned.

Verily handed him two blue ribbons that were hanging from the marquee's rafters. 'Here, congratulations on winning.'

'Care to explain, please? Now.' He held the ribbon in his hand and frowned at the men drinking his beer. 'How can I win something I never entered?'

Molly patted Alex's shoulder and said, 'Hon, it's your win too. Verily just pulled an Agnes on you and entered on your behalf. We told no one it's your beer, but then again everyone knows you're living together. Congratulations, Alex, on winning first prize for your Rosella beer, even if you're the only one who entered that part of the competition. However, you did win the Rosella Festival's *Best in Show* blue sash for overall originality for your product involving rosellas. You'll get to collect your trophy later at the presentations after the game, when they present the Rosella Cup. Well done, I've never been prouder of the pair of you.'

'But that's my beer.' He pointed to the beer the men were drinking. 'Verily?'

'Technically, it isn't your beer.' Verily hooked her arm through his and guided him to the side of the tent. 'Hi honey, how was your trip?'

'How? Oi, tell me you didn't do an Agnes with the beer, like she did with Molly's jam.'

'It's not like that at all.'

'Well, technically you did come up with the idea of using rosellas, and you did bottle it all and picked the rosellas with Molly.'

She grabbed his hands and stared at him with that determined focus he adored. 'It's your beer, Alex. I'm not claiming it at all, I entered in your name and everything. That beer those men are drinking is what you kept paying me to work for you. I told you it was stockpiling in the storeroom.'

He thumbed up the brim of his hat and stared back at the empty crates and the large eskies full of beer with ice. 'I gave you that as a gift, that's your wages.' He hadn't realised he'd given her that much. 'I'm sorry I couldn't pay you in cash.'

'Don't be, or I wouldn't be able to share what I had.'

'You're giving out free beer? No wonder the line is long.'

'It's a taste-testing session. You wouldn't do it.'

'I didn't want to be judged, not until I was ready.'

'I know. I get that, I do. I practised for years on my own in my dad's yard pitching a ball at a stupid tyre until he practically dragged me to try out for the school team.'

'Molly told me that story.'

'I kept saying I'd only try out when I was perfect.'

'You were, you *are* perfect,' he said stroking her soft hair.

'Aww.' She wrinkled her nose at him. 'You're procrastinating too. I know you said you didn't want to use what you had in the shed for a taste-test, which is understandable. So, this is my gift to you. I'm sharing my stash with the town—Alex, they like it.'

'What?'

She grabbed a handful of papers from the box and held it out to him with handwritten comments against his batch numbers. 'They like it. I've had requests all morning about where they can buy some. You have that stock in your shed, and the Publican wants to talk to you about getting some for the pub.'

'Really?' It was his dream to stock the pub.

'The Publican had this guy with her who's staying at the pub for a few days. He's from some liquor store and sounded just like you, going on about the different beer and flavours.

He couldn't stop raving about the unique Australiana qualities of your Rosella Sour IPA. Here's his card, he wants to talk to you.'

Alex read from the business card, 'Territory Liquor Distributor?'

'Yep, that company can deliver stock Australia wide.'

'No way, I only wanted to do the pub, not—' Alex watched the men he knew drinking his beer, put down their comments, slip the paper into the box, then pat him on the back as they walked past. 'Which brew did you use?'

'I brought the ones you said were your top five. The Rosella beer they like most. You need names for your beer types. I've only been keeping track of their comments using your batch numbers.'

'How about Rose's brew for the Rosella beer? That's if we decide to go ahead.'

'After my mum?'

'Yeah, and it's your middle name, and for Molly's sister. Keep it in the family, our family.'

'Oh, wow.'

'You're cute when you're speechless, you know that.' His arm hooked around her neck pulling her closer and kissed the love of his life. Sure, it started slow and sensual, but when she melted into him with the husky hum it almost drove him crazy. His mouth went into overdrive lapping up her taste he'd missed, trying to recapture all the time they'd spent apart in one lip-locking moment. She was his air and everything he'd ever want, there was no more leaving her behind, because baby, he was home!

'Oi, there's children present, mate,' called out one of the men in the queue as a few whistled at them, with no child in sight.

Damn! He'd forgotten where they were.

'So, I'm forgiven for doing this and not asking?' She said with a sigh, leaning into his chest staring up at him with those sexy bedroom eyes that reflected the world. His world.

'You know I would've said no, but I'm glad you did it.' He could do anything with her. 'So, have you made up your mind yet? Do we stay or go?' It looked like they were staying. But Verily had the skills for being unpredictable, a by-product of her time as a professional player.

Agnes stood at the front of the tent and blew her whistle, making everyone flinch at the echoing sound. 'RIGHTO YOU LOT, THIS GROG SHOP IS SHUT.'

'AWW,' the men cried, echoing along the long line outside.

Agnes silenced the men with one glare as her curly bob shone under the sunlight. Gone was the mono-brow, thongs and footy socks, replaced by shiny sparkly thongs and painted toenails, baggy slacks, and fitted shirt, but she was still the same coach.

'Wow, look at Agnes.' Alex blinked a few times at the coach. 'Speedy told me about it, and the rest of the girls sent me photos, but I don't believe it.'

'Should I be worried you're getting photos from other women?' Verily asked.

Alex hooked his arm around her shoulders and brought her close. 'Puhleese, they're like my sisters, when I have the goddess at the end of my hallway. How soon can we go home?' Nuzzling into her slender neck he kissed her jawline, making his way back to those soft lips for another one of those kisses.

'BOUT TIME YOU SHOWED UP, BOY.'

'Agnes.' Alex winced at the blast of a whistle.

'WE HAVE A GAME ON. DUSTY DINGOES OUT YOU GET. HUSTLE, HUSTLE, HUSTLE.' Agnes shut the eskies and snapped them shut with a lock. 'YOU CAN TALK TO MANAGEMENT AFTER THE GAME.' Agnes put the key in her top pocket and glared at the crowd of men, making them soon disperse.

'Good luck out there. I'll be watching with Molly.' Verily kissed Alex's cheek. She scooped the men's feedback into the box, tucked it beneath the table as the rest of his team closed up the tent.

'Where will you be?' Alex reached for her hand, admiring the way her dress hugged her curves. The sweatpants were rare now—except for her morning runs.

'Just look for Molly's brolly.' Verily hooked her arm through Molly's, both shaded by the bright yellow umbrella that matched Molly's dress. Alex watched the pair of women he adored disappear into the crowd.

His life was great and getting better every day.

He stood there until she'd disappeared and that weight of loss bore down on him, missing her. He hated that feeling, only making him more determined to follow her.

'Dad? You're here?' Alex blinked at Neville, stepping in front of him through the crowd.

'I was hoping to catch up. I, ah tried that beer of yours, son. Molly made me.'

'And?' Here it comes.

'Not bad. Not bad.' He patted Alex's shoulder and grinned. '*It's bloody good!*'

'Really?'

'Yeah.'

'Why are you in town? I didn't think you'd bother with the Festival.'

Neville sighed, crossed arms over his chest and stared at the dirt beneath their boots as the crowd passed them by. 'I'm here to tell you I've made my decision on the house. I'm the same as you, that place was never a home without your mother.'

'Is that why you were never home? I thought it was because of me, that I'd disappointed you—'

'It was never you, son. It was me. I couldn't cope after your mum was killed. It was like a cold knife in my guts that would twist every time I drove up that hill to not have your mother there to greet me. My heart used to wanna burst at the site of that house where your mum's garden used to be filled with her flowers along the front wall, where she'd be standing there at that front door waving at me. There'd be clothes drying on the clothes line out the back, the aroma of her cooking filling the air, but it was her laughter that used to fill that house most. Every time I'd hear her laugh, it made me smile.' Neville sighed, sliding his hands into his jean's pockets. 'That house hasn't been a home for a very long time...'

Which is why Alex was more resolved to follow Verily.

She was all he thought about, not obsessed, but she was his personal brand of home he'd follow anywhere. Yet, he'd miss the town, the people and the place too. Maybe they would come back, but he was making sure he put his family first. Always.

'You're right, son, it is time to move on. So, I'm gonna put the house on the market. Unless you want it?'

'No, I have my home.' And her name was Verily.

'You look happy.'

'I am.' He had a beautiful lady and his beer had won two blue ribbons, even if it was from the local show. He'd always wanted to have someone drink it, and they had. *Dream achieved!* 'What are you going to do with yourself, Dad?'

'I'll get a small place somewhere along the highway where I can park the truck. Do you still want to drive the other truck?'

'Are you selling them both to buy a new one?'

'No. Mine is fine and it'll keep me until retirement.'

Alex pulled the truck keys from his pocket and out came the business card from the liquor distributor. He was so close, but was he ready to take that leap for the brewery? 'Here, Dad. It's parked up at your place.' He handed his dad the keys to the truck and didn't feel sad at all about leaving that part of his past behind.

'Don't you still want to drive?'

'I'll do the short runs, but only after the harvest.' If they stayed.

Only Verily and Molly knew of the question he had yet to have answered. They'd agreed that they didn't want anyone influencing their decision.

In case they left, someone else could manage the harvest if he ended up in a plane seat beside Verily, and Alex was perfectly okay with that. It was good to let someone have the reins for a while and Verily needed to do this after living a life following everyone else's orders too. She needed to make this decision for herself.

Neville looked at the keys in his callused palm, then up at Alex. 'There's enough work to keep the truck here, you've got the room to keep her safe and it's handy for the Railway Station. Maybe you'll let me park up and use your shower now and again?'

'Anytime Dad, Molly's the same.' It was the way his father lived, and he'd accepted that a long time ago, but he wasn't ready to tell his dad yet if they were leaving. Not in public anyway.

'You know, all those years Molly and her family wouldn't accept any money from me for looking after you.'

'Really?'

'Yeah. Molly kept saying she was your godmother and did it for your mother. She has a good heart.'

'How come you never hooked up with Molly, if you had a crush on her sister?'

'Molly? Nah, she was your mother's best mate and just a mate. Always will be. She's got enough men chasing her, she doesn't let too many know about.'

'Since when? Don't tell me.' Alex cringed, it'd be like talking about his mother and sex.

'OI, WE NEED THE CATCHER,' hollered Agnes,

parting the crowd around her.

'That's not Agnes, is it?' Neville asked.

'Molly and the team did a makeover on her. Don't ask me, I stayed right away from it.'

'I'd heard their feud was over. D'ya reckon we've got a chance too?'

'For what, makeovers? You do know that involves waxing and make-up.' The two men chuckled.

'Nah, I meant to chat over a beer, like as a father and son thing. I'll admit, I did want the partnership thing hoping in a few years you'd buy me out and I'd retire. I never did ask what you wanted, I'd just assumed driving trucks was it, coz that's all we ever talked about.'

'I'd rather we had a beer and talked over other things.' He held out his hand to his father. Neville clasped onto it, then reached over and hugged Alex, patting his back.

'I know I never say it, but I am proud of you, son. We'll talk soon. Have a good game, I'll be watching.'

'Thanks.' He felt like a little boy all over again because his father had never watched any of his games. 'See ya after the game, Dad.' Neville nodded at him, and with a relieved grin, Alex jogged to meet his team as they got ready to play their final game of the season.

TWENTY-SIX

They'd sent the visitors into bat, and the Dusty Dingoes returned to the field. The scores tied as Speedy stood on the pitcher's plate in the centre of the diamond and prepared to pitch. She nodded at Alex who nodded back ready. She swung her arm around, released the ball, and with a resounding slap, it landed in Alex's catcher's mitt.

'*Strike one,*' shouted the umpire.

'*Goooo Speedy, you can do it,*' shouted Verily with the rest of the team and the town behind her in the grandstands. From the playground, the Kimble's mob of kids banged drums, tooted their horns, waving streamers like a miniature cheerleading squad with war paint slashed across their cheeks. All of them, boys and girls wore multi-coloured tutus that bounced with their cheers. They certainly stood out.

Ball in hand, Speedy lined up for the second swing, she threw underarm and again, *slap*. It landed in Alex's glove.

'*Strike two,*' shouted the umpire.

Again, the crowd cheered as Speedy wiped her hands up and down, up and down on her uniform. She'd made the second strike a few times now. Was this her chance?

'Come on, Speedy, you can do it...' Murmured Alex as he crouched low to receive. Speedy did the nod, he nodded back, just like Verily had practised with him. Five seconds later Speedy's arm windmilled, and she released the ball…

It was a corker of a shot, spinning sideways. The batter took a swing and missed but Alex caught it—just.

'STRIKE THREE—YOU'RE OUT,' cried the umpire.

'*I did it. I did it. I did it.*' Speedy jumped up and down, her teammates joining her in the centre.

'Well done, Speedy.' Alex picked up his little cousin and threw her in the air as the crowd cheered. He was delighted and proud for her, not that he'd won his bet, but that she'd tried so hard for this moment.

He searched the crowd for Verily who was seated beside Molly and her bright umbrella. Verily had covered her mouth with her hand as if to contain herself, but her eyes and cheeks were shiny from tears of joy. He waved at her, she should be proud of what she'd achieved for Speedy.

'Can we please get on with it,' called out the umpire.

'Sorry, it's my first strike. Did you see it?' Speedy asked.

'I did, congratulations. I'm sure it won't be your last. Let's move this game along, please,' the umpire said, tapping his watch.

Back into their positions on the field, a new batter stood at the home plate. Speedy took her spot and pitched. The ball got smacked to the outfield for super-mum Karen to chase as the batter sprinted to the first base.

The second batter took her place on the home plate and prepared to swing. Speedy pitched, the batter bunted the ball short in front, tossed the bat into the dirt and bolted for first base. The other member of their team ran to second while Tess, without her hot-pants but in proper baseball pants, ran forward as short-stop and scooped up the ball, but the opposition runners were safe on the padded plates.

The third batter stood on the home plate with a bat ready to swing. Speedy pitched, and the batter hit hard. Bat down, the batter ran for the first plate, as the other batters ran to the next plates, and the ball slammed straight into Speedy.

'OW.' She cried out holding her arm and collapsed on the ground.

'Speedy! *Timeout.*' Alex tore off his helmet and ran to his little cousin on the ground. 'Jenny?' He called for the bush nurse as he lifted Speedy from the red dirt. Speedy gripped her right arm, wincing in pain.

Jenny dropped her glove and knelt down beside Speedy. 'Okay, Speedy let me take a look.'

'Ow,' Speedy cried out, pressing her back to Alex's chest.

Verily ran over with Molly beside her. Agnes, with new dress-thongs crunching under the dead grass also met them in the centre carrying the first aid kit.

'Speedy are you okay?' Verily asked.

'It's my pitching arm, it is,' Speedy whined as sweat and tears trickled over her reddening face.

'Wriggle your fingers, Speedy,' asked Jenny and Speedy complied while wincing. 'I don't think it's broken but you'll have one beauty of a bruise.'

Verily crouched beside the girl. 'Speedy, you've just been given the hellfire christening.'

'I have?'

'Yep, you're a true softball pitcher now with a war wound like that. I've suffered the same. They say the sign of a good pitcher is when the batter tries to take you out of the game, so welcome to the club, my friend.' Verily held out her hand and Speedy shook it with her left.

'I am, aren't I?' Speedy grinned through her tears.

'Can you pitch, Speedy?' Tess asked.

'Noooooo,' wailed Speedy, gripping her upper arm. 'I want to, but I can't.'

'WHICH ONE OF YOU PRINCESSES IS GONNA PITCH IN HER PLACE?'

'It's not just that, Agnes,' said Molly. 'They need another player to put on the field.'

'We'll pinch some kid from the crowd or one of Karen's crew,' said Bella.

'That won't do,' said the umpire, peeking over from the back of their group. 'You need a full team of players at least older than twelve. There are rules for bringing ring-ins into this game.'

'Then how come the other teams have their fancy dodgy cousins, with all their special softball skills, showing up for the finals like those playing for first and second place? We're only playing for third, you know,' Molly said to the umpire.

'Players must live in the town, or have a resident to verify they live in town—'

'Which we know they don't.'

'—and show up to at least one game and practise before they can play in the last game of the season. I'll tell the other team to go have a break while you work out your issues.' The umpire blew long and hard on his whistle then showed the T sign with his hands to the opposition standing by their tent. *'Injury break—thirty minutes.'*

'Come on, let's get you into the shade, Speedy.' Alex scooped up his cousin and carried her to their team's marquee.

In the shade, they gathered around Speedy who sat with ice on her arm. 'I look like you with your shoulder, huh, coach,' she said to Verily.

'I'm no coach.'

'BUT YOU CAN PITCH!'

'Nice try, Agnes, you heard what the umpire said about games and practises,' said Alex.

'I'm not a player,' Verily muttered, dropping her head.

'Hey, it's okay.' He stroked her soft, messy hair.

'NO. YOU'RE AN ASSISTANT COACH THAT PLAYS.' Agnes pointed at Verily and everyone inside the tent stopped and stared at Verily.

'Agnes is right,' said Molly, stepping forward.

'OF COURSE, I'M BLOODY RIGHT.'

'Agnes plays catcher when Alex isn't here,' Molly said to Verily. 'And, you've been to nearly all of the team's practises here and at home and most of the games. As the team's secretary, I can vouch for your attendance and your position as an assistant coach, and, everyone knows you're recovering from an injury and haven't been able to play.'

'No.' Verily stepped back from the pair of middle-aged women.

'GIMME FIVE MINUTES WITH THOSE UMPIRES AND I'LL GET THE ALL CLEAR, YOU WATCH.'

'No, I can't.' Verily searched for the nearest exit.

Agnes stepped in closer, blocking her path. 'WHAT, YOU WANT A KIDNEY TO PLAY? I HAVE A SPARE.'

'Agnes, let me,' said Molly, waving her hand at Agnes to step aside.

'Oh no, you don't.' Again, Verily stepped back from her aunt and into Alex's side as he slid his arm around, her holding her in place.

'No, let me,' said Alex grinning at his lady. 'Princess…'

'Oh, this is just great.' Verily couldn't say no to Alex and he knew it. 'I can't, I haven't got a thing to wear. That makes me sound like such a girl, huh?' She giggled and tried to step away, but he kept her in place.

'You are a girl… mine.' He kissed her nose, admiring her appearance, but she needed more to play in than a cotton dress and strappy sandals. 'Molly, go see Fitzy for a ride in his chopper.'

'Why?'

'You're going to fly home to collect Verily's gameday bag. It's on the back veranda.' She was living with him now, where her clothes hung on the line at the back where they rarely entered the cottage dressed. 'Go, Molly, we've got twenty minutes, we want that glove, helmet and everything else in that bag.'

'Ooh, how exciting.' Molly dashed out the door with her umbrella in the air as if it was a sword leading the cavalry's charge.

'Agnes,' said Alex, 'go sort out the umpires about allowing our team's assistant coach to play.'

'THEY'LL BLOODY AGREE; YOU'LL SEE.' With a bounce to her new bob, Agnes left with a flip-flop-flip-flop from her sparkly new dress thongs.

'Alex, I can't,' Verily whined, trying to slip his grip.

'You can. You said you can't do a full game, and we're in the last part. You also said you wouldn't because of Speedy. So, Speedy?'

'Yes, Alex.' Speedy looked up with ice on her upper arm, where a large circular bruise was forming.

'Do you give permission for Verily to pitch in your place for the rest of the game? This is a onetime only offer. A never to be repeated deal.'

Speedy's eyes lit up brighter than the min-min lights haunting the highway at midnight. 'Are you kidding me, I'd love it, I would.'

'I can't,' again, whined Verily.

With his arm around her shoulders, he held her close to his side. 'Yes, you can. Jenny, you'd better get some extra ice and painkillers for this. Tess, go see that cop that's sweet on you and see if he's got a speed gun handy in that cop car of his. The rest of you mob, chillax while I have a conversation with our team's relief-pitcher.' He grabbed Verily's hand and walked her out of the tent.

'What the hell are you doing requesting a speed gun when I can't throw that fast.' Verily shook herself free.

He grabbed her before she fled. 'Yes, you can. You've been practising with me for over a month and you're stronger than you realise. Hear me out, *please*,' he pleaded, and she stopped wriggling and turned around to face him.

Smoothing the sides of her face free from her messy hair, spotting the fear in her eyes made his stomach drop. 'Hey, I'd never put you in any harm and there's nothing to be afraid of.' Had she lost her nerve to play too? 'Look, we've got a loaded playing field and if this goes down, we might actually win our first game in nearly ten years. We have nothing to lose. We've got no chances of winning the Cup, and if we don't have another player, we'll lose by forfeit, anyway. Besides, I'd like to at least brag I got to play one game with you. This might be my last game and only chance to catch for you.'

'I don't know.'

'You said you couldn't with Speedy, but you have her permission. We know Agnes will get her way with the coaches or we'll be banned from playing for life.'

She stood with screwed lips thinking hard. 'I'll just be another dodgy cousin here on holidays.'

'So, the decision is we're going?'

'Oh my god.' Her sleepy eyes widened.

'What?'

'My whole life, my whole playing career, I'm that dodgy cousin.'

'How big is your family?'

'Don't you get it? I play from contract to contract as the hired gun, that's been my whole career.'

'*Was* your career. Today there is no contract or money, you're paying for the privilege.' Would she dare? He wasn't going to let her give in. 'Haven't you always said, if you could, you'd do it one more time?'

'Do you want to go?'

Nice change of topic, princess! 'I've already returned the truck keys to my dad.'

'Already?'

'When you ran away from me from that time Dad shouted at us, I knew I couldn't let you go. I'm happy to stay and I'm okay to go too. I've actually been feeling pretty good letting you make the tough decisions, it's like a weight's been lifted.'

'I can see that.'

'For me, it's been a good decision. How many sleepless nights have you had worrying if you're making the right ones?'

'Lots, except the dragon fruit flowering night.'

'I'm glad you got to see that, it's pretty special, but so are you.' He said holding her in his arms he rested his forehead against hers.

'What if I said I'd cash in my airfare and we use that as freight costs towards your brewery?'

'What? I thought you gave all my beer away.'

'I did, only what was mine, to test it and they liked it and I've always liked it. The rest is still in the shed, but it's your dream too and I've learned to invest wisely. If you're willing to commit to me, it's my turn to do the same.'

'What, why?'

'My dad sacrificed his career for me to help me get to where I wanted to go. I got there because of his support and his sacrifices. So now, I believe it's my turn to support someone else to help them achieve their dreams goal. Yours, Alex. I want to prove I believe in you, that I'm willing to invest my time and everything I have into our future too.'

His over full heart pressed against his chest spreading an inner warmth through his body, just to hear she'd be willing to support him. He could see she meant it. 'We're a team. You and me, equals. You get that, right?'

'You know me, I'm a highly-seasoned team player.'

But she still needed to make that step free from contracts, coaches, terms and conditions and training schedules set by others. Verily needed to make her own terms, her own rules and guidelines that they would live by, committed as a couple. He wanted her to be very much a part of the decision-making process, every step of the way and that started with this one question. 'So, are we staying?'

She shrugged.

He frowned. 'Nick-off.'

She laughed with the sweetest smile. 'I don't want to be a dodgy cousin anymore.'

Decision made and relief and joy swamped him, but her smile that reached her eyes, told him she'd made the right choice for herself as well. 'There's that cheeky smile I'd missed.' He cupped her cheeks with his palms and leaned in to kiss her.

Above the gum trees, a small muster chopper roared with a flurry of dust as Molly waved from her seat in the sky. The team watched from the shade of their tent. Agnes argued with the umpires over by the home plate where they busily flicked through the rule books. Men and women leaned against the barriers that made up the racetrack, their wide-brimmed hats shading their eyes from the sun. Kids blew whistles, parading in their tutus as they played in the playground with the smell of the barbecued foods filled the air. Hands where shook, backs slapped, hugs swapped, but they all wore smiles greeting a neighbour or an old friend who'd come to their small town festival.

'You can see it, can't you,' whispered Alex with his arm over her shoulder. 'You asked that question the first time I drove you into town, what made Elsie Creek a town. It's those people there who make a town, and I think it's about time they met their latest resident, don't you?'

TWENTY-SEVEN

er hands trembled as she tightened the laces on her cleats and slammed their spiky soles into the dust. 'Can you strap me up? Just put strips across my shoulder.' Verily unrolled the sticky plaster and tore off the end with her teeth.

'Should I get Jenny to do this?' Alex asked.

'You can do it.'

He took the tape and pressed it gently over her shoulder covered in crisscrossing tracks of scars. 'Are you nervous?'

'Oh, yeah.' She nodded, swallowing a couple of anti-inflammatories and washed them down with hard gulps of water. 'Mind you, I've never taken drugs before a game.'

'I'd never realised how cute your arse is in this uniform.'

'Tight for the game and it's got protective padding.'

'What about padding for your arm! I don't want you risking it when you've come so far? Maybe we should cancel—'

'This was your idea.' She rummaged through her bag and pulled out her long-sleeved shirt.

'Would you hate me if I said stop, I mean, it's like you're going into battle.'

'You were the one who talked me into this.'

'Yeah, I did, eh?' He grinned as he helped her slide on the team shirt and held out her helmet. 'You'll be wearing this and I don't care about the helmet hair.'

'I never played without it.' Hair in a ponytail she put on the helmet. Grabbed the soft hand-towel she tucked into her back hip and slid her fingers into her glove. It felt so alien, and yet so familiar to be standing in uniform again. 'How long are they giving me to warm up?'

'Five minutes. Let's go, my little softball princess. I've never been prouder. Hey, you do realise this is like one of those wish-list things I'd never expect to come true.' By the hand, he led her from the tent.

Her eyes adjusted to the bright sunlight to meet her waiting team. She was a player again.

'Umpire.' She gave the umpire a nod as she approached. 'Thanks for letting me play.'

'My, pleasure, I'm a huge fan.' He shook her gloved hand with two hands.

'Ah, thanks. May I have the ball please, I'd like to warm up.'

'Yeah, sure, I'll be right here. Did I hear you were chasing down a speed camera to tape this?' The umpire asked Alex.

Alex turned around and there were the town's police in their blue uniforms, standing with the broad-shouldered Sergeant holding up a large white speed gun. 'You can set up over there, Marcus.' The police officers ducked under the barrier. 'This is gonna be fun.'

'Fun for who?' Verily mumbled.

'Hey, I'll be right here, it's just like we practised. I'm sure you've played in bigger crowds, it's just the town. Now, make me proud,' Alex tapped her on the backside and took his place on the home plate.

'Can someone please get that water buffalo off the playing field? We play ball in five,' shouted out the umpire.

A few kids squealed with laughter as they ran onto the field with bright-coloured flowers in hand and tried to coax the water buffalo. Today, Cecil was dressed in dusty red ribbons that flapped from his horns and tail, displaying *Welcome to Elsie Creek's Rosella Festival* painted on his broad sides. His companion, the red chook, balanced on his back as they led the buffalo off the field and the Dusty Dingoes took their positions.

Verily walked across the dry hard ground where heat waves rose beneath the outback sun as she approached the pitcher's plate.

It was the longest solitary walk in her life.

This was worse than the first time she'd stood before a world class audience.

Here, it might seem a small outback town, playing softball next to the rodeo rails with a water buffalo as their mascot, but it was a home crowd. She couldn't remember ever playing before her own home crowd before.

While on the mound, her team got into their fielding positions. She scratched at the dirt with her cleats going for the perfect position. Digging her heels in, she looked at Alex who nodded.

She rolled her arms a few times, and swung them across her body to stretch, nodded back at him and threw the ball. He caught it; she threw it back. Again, he caught it, she threw it back, just liked they'd done countless times in the orchard, out the back of the Picker's Cottage, or on their own private softball diamond beneath the windmill.

'TIME,' cried the umpire.

Verily inhaled sharply and gripped the ball in hand trying to beat down her nerves to silence the voice telling her she was a failure. She could do this, she had to. Because she wanted to—and that snapped her focus into play.

A new batter approached the plate and took up her position.

Verily only focussed on Alex who gave her the signal, and she inhaled, swung her arm around and with the sling of her wrist the ball flung free and *whack*—straight into Alex's hand.

'*Strike one!*' Shouted the umpire.

'How fast, Sarge?' Alex asked the speed gun groupies behind him as he tossed the ball back to Verily.

'Sixty.'

'My girl's still warming up.'

'Excuuuuse me, ladies and gentlemen,' called the MC over the speakers, tapping the microphone, its squeal made everyone wince. 'Sorry, 'bout that. I just wanted to draw your attention to the Dusty Dingoes relief pitcher and their playing-assistant coach. For those unaware, we'd like to welcome the return of our town's most famous resident who is an Australian bronze medallist; five-time world champion pitcher; three-time world record holder for the fastest female pitcher, averaging a game speed of a hundred and ten kilometres. I give you Elsie Creek's mango farmer, Verily Wayfaren.'

'*Bloody hell, who told,*' called out Bella from the outfield.

Up at the speaker's tent, with her bright yellow brolly, was Molly, waving.

It was like a flashback to the many countries, games and other softball tournaments all over the world. When Verily had stood in the middle of the field to pitch, she'd look up and there she was, Molly with her brolly.

Molly had been there for all her celebrations, flying in for the big events. It was Molly she called to share the good, and the bad over the phone when she couldn't talk to her dad. It was Molly she thought of at Christmas and even Mother's Day.

Verily may have come here to find the connection to her mother, but it was Molly all along, her aunt. Molly had been her long-distance mother figure, that voice of reason, all her life.

It's what she'd been searching for, that connection to family and she had it. Here, in Elsie Creek with Molly, and now with Alex. Why would she ever want to leave?

She looked around at the team who'd supported her, the coach she'd warred with, the water buffalo she'd led with a bunch of flowers, and the townspeople. She no longer felt like an alien in a foreign land and truly believed she was home.

'Let's do this.' She nodded to Alex, wiping down her

pitching hand and ball on the soft cloth, getting her focus back on the game.

'Secret's out babe, time to show the real stuff,' called Alex from the home plate.

'No more secrets.' It was showtime.

'I'm dead,' said the batter, stepping back from the plate.

Verily hung her head and took deep breaths to regain her focus. She looked at Alex who nodded, then she let her arm swing and let the ball loose.

'Strike two,' shouted the umpire.

'EIGHTY-TWO CLICKS,' hollered the sergeant. He stood over the younger officer holding the speed gun. A third officer ran with arms full of bullet-proof vests and helmets. All three slid on the flak jackets and full-face helmets and crept closer behind Alex and the umpire.

'Told you she was only warming up,' said Alex as he threw it back to Verily who shook her head at the police officers.

If only her father could see this. He'd laugh from his familiar spot on the sidelines, enjoying himself. She sighed, looking over at the team and the crowd laughing at the water buffalo, the police, and the unique players who'd showed up to every game.

She'd finally found her fun with the sport and let loose with her third pitch. It flew fast and slammed straight into Alex's mitt as the umpire called out, 'STRIKE THREE, YOU'RE OUT.'

'NINETY-NINE KILOMETRES,' shouted the sergeant as the other officer held up the speed gun.

'*Time out,*' called the opposing coach as the batter left the home plate, dragging her bat behind her.

With the softball in hand, Alex jogged to meet Verily in the centre. 'How are you holding up?'

'I'm okay. *What the hell?*' Verily glared at the incoming player. 'What is *she* doing here?'

It was Sherice, all shiny with her blonde hair and hip-swinging sway. Buttons low on her shirt and long, lean legs standing at the home plate.

'Honey, we talked about this,' Alex said, facing Verily.

Verily squinted past him to private enemy number one. She'd hated what Sherice had done to her, to Alex, and to Tim who she'd gotten to know as a friend.

'Don't even think about it. You'd break her leg at the speed you throw.'

Ooh, it's gonna happen. 'Just be ready to catch.' She patted his shoulder, took the ball and headed back to the pitcher's mound. She scratched at the dirt for that solid stance of power and the perfect pitching position.

'*Play ball,*' shouted the umpire from the home plate. Sherice tossed her shiny hair in the sun, then waved at the cops crowding the home plate.

Verily just let the hatred build-up as she focused on her target. 'Keep that catcher's mitt steady, Alex.'

'Right, well, not gonna argue with you now, but don't you...'

She glared at him. The time for talk was over, it was time to play.

Alex hurried to the home plate and from his jeans

pocket he pulled out a piece of thin flat plastic padding. 'Just letting you know, Umpire, I'm not cheating. I'm just putting some extra padding into my glove because her Satan Screamers sting.'

Verily stood on the mound. She twirled the ball in her fingertips, ignoring her shoulder's pain, allowing hate to drive her. She'd been playing until now, and the one thing she'd learned is that when you play the game you played it with everything.

Seconds after Alex's nod, she swung with all her soul and released the ball. It flung free and WHACK.

'A HUNDRED AND SEVEN KILOMETRES,' called out the cop in the back.

'That'd be a strike, umpire,' Alex said, holding out his glove.

'Ah, yeah. Strike one, then. Have I got enough padding on me?' The umpire looked at his chest plate and helmet then back at the cops in full riot gear.

'I didn't see it,' said Sherice.

'You're lucky Verily isn't aiming at you, for what you did to us. You never upset the pitcher, especially with my lady's aim.' Alex grinned and threw the ball back to Verily.

Verily could never backchat in games. She was never allowed to say a word, but she knew how to psyche out a batter when they faced her and let them know they'd riled her up. It only made her try harder.

On the Pitcher's plate, Verily lined up her perfect lifelong practised position and then, with head tilted she stared at Sherice.

'Why is Verily smiling at me like that?' Sherice asked, gripping her bat.

'*Oh crap,* it's another one. Get that speed camera ready you mob, it's coming.' Alex squatted down with mitt in position. He squinted and gave a nod and she threw it so fast he didn't see it.

But they all heard it. *Whack.* Ball against leather.

'*Strike two,*' cried the umpire.

'A HUNDRED AND EIGHTEEN KILOMETRES,' shouted the sergeant through his protective face-shield.

'She's breaking the town's bloody speed limit there, Sarge,' called out one of the men leaning against the fence with the rest of the crowd.

Again, Verily lined up. This was it, her last shot. She let loose her screamer that powered through her shoulder, and the ball catapulted across the paddock.

Smack.

Sherice swung the bat.

'Bit late to swing don't you think, Sherice, I've already got the ball.' Alex showed her the softball in his mitt. 'If you want to stand there and fan the team, by all means, keep on swinging.'

'STRIKE THREE, *you're out,*' cried the umpire who turned around and asked the cops beside him. 'How fast was that one?''

The sergeant raised the visor of his riot helmet and showed the speed camera's numbers. 'A HUNDRED AND TWENTY-NINE. If she goes over a hundred and thirty, I may have to book her.'

Alex jogged to the centre with the softball as the rest of the team joined them. 'Are you okay? You were packing some heat.'

'I just want to finish this.' Her arm and shoulder burned, the pain was piercing through to her fingers, but she also knew the game and the team that surrounded her.

She couldn't pitch.

But she didn't need to play with everything because this wasn't about her anymore. It was about those who got to this place, the team, not her. All season she'd been sitting on the sidelines and had fun, painting her nails with Molly, blowing whistles and banging drums with the Kimble's kids, and even heckling with Agnes.

It was time to give the order in the play as a coach and not a player. She believed in them like they'd shown their belief in her.

Verily said, 'Look, from here on out guys, it's game. Bases are loaded, and we only need one more batter to get out to win this game. It might not be the Cup—'

'But it'll be our first game in ten years,' said Bella.

'We can win if you strike them out,' said Mindy with her sister Mandy nodding beside her.

'I can't.' Verily winced holding her shoulder. Alex frowned as he put his large palm on her shoulder. 'Don't make a fuss, they're not allowed to know. We can do this. As a team, we can do this. We've all practised the plays and now it's all about strategies.'

'Strategy? This isn't chess,' said Jenny.

'What'll happen now is their coach will tell the next

batter to just swing blind and hope it'll connect. They will also steal home as soon as the batter swings.'

'Do you think they will swing blind?' Tess asked.

'They can't see it,' said Alex with an arm around Verily as she leaned into his body heat to support her shoulder. 'The umpire didn't see that last throw and Sherice swung after I caught the ball.'

'If I was their coach, it's what I'd be telling them to do as their next play. You can see he's making the signals.' She nodded to the coach hand-signalling to the opposition players on the loaded plates. She was also a coach who had the home ground advantage and an intimate world-class knowledge of the rules. 'Did anyone call time?'

* * *

'No,' said Alex and looked around with wide eyes. He knew what she was up to because they'd talked game strategies while playing catch in the yard.

'Allow me to introduce you to a faker's play. Everyone, come in closer.' They huddled in the mound as Verily drew in the dirt and explained the tactic.

They gave a cheer and ran back to their positions on the field. First, second, and third bases were loaded with opposition players who kept their toes to the mat, poised, and ready to run. Alex took his spot at the home plate beside the umpire.

'How's your hand?' Asked the umpire.

'It stings.'

'How can you see it?'

'Verily aims for my glove as her target. She aimed for my nuts once, so I've learned pretty quickly to catch.'

'I can imagine,' said the umpire. 'I saw Verily play in the world championships, no one got past her.'

'Gee, that's just great,' whined the new batter. 'How come she's here? Just for the game?'

'Verily lives here. She was born in this town and Elsie Creek is her home. She lives with me on her family farm as a fourth-generation mango farmer.' Alex was looking forward to making the fifth generation and watching them grow and he'd make damned sure he was home for that. He did not want to miss any family time by being on the road like his father.

Alex took his position and nodded to Verily, she nodded back and swung her arm trying to hide her wince. He could see her pain and it took everything inside him to not stop the game, but he didn't. She wouldn't let him if he tried.

'*You're out,*' cried the umpire at first base where Mindy had tagged the opposition team runner with the softball she'd hidden in her mitt from their meeting at the pitcher's mound. No one had seen it until she showed the umpire on First base and tagged the runner.

While everyone was still watching with confusion, Mindy then threw the softball to her sister on third base who tagged the next player. Mandy threw it to Tess and in her leggings, she slid across the ground and with the softball stretched out, she tagged the third runner halfway to the home plate.

'*You're out,* GAME OVER, *Congratulations Dusty*

Dingoes,' cried the umpire at the home plate with a wave of his hands in the air.

'But, but…' The batter stood on the plate blinking. 'She didn't pitch, is that legal?'

'It's a faker's triple play, I haven't seen one in years. Well played, I kept wondering why that other team never stole home sooner.' The umpire shook Alex's hand with vigour.

'Our assistant coach has a few tricks up her sleeves with the game.'

'I imagine. I'd heard she was starting a coaching clinic in Japan, is Verily going to do that here?'

'Is there a market for it?'

'If you ran it in the dry season, softballers would come in droves to escape the southern winter and learn how to pitch from an expert, and that is an expert you've got there, mate. Shame about the accident doing in her pitching arm.' The umpire pointed to Verily who was in the centre where Agnes handed her a chunk of ice for her shoulder while Jenny put a sling around her neck and wrist.

Alex hated the sight of that, but he also saw she was still smiling.

'Here, take my card,' said the umpire. 'If you ever need a hand to set it up and the rules and regulations for running a softballers coaching clinic, I'll help. Our organisation would love to support it. Heck, I could give you the name and number of sixty softball mums who'd pay to bring their kids to learn today.'

'You're kidding?' Alex stared at the second business card handed to him that day.

'I'm serious, mate. You could use this ground for coaching, it's got all the public amenities and they could camp here while Verily ran that clinic.'

'That'd be good for the town.' Alex could see Molly managing that part with Agnes, who was talking about moving her van in to become the new caretaker of the sportsgrounds.

The umpire asked, 'You don't suppose I could get her autograph on a game ball and a photo with her?'

Alex's mind whirled into gear, Verily could do this coaching clinic if she wanted. She'd coached Speedy, she'd coached his team to win its first game in a decade. She'd only struck out one player, the rest was a team effort.

But Verily wasn't into talking with people or player's parents, she talked to players as a player and was good at it. Players understood her, and Alex didn't mind a chat and was getting good at networking and was used to fielding phone calls. They could do this, as partners, as a team. 'I'm sure *we* can organise something, I'll bring Verily to you.' She might listen to the umpire. It was also something extra they could consider for their future because he knew how much she loved the game.

'Great, I'm gonna get a beer. I've heard they've got this Rosella beer the men have been raving about. I'm keen to try it, to celebrate.'

'Celebrate?'

'Heck yeah. I got to umpire a world champion out here in the middle of the Territory, and mate, that doesn't happen every day in my world.' The umpire left shaking his head with a wide smile. The opposition packed up their gear, while the Dusty Dingoes danced in the centre as the home crowd cheered.

Alex kicked at the home plate with his boots, pulling it free from the dirt, he approached his team where he was hugged by the women who were like his sisters. Finally, he found his lady among the happy crowd. 'I know you're sore, I can see it.'

'But it was worth it.' Verily smiled as she hugged him. 'You guys are brilliant. You deserve the win, and you might win more next season. Isn't that right coach?'

'YOU BETCHA DINGO'S DONUTS WE WILL,' shouted Agnes, and the team cheered.

Alex pulled Verily closer into her arms. 'So, next season, huh?'

'And the season after that, and the season after that. What are you doing with the home plate?'

'This is my game souvenir of playing with you, it's also going to be our new back doormat.'

'Why?'

'So you'll always know whenever you cross this plate you're home and safe.'

'Aww, has anyone told you that you're just perfect?' Her good arm over his shoulder, the home plate rested between their chests. 'I love you, I do.'

'Love you too. Now shh, I'm trying to kiss you.' And he did, pressing his lips to hers he kissed her in the middle of the field because the rest was just background noise. He wrapped his arms around her in the centre of a cheering team who were more than just a team they were part of a town.

The water buffalo, Cecil, carrying his red chook high on his wide shoulders, wandered from the sports ground and down the one and only main road of town. His hoof-steps echoed as he clip-clopped past the hairdressers, the supermarket, the post office, the craft store, the hardware store and the mighty two storey pub. Like the rest of the shops that lined the main street, they were all closed for the day.

The echoes of the partying townspeople were behind him. The train tooted in the distance on the left and Cecil raised his large head to listen to the rattle of the carriages riding the rails.

Fluttering in the breeze were ochre-coloured ribbons, wrapped around his horns as the paint and glitter sparkled across his coat. With a swish of his tail, the red chook clucked on his back as he strolled toward the sinking sun on the distant horizon of the never-ending road. For there was nowhere else like Elsie Creek, that may be just a speck on a map, but it was a place that many champions called home, making it a tru-blu Aussie diamond in the middle of the outback dust.

THE END

For now…

Did you like the story?

If so, *your opinion* matters to me!

I'd love to read your review on

GOODREADS & BOOKBUB.

Or share a cover of this book on social media so I can
see how far this story has travelled!

Please add **#Escape2HEA** for me to find you.

With much gratitude,

Mel.

MelAROWE.com

Thank you!

Thank you for reading this story of the fictitious town of *Elsie Creek*. She may not exist, yet there is a part of her found in the Northern Territory townships, roadhouses, dusty sports grounds, crocodile-crowded boat ramps, and even in the rural pubs sparsely scattered across northern Australia.

Having had the privilege of playing an outback softball game with a group of women of all ages and nationalities, I admire all those NT softballers who travel extraordinary distances just to play their games. You truly are shining diamonds in the Territory dust.

Thank you to the NT's Adelaide River pub and this tiny township's committee that runs the annual Rosella Festival that also gave me the idea for this story. I gladly make the trek to stock up on the best homemade rosella jam in the Territory.

Thank you to the amazing *Handbrake* for not disowning me, and thank you to my sister for her support. I know neither have ever read a word I've written, so I'm putting this right here in case you do dare to indulge.

Thank you to the writer friends I've met online who've helped me so much when I live in a world where finding decent Wi-Fi is like discovering gold. And on top are the sparkling gems scattered across Australia Suzie Frewin and Claire-Louise Holderness. Ladies, I can't thank you enough!

Thank you to my fabulous first readers team, I'm am truly blessed to have you join me in my writing journey.

Thank you to the quirky, colourful, and exceptionally extraordinary people I've met while working and living throughout northern Australia. The experience has been—and continues to be—priceless.

Thank you, because I can, because I did, and because I continue to do so ...

Until next time,

Mel A. Rowe

MelAROWE.com

About the Author

Australian Bestselling Author, Mel A ROWE, creates escapes for you to enjoy from the comfort of home.

Delivered with a dash of drama, witty humour and quirky family units, Mel is known for reinventing romantic versions of *home*, taking her common characters on uncommon journeys that lead from boardrooms to billabongs as they try to find their own HAPPILY EVER AFTER.

Living in Northern Australia, Mel enjoys random outback road trips, fumbling with her camera, annoying her family with her bad singing, and making new friends in the middle of nowhere— except for water buffalos. She's been chased by a few.

Feel free to contact Mel as her word journey continues at…

MelAROWE.com